JUMPER'S HOPE

CENTRAL GALACTIC CONCORDANCE BOOK 4

BY CAROL VAN NATTA

WWW.CHAVANCH.COM

JUMPER'S HOPE
Copyright © 2016 Carol Van Natta
First Ebook Published October 2016
Published by Chavanch Press, LLC
ISBN: 978-0-9831741-8-9

Cover design by Gene Mollica Studio
Edited by Shelley Holloway
Author website: Author.CarolVanNatta.com

DESCRIPTION

* * * * *

Two retired elite special forces veterans discover their battles aren't behind them after all. Someone considers them loose ends, and will stop at nothing to erase their knowledge of a secret government project. Their service left them both with wounds that will never heal. Do they still have what it takes to survive?

Kerzanna Nevarr's elite special forces days of wearing Jumper mech suits and piloting Citizen Protection Services' ships are long gone. The dark legacy of her service forced her to learn to live a quiet life. And she had to do so alone, without the lover who died before her eyes.

Jess Orowitz, veteran of CPS's secret spy organization, Kameleon Corps, made the mistake of trusting his superiors. He's paid a horrific price—fractured memories, constant headaches, and the death of the only woman he ever loved. Retirement on a quiet farming planet has kept him in an emotional deep freeze, but safe.

But now, Kerzanna is being hunted for reasons she can't guess, and even more stunning, the man who helps her escape is Jess, her supposedly dead lover. For Jess, discovering Kerzanna is still alive is only the first of the lies and betrayal he uncovers.

Worst of all, their hunter is someone with CPS intel and lethal resources. Someone who believes the only obstacles standing in the way of success are one broken-down ex-Jumper and a fractured Kameleon.

Together, are they strong enough to escape death one more time?

* * * * *

CHAPTER 1

IT TOOK JESS Orowitz a lot longer than it should have to realize the injured pilot he and his neighbor pulled from the flitter wreckage was a dead woman.

She groaned as they set her down as gently as they could on the glascrete surface of the public flitter port's landing pad in front of an older, gaunt man who was slowly opening his large medic kit.

Jess's farming neighbor, Bhalodia, the man who had called Jess to the scene, stood and moved back, rocking side to side on antsy feet. He'd dressed up in his only white tunic to come to town, and now it was ruined by a smear of bright red airfoil lubricant on his sleeve.

"She one lucky pilot." His English was more pidgin than Standard, but he got by similarly in at least twenty other languages besides his native Thai. He pointed a thumb over his shoulder toward the hot, still-sparking remains. "Broke flitters usually tumble, not slide."

Jess knew it had been the pilot's skill that avoided the buildings when landing what was left of her ruined flitter, but he was too stunned to speak. Kerzanna Nevarr, the only woman he'd ever loved, the woman who'd been killed four years ago in a full-city riot on a distant planet, was alive. He stayed on his knees and had to remind himself to breathe.

Considering the Central Galactic Concordance had more than five hundred settled planets across the galaxy, hundreds of thousands of cities, and hundreds of billions of people, the chances of the two of them reconnecting again in a tiny town in farm country on a back-of-beyond planet were impossibly remote.

And yet here she was.

Her tangled dark blonde hair was much longer and curlier than he remembered, and partially covered the decorative Jumper tattoos on the side of her neck that led to the skulljack interface just behind her ear. Her nose looked straighter, and the thin scar that had bisected her right eyebrow was gone. He wondered if her eyes were still as blue as the summer sky. Cosmetics made it easy to change eye color on a whim, but Kerzanna had never paid much attention to fashion. Under the bloody, torn casual pants and loose jacket and top she wore, all shades of brown and cream, she was still tall and looked well muscled. Maybe she'd been one of the lucky Jumper veterans to escape the long-term side effects of the mech implants and enhancements.

"Pssst!" Bhalodia hissed quietly in Jess's ear, startling him. "Told you. Pitt chemmed again." Bhalodia tilted his head toward to the medic.

Pitt looked like he was performing a slow-motion dance interpretation of a medic assessing a patient, but unfortunately, it was real. Kwiksloe addicts thought their consciousness was expanding at half the speed of light, but it was just an illusion brought on by a depressed nervous system. It was why Bhalodia, who'd known Jess was still in town for a meeting, had pinged him to come to the crash site and prevent an unnecessary death because of Pitt's impairment. Jess could be a medic when needed, though he paid a price for it.

Markalan Crossing's town constable, Castro, walked around the corner of the main hangar building, then broke into a trot the moment she saw them. She was mostly good at her job, unless it had anything to do with her lover, Pitt. Bhalodia muttered disgustedly as he turned away from Jess and toward the flitter wreck. Bhalodia had served eighty-two years in the Central Galactic Concordance Military Ground and Air Divisions before retiring to his sprawling family farm on Branimir, and had zero tolerance for the situation with Castro and Pitt.

Castro's habitual frown deepened as she took in the status of the flitter and the pilot, then became deeply pained as she realized Pitt's condition. She gave Jess a warning look as she put her hand on Pitt's shoulder and waited for him to notice and look at her. "Sweetie, I ordered a medevac. Maybe you should wait and let Orowitz and Bhalodia take her to the clinic."

Jess struggled to stay still during the ten long seconds it took Pitt to process her words and respond. "I'm-m-m… g-o-o-o-d…" He gave her a slow, sunny smile that said she was his entire universe.

Castro visibly melted and smiled tenderly back, even though she undoubtedly knew the kwiksloe gave him tunnel focus. "All right, sweetie. I trust you." She stepped back and glared at Jess, daring him to say one word. Her hand strayed as if by accident toward the needler on her quick-release belt. Something about her said she was microseconds away from unloading a full clip into anyone who interfered with Pitt.

Kerzanna needed immediate, competent assessment, and Pitt was useless. Jess sat back on his heels and dropped his gaze so Castro wouldn't see any changes in his expression when he reached for the part of his mind that was Jess-the-medic and let it take over. The familiar sharp pain became a familiar dull headache as he let his professional gaze catalog Kerzanna's injuries. He ignored the superficial cuts and contusions and focused on the probable head injury and possible cracked sternum. Her wheezy breathing suggested lung impairment, likely from smoke inhalation or possibly from an intruding broken rib or crash debris. Jess-the-medic's hands twitched when Pitt carelessly thumbed her swollen cheekbone and drew a grunt from her. The idiot was wasting time with a manual assessment instead of using a scanner.

Jess-the-medic wished he was a minder healer, able to help Kerzanna with just his mental talent, or at least a telepath, so he could tell Pitt what to focus on first, but he was just an ordinary man. Or as ordinary as he could be after the Citizen Protection Service's secret Kameleon Corps program left a few extra people in his head. He would diagnose his mind as fractured, except he was one of the fractures.

The medic kit probably contained inhib in its pharma supplies, but even if Castro would let Jess administer an emergency dose to Pitt, it'd take fifteen or twenty minutes for him to gain even minimal coherence. Kerzanna's pallor suggested shock, and despite what Jess-the-man thought, it was obvious to Jess-the-medic from the subtle degradation of muscle mass and the mechanical stiffness of her joints that Kerzanna suffered from Stage Three of Pelker Thomré Vadembo Syndrome, colloquially known as waster's disease. On average, Jumpers with eighteen years of service and six years into retirement were in Stage Four, so she was better off than most. Jumpers were supposed to only get treatment at CPS clinics, but all competent medics knew the basics, despite the CPS declaring it to be classified data and blocking commercial publication of any information on it.

Pitt had apparently noticed the shock, because he pulled out the standard oxy-stim jet from his kit and pressed the activator. Jess-the-man clasped his hands together to stop his medic self from touching Pitt and getting a chest full of needles from Castro. "Don't give her that. It could kill her."

Jess-the-medic's authoritative tone got Pitt's attention. His hand stopped centimeters away from her unprotected neck, puzzlement slowly blooming in his expression. Jess gave him a hard look. "She's an ex-Jumper. Probably has PTVS." Because Castro was still standing there instead of examining the downed flitter like she should have been, he added, "Waster's. The adrenal compound in the oxy-stim could stun her nervous system, make her forget how to breathe."

Castro narrowed her eyes. "How do you know?" She stabbed a pointing finger at Kerzanna. "Do you know her?"

Jess-the-medic tilted his chin toward Kerzanna's head. "Jumper tattoos, old style. Hair is too long for regulation. She wasn't jacked in when we pulled her out of the flitter, so she's decommed. Retired." His professional history, if Castro cared to check, showed he'd been in the Citizen Protection Service as a base quartermaster and emergency responder for thirty years. In most cases, it accounted for any unusual knowledge he had, including medical protocol for a member of the CPS's elite division of special forces. His personal history was none of Castro's business.

Castro's left wrist gauntlet lit up, and she subvocalized a response. "Medevac capsule's here." She turned to the north and cupped her hand over her eyes to shade them from the noonday sun. "We're lucky to get it. A mine accident has most of them tied up."

While they'd been talking, Pitt's face had slowly become a study in despair, perhaps because he'd recognized the serious mistake he'd been about to make. He looked slowly at Castro, his lip trembling and his eyes brimming with unshed tears, then at the jet in his hand. With an unexpected burst of speed, he plunged it down onto his thigh and gave himself a full dose.

"*Merde!*" growled Jess, too late.

"Billy!" yelled Castro. Jess-the-medic grabbed the jet as Castro dove to catch Pitt as he toppled sideways. He was already starting to twitch. Without treatment, it would soon escalate to a full-blown, lethal seizure. Oxy-stim was even worse for kwiksloe addicts than it was for Jumpers with waster's. Jess-the-medic dropped the jet and leaned across Kerzanna's legs to paw through the disorganized medic kit, looking for a stim counter-agent.

The automated medevac capsule descended to the landing pad. Bhalodia stalked toward it, silently sneering at Castro as she cried, cradling Pitt's head and shoulders in her lap. "Billy, baby, what were you thinking?"

Jess found a sedative jet and adjusted it for a child's dose, enough to blunt the stim. Too much, and Pitt would crash. He punched the jet into Pitt's thigh, next to the first injection site.

"What was that?" growled Castro, trying to pull Pitt's shuddering form away.

"Dormo. Sleep med." Jess-the-medic glanced at his original patient, the woman who had Jess-the-man tied in knots. Thanks to Pitt's idiocy, she was now the lower priority patient for emergency transport to the regional medical center, but she still needed treatment. He rose to his feet and helped Bhalodia guide the capsule as close as they could get behind Pitt.

"Castro," said Jess-the-medic, squatting down in front of her again. "Pitt needs to go to the medical center. Now."

Castro shook her head stubbornly. "No. He'll be good after some inhib."

Jess-the-medic shook his head and started to speak, but Bhalodia beat him to it. "Okay, okay, good. You do like always. He die, we get new medic. Not chem addict. " Bhalodia walked to the far side of where Kerzanna lay and lifted her outstretched arm to cross it over her, in preparation for lifting her, then gave Castro a sharp, sly look. "I bet we get new constable, too."

Once the medical center confirmed the kwiksloe, which was illegal on Branimir, Pitt's career as a medic would be over. If she didn't let him go for treatment, he'd die, and her career in enforcement would definitely be over. Castro's star lane choices were rocky, but she'd made her own star chart.

She glared at Bhalodia with all the hate and resentment she should have been directing at her addicted lover, but she relaxed her arms to let go of Pitt.

Jess-the-medic told Bhalodia to make sure the capsule stayed grounded, then scooped up Pitt's quivering body and climbed to his feet. Fortunately, Jess was a big man, taller even than some Jumpers, and Pitt was short and thin. With Bhalodia's help, he got Pitt into the capsule, entered what little data he knew about the patient, and sent it on its way. Medevac capsules had extensive built-in diagnostic and treatment capabilities, plus real-time communication with the medical center, so Pitt would probably live.

Jess-the-medic returned to kneel beside Kerzanna. He opened the medic kit wider to root around through the haphazardly arranged contents until he found the scanner. He directed it toward her chest and the suspected lung injury. Thankfully, although the scanner showed a cracked sternum, her ribs were only bruised and her spine was normal. Her residual Jumper reinforcements, plus the cybernetic right ilium and femur of her hip and thigh, had probably saved her from worse damage. The concussion was another matter. "We're going to need the autodoc in Pitt's office."

Castro stood and brushed the tan prairie dust off the back of her dark uniform pants. "I can't let you in without Pitt there. Just because you had first-responder training doesn't mean—"

Jess rose to his feet and invaded her personal space. "Yes, you can." He didn't like using his two-hundred-centimeter height to intimidate people, but Castro was endangering Kerzanna. He let his eyes reveal a bit of Jess-the-bomber, the man who'd laugh while his enemies died in a fire, as he stared at her unblinkingly. The pain in his head doubled, and he let her see that, too.

Castro stumbled back two steps before she caught herself. The fear in her expression gave way to stubborn challenge, and her hand drifted toward her needler, but she nodded once. "I'll escort you."

Jess-the-medic turned and squatted onto his heels to close the medic kit. He looked around for Bhalodia and smiled when he saw his neighbor bringing an antigrav loading cart from the flitter port lobby. Not the most dignified of gurneys, but Kerzanna weighed too much for even Jess to carry her very far. She was slender and fit for her size, but she was only about ten centimeters shorter than he was, and she had biometal-reinforced bones.

As gently as he could, he lifted her onto the cart, which dipped alarmingly until they got her weight centered. From the smell, the cart has last been used to haul fresh compost. He slung the medic kit's strap across his shoulder and pushed the cart's handle to get it moving toward the walkway. Pitt's medical clinic was close, and staying outside would be faster than going through the port building. Markalan Crossing was small enough that most everything was only a block or two away.

Bhalodia started forward, then hesitated. "I get bag. Meet you soon." He turned and walked toward the port office.

Jess didn't have time to wonder what Bhalodia was up to. Gravcarts were finicky and hard to control over irregular surfaces like old outdoor walkways, so he concentrated on keeping it level. Kerzanna was lucky to have stayed unconscious for so long, because she'd obviously taken a beating when trying to keep the flitter on course for a survivable landing, and the rough cart ride wouldn't be easy on her.

Castro let him into the town medical clinic's treatment area and helped him lift Kerzanna up and into the autodoc that took up most of one wall. The room's garish gold-accented purple color scheme was courtesy of a previous medic with absolute zero design sense. Jess-the-medic arranged Kerzanna's arms and legs so the unit could treat her more easily, glad it was long enough to fit her comfortably. When the town's old autodoc had finally come due for replacement, the farming families in a fifty-kilometer radius had contributed extra funds to get a modern, upgraded model. It was their best defense against Pitt's incompetence. Jess quickly entered the patient history he remembered and his suspicion about the Stage Three of waster's, then sealed the lid and started the treatment cycle.

Jess-the-medic turned to look at Castro, expecting questions. His head was pounding, but he couldn't leave until Castro did. Jess-the-man wouldn't know what to say.

Castro entered a sequence on her right wrist gauntlet as she subvocalized into the earwire she wore along her jawline, then gave Jess a hard, resentful look. "How much longer?"

Jess-the-bomber stabbed his way into Jess's brain. *Don't give her a professional opinion!* Jess covered the sharp pain by turning to look at the autodoc's readout. "It says nine minutes for the initial report. After that, it's anyone's guess."

Castro bit her lip and rocked back on her heels, her eyes darting between the autodoc, him, and the front door.

"Someone should be here when she wakes up," said Jess-the-bomber, shoving his hands in his pockets. "Any news on Pitt?"

His words had the desired effect on Castro. "No. I need to be... I can't stay."

Jess-the-bomber shrugged, as if he didn't care one way or the other. "I can, at least until you get another medevac here." He tilted his head toward the sealed autodoc. "She's not going anywhere."

Castro frowned, clearly torn. At last, she turned and took a step toward the door, then turned back and glared at him. "If anything is missing, I'll be targeting you first." Her attitude said she'd be targeting him, regardless, if only because he'd called out Pitt's negligence.

Jess-the-bomber shrugged again. "You know where the farm is." The clinic had nothing of interest to him.

Castro hesitated a moment longer, then strode out the door.

Jess-the-man made Jess-the-bomber and Jess-the-medic retreat, leaving him with a splitting headache and stiff shoulders, a room full of painkillers that didn't work for him, and a deluge of powerful memories all centered around the woman in the autodoc. A wave of icy nausea chilled him.

He staggered outside into the sunlight and leaned against the side of the clinic, dragging in deep, cleansing breaths of fresh air.

CHAPTER 2

KERZANNA NEVARR DREAMED she was dreaming, which even her dream self knew was weird.

In her dream, she dreamed of flying, but without a planet-fall mech suit. The wind and the empty sky exhilarated her. The brown and green plains below her transitioned to the northern ridge of blue mountains on the horizon, where Branimir's multitude of mines operated. Her chest hurt a little, but that was probably the thin air in the high altitude. Below her, a small town drew her eye, and she dove for it, but her dreaming dream ended, and she woke in the tilted-back nav pod pilot's seat of a private interstellar starship. Too soft for military, too purple. Too filled with dead people.

Well, one dead person, standing to the left of her seat. Jessperin Orowitz, her very dead ex-lover. She remembered his messy death, but her dream self didn't care about facts. The love of her life was back, and she was happy. She reached out for his hand, and his fingers curled around hers.

She smiled at his always too-serious expression and gazed into his mismatched green and brown eyes. His brown face looked good with its bronzed highlights, as if he'd been kissed by the sun. His wavy black hair was long at the top and back and cropped close at the sides. The scruffy beard she'd often teased him about was gone, making her want to kiss him to see how his smooth skin felt. She squeezed his warm, capable fingers. "You look pretty damn good for a dead man."

A surprised look crossed his face. He cocked his head a little, then brushed gentle fingers across her cheek. "You're dead, too."

"This is the afterlife?" She looked down at her inert torso and legs, then back to him. She sniffed her shirt. "Smells like shit." She giggled at her own joke. Life—and death, apparently—was funny.

She smiled up at him. "I moved to Branimir for you, since you never got the chance." Once she'd finally fallen off the CPS's detain-and-restrain list, she'd looked for a quiet place to ground herself, and remembered Jess's plans before she'd derailed them. It seemed a fitting way to honor his memory. "You'd like it."

"What about you?"

She shrugged. "Branimir has been good for me." She'd outgrown her family's rural ranch community and left as fast as she could for brighter lights, so a planet known for farming, mining, and business-centric minimalist government wouldn't have been her first—or even hundredth—choice. Jess's death and her health changed her priorities.

She knew her dream would end soon, and she needed to tell him something. "I used to hate you for splitting us up that day. You spied on the Minder Veterans Advocates for the police, and got yourself killed right in front of me, but I'm not mad any more."

"Why not?" His voice caressed her ears. She remembered her body twined with his, fitting perfectly, skin to skin, and the steady rise and fall of his chest, drawing in the scent of him with every breath. She sighed. "Because I lived. I had to forgive myself for bad choices, and that meant forgiving you for making better ones."

Jess smiled, and made her want to get a lot closer. His smile always had that effect on her, even on a crowded public transport.

She gave him her best sultry look. "Let's get naked." She struggled to sit up, but something was tying her down. She tried to move her legs, but couldn't. "Afterlife tanks."

She looked more closely at her restraints and realized they were medical lines. Oh, frelling hell, she was in a goddamn autodoc. Or as she liked to call them, control freaks. "Why am I here?" Another question arose. "*Where* is here?"

"Easy." Jess touched her face again, and she turned her cheek into the warmth of his hand. "You were piloting a high-low flitter and stuck a hard landing at Markalan Crossing's commercial landing port. You're in the town clinic."

At least she wasn't in a Jumper treatment tank. The town's name rang a bell, something about a meeting, which was odd. She did most of her business at the mines, the ore processing plants, and Branimir's only spaceport, not in the middle of crop farming country. More flashes of memory bubbled to the surface, of flying a flitter, pinging for a traffic control system, an explosion behind her, of grabbing the manual controls, loose objects, tumbling sideways. She tried to sit up again, but the autodoc lines kept her immobile. Adrenaline started to spike, then leveled off. The autodoc's happytime drugs made it all seem like a hilarious tri-D show.

It wasn't funny. Dreaming of Jess again wasn't funny, it was heartbreaking, but the autodoc didn't care. It wanted her to be happy, so it pumped her full of happytime drugs so she'd be farkin' thrilled while they replaced yet another part of her with cybernetics, since cloned parts didn't work for Jumpers with waster's.

And there was the proof. A medic in white with a red armband approached and peered at her. He was shorter than Jess, but who wasn't? "No more biometal," she told him, but he shook his head and vanished, leaving only her dream lover, looking haunted and sad. His fingers slipped out of her grasp, and he faded into the darkness before she could say goodbye. Dammit, not again.

All things being equal, she preferred the afterlife. A tear slipped from her eye as the darkness closed in and took her sinking into nothingness.

Kerzanna woke with a jolt, chest arching skyward in response to lightning in her veins. She sucked air like a ramjet engine as her heart pounded. The blackness receded from her vision to reveal a decorated purple ceiling and walls. She was on a bench… no, an open autodoc bed. She lifted her arms in time to see microneedle threads withdrawing from her skin. An insistent beeping cut off abruptly.

She began her survival checklist. First, adrenaline spikes were the enemy. She concentrated on her breathing, ensuring she wasn't taking in more air than she needed, and expelling it all before inhaling again. For the next few breaths, she took inventory of how she felt, relaxing any tension she found as she went over each part of her. The lights brightened, or maybe her brain was coming fully online.

Next, status. She'd been in a rented flitter. She remembered fighting the manual controls to control the axis and skid the flaming hulk down onto the landing pad, but nothing after that. No clue as to what had damaged the flitter. So how did she get to the autodoc? Hazy memories stirred of a short, older medic and…

"Jess." She barely whispered the name. She'd spent countless meditation hours trying to let the memories fade with time, but all it had taken was one injection of happytime drugs to bring them back. Goddamn autodocs.

She doggedly went back to her checklist. Health. Her head ached like she'd used it to smash asteroids. Her chest felt heavy and tight. She started to look down, but her stiff neck told her she'd regret it. She slid her hand up and discovered what was probably a bone regenerator adhered to her sternum, in the valley of her breasts. A quick check of her internal systems said the cybernetic central processor lodged under her breastbone was online and responsive. Some thoughtful medic had put a soft knit blanket over her for modesty. Jumpers gave that up in recruit training, but she appreciated the gesture.

"How are you feeling?" The man's voice was professionally caring and so like Jess's, down to the faint French accent he sometimes had. No wonder the happytime drugs had dredged up his memories.

She snorted. "Like I crashed a flitter." Medics were all the same. How did he *think* she was feeling? "How long have I been in here?" She patted the autodoc bed.

"Forty minutes." She heard the sound of a throat being cleared. "I'm sorry, but there's no time to ease you into this."

"Ease me into wha..." Her voice failed as Jess Orowitz, the man of her recent dreams and old sorrows, stepped into full view. She cleared her throat. "Oh, frelling hell."

He had to be real this time, because she hurt too much to still be in autodoc dreamland.

The demons of chaos had ignored her for the last few years, but they were back in her life with a vengeance. Never mind the unforgettable memory burned into her psyche of his execution death on a bloody sidewalk, or that for two years, she'd been on a CPS detain-and-restrain list for the events in the Mabingion Purge "police action"—a galaxy-famous debacle—that led up to his death. Reality was standing in front of her, in loose, olive-green cargo pants and a form-fitting orange knit shirt that hugged his wide shoulders, well-defined chest, and narrow waist. "You're alive." Her fingers tingled with the urge to touch him just to be sure.

Maybe she was in end-stage waster's disease, a prisoner in her own body, and her sense-deprived brain busy hallucinating to make up for it. If so, someone should tell her stupid brain to quit with the aching head and chest.

"You're alive, too. I was told otherwise. The police report and holos of your body were graphic." His expression was haunted. The lid of his right eye, the brown one, drooped slightly every few seconds, and the one over his left, green eye twitched faster, at heartbeat speed. His head must be hurting, meaning the crowd of voices in his mind hadn't gone away. She would have wished otherwise for him.

His shoulders hunched as he shoved his hands in his pockets. "What name do you go by these days?"

"Kerzanna Nevarr." She twitched a corner of her mouth, realizing he was testing her. One of the stronger voices in his head—the one that sounded a bit Nordic—was paranoid to a fault. "Malory Solis sends her regards."

Solis was the cover identity he'd hastily cobbled together for her the last day they'd been together. At first glance, Jess looked like a handsome but thick-headed security enforcer or a heavy laborer, and he wasn't a people person, but that all hid an inquisitive mind and stellar data manipulation and coding skills. The ID he'd created had gotten her off planet and held up well on a succession of frontier planets, where the CPS had little official presence, but wasn't above non-judiciary rendition if they'd discovered who she was.

A bit of his tension eased. "Sorry for the emergency re-entry from the autodoc. I woke you early because a friend looked at the wreckage of your flitter and said it was sabotaged. I wanted to give you the option not to be here in case someone comes looking." His right eyelid twitched more noticeably.

If she'd had any doubts that it was really Jess, the twitches would have reassured her. The best body shops in the galaxy might have been able to make someone look exactly like him, for whatever bizarre reason, but she'd bet they wouldn't know how to duplicate that behavior pattern.

"What should I call you?" Axul Larsson had been the identity he'd created for himself to escape the mass police and CPS arrests of the riots that came to be known as the Mabingion Purge. The mischievous game Jess had invented for himself, of creating mythical people and events and finding sneaky ways to get them into official data hypercubes, had turned out to be quite useful.

He ducked his head diffidently. "Just Jess."

Memory slammed hard of the first time he'd walked into the Jumper-friendly pub she'd been working at five years before. He'd caught her attention immediately, especially when she realized the tall, handsome man wasn't a Jumper, and was shy but sharp. It had taken two more visits before he'd told her his name, with that same look and those same words.

She shook her head. Distracting side trips to the memory gardens would have to wait. "I don't know who would be looking for me. I've done nothing to make anyone's hit parade." She frowned, remembering she'd said something similar to him four years ago, right before everything had gone horribly twisted. He'd probably figured out she hadn't told the whole truth back then about what Minder Veterans Advocates had been doing, and her involvement.

She took two deep, centering breaths, then carefully sat up. The pain in her head and chest had teeth, but nothing a Jumper couldn't handle, and she didn't feel dizzy. The blanket fell, but the bone knitter stayed in place. She tapped it. "How much longer should it stay?"

"Four hours, minimum, six hours would be better. Your bone sternum has a sixteen-centimeter crack. The underlying biometal is thinner than usual, but your central processor appears undamaged." The subtle French accent was back. "Where are you going?"

"Right now? The fresher." All medic centers had at least one. She swung her feet off the bed and to the ground. She tensed her legs briefly to make sure she could feel them both, then stood up. She was grateful that Jess stayed where he was, instead of trying to help her. Maybe he remembered she didn't like being crowded. Her favorite brown pants were torn and blood-stained, and smelled faintly of manure. The medic had probably cut off her shirt and bra to make room for the bone knitter. "Did my luggage survive?"

Jess tilted his chin toward an exam table to his left, where her bag, a portable case, and her few extra clothes were spread out. She'd only planned for an overnight stay, if that. She couldn't wear a bra over the bone knitter, so her breasts were on their own for a while. She grabbed the loose-knit top she usually slept in and discovered new rib-muscle pain when she pulled it on over her head. The pilot seat's web had kept her from bouncing around the flitter's cabin, but it hadn't kept things from bouncing into her.

She relieved herself in the fresher and winced at the sight of her bruised and swollen jaw and cheekbone in the mirror. She'd need a trip to a Jumper-certified medic clinic to get them fixed. Autodocs only cared about the big stuff, and civilian clinics couldn't treat her.

Simple physical activities like washing her face, rinsing her mouth out with mint-flavored orajet, and tying back her gunky long hair helped flush some of the cobwebs out of her head. She owed Jess honesty and distance.

He was leaning against the wall by the autodoc when she got back. His hands were in his pockets, and his face was enigmatic. She wanted to watch him, talk to him, see if real life on Branimir met his expectations, but there was no time.

She grabbed her socks and boots from the table and sat in the room's only chair to put them on. "I don't believe the sabotage was targeting me. I don't owe money. I haven't had a relationship since we… in years. I'm not involved in any organizations, unless you count the Branko Regional Commerce Council, and I'm only in that because I inherited the membership when I bought a mining transport business. We endorse governor candidates and argue about trade rules." She paused to give him time to speak, but he'd never been much of a talker. His expression gave her no clue as to what he was thinking. He didn't used to be so guarded with her, but she couldn't blame him for not trusting her.

She shook her head and started stuffing her belongings into her bag. "But even if I wasn't the target, you're right. Someone could come looking to clean up the mistake, which means you, the medic who treated me, and your friend who investigated the flitter could be in danger because of me." She sealed the bag and opened the portable case to check that the mineral test equipment had survived. Her spare percomp was terminally cracked, but everything else looked good. "So, point me to where I can rent something that flies, and I'll lead the trouble as fast and as far away as I can."

She closed and sealed the case, then turned to watch him, letting the silence settle. Only after his death… not-death, had she realized she'd rarely given him time to think or choose his words, not even once she'd figured out he had a frelling *committee* in his head that rarely agreed on anything. However much they'd been in love at the time, her volatile temper and impatience hadn't been good for their relationship. Or, as it turned out, her health, once the waster's disease really took hold. Controlling herself, redirecting her angry impulses, learning to choose her battles, had been hard-won lessons while on the run. She was still learning them.

"That's too predictable." He pulled his hands out of his pockets and stood up straight to meet her gaze.

She raised an eyebrow at him, but said nothing.

"Worst-case scenario. They targeted you, personally. They find out you're alive, and expect you to find a way to fly out. A rental is too easy to trace, because it'll have to be delivered from Szmarko." The corners of his lips sketched a smile. "The only rental in Markalan Crossing is an articulated-tandem ground hauler with a top speed of six kilometers per hour."

He'd obviously been giving it some thought, and her brain was still stuttering. Although the prudent part of her argued that people could change a lot in four years, she was inclined to listen. She'd always listened, although she hadn't always agreed. "What do you suggest?"

He waved toward the clinic's door. "I'll drive you south to Omicono City in my ground hauler, where I'll rent a flitter, to keep your accounts quiet. We'll go straight to the spaceport and take the first interstellar ship off planet. They can't kill what they can't find. Best-case scenario, it was an unlucky accident, and we get an off-world vacation for a few days."

She was nonplussed. She knew he didn't trust her, and for good reason. "Why would you do that for me?"

He crossed his arms. "Because I'm the random factor they can't easily trace." He frowned. "Because it torques my jets that the CPS went to a lot of trouble to make us each think the other was dead. I want to know why."

CHAPTER 3

JESS STUDIED KERZANNA as she considered his plan. Somewhere in the past four years, she'd learned to keep her thoughts and emotions off her face. She'd already surprised him by not rejecting it immediately, and not losing her temper at the whole situation. The Kerzanna he remembered chafed at retreat and devious tactics, and detested owing anyone anything, for reasons he'd never fully understood. She would never believe that he was seizing a chance few ever got: a do-over of the choice he regretted most.

She'd taken the news of his not-dead status in stride far more quickly than he had hers. He'd always admired her practicality and ability to prioritize the essentials.

She frowned. "The local police will have questions."

Jess snorted. "Constable Castro is busy." He described what had happened with Pitt, and how Kerzanna ended up in the local clinic's autodoc instead of evacuated to the regional medical center's emergency ward. "The port manager probably took a data cube's worth of holo and flat images of everything and has already cleared the landing pad for business. The pieces of the flitter are probably in a storage hangar for Castro and the insurance assessors to look at later."

She frowned. "What about the medic who treated me, then? Short guy, Asian."

"I treated you." He visualized the events from her perspective. "The short guy is probably Bhalodia, my neighbor. He brought your bags over." He'd come in while Kerzanna was in autodoc twilight. She'd been thrashing around, and Jess had belatedly remembered her claustrophobia. Opening the clam-shell top had soothed her.

He had been distracted by the nonsensical things she'd said about the afterlife and him spying on Minder Veterans Advocates, the veterans' activist and support group she'd been heavily involved with back in Ridderth. When she'd held out her hand to him, he'd slipped his hand in hers without thought. Despite his rational-brain reservations about the whole situation, at a very fundamental level, his body remembered hers. The curve of her face still fit his palm.

Bhalodia had bluntly shared his opinion that the flitter had been sabotaged with badly positioned explosives, and Jess trusted the assessment. Bhalodia had been fixing and flying military flitters for longer than Jess had been alive. On his way out the door, Bhalodia also told Jess that if he was smart, he'd go back to his farm and stay out of it, like Bhalodia planned to do.

The part of him that was Jess-the-bomber agreed and pushed him to leave Kerzanna in the autodoc. *Let her think she was dreaming. Her trouble isn't ours.* Jess-the-man shoved the bomber into a corner of his mind and ignored him. He didn't used to be able to control the bleedovers nearly that well, but he'd stubbornly kept trying until he'd found techniques that worked for him. Apparently, he needed to work on control for cases when dead lovers came back to life.

She stood. "I'll go with your plan on two conditions." She held up a thumb. "One, I'll pay you back for every expense, and none of your 'I lost the receipt' crap." Her chin jutted forward pugnaciously. "Fuel or recharge for your hauler, too."

He nodded, even as he suppressed a sigh. The CPS paid Kameleons extremely well—one of the recruitment incentives—and he'd accumulated even more money to hide away as a game, not because it meant anything to him. It bought him a quiet farm, but it couldn't buy him a quiet mind. It couldn't buy him a better childhood or different star lanes for his life. "I'll send you an invoice once we're sure no one's tracking your accounts." Branimir was famous for being purposefully uninterested in personal transactions of any sort, from finances to travel to information queries, and kept the bare minimum data required by the Central Galactic Concordance government. However, with a bit of effort, he could trace financial transactions, so he had to assume others could, too.

She nodded and held up her index finger. "Second, you drop me off at the spaceport, then you go home. The last time you got involved in my drama, it got you killed." She huffed with exasperation. "Okay, you lived, and so did I, but you know what I mean."

He nodded once. He'd wait to argue with her about the second condition once they got to the spaceport.

She winced and rubbed her neck. "As much as I hate autodocs, at least they have good painkillers."

Jess eyed the autodoc, then the clock. "Sit a minute while I frag the autodoc's memory of treating you."

It was a testament to how much she was still hurting that she sat without argument. Jumpers were notoriously unwilling to admit weakness, even if they'd just crashed a flitter, and she was a Jumper, through and through.

He easily cracked the autodoc's security by means of a diagnostic side gate, then told the unit the last use had been a test. Autodocs red-flagged deletions of treatment records in a dozen reports, but this one logged tests once and ignored them. Just to be thorough, he tweaked the record's time stamp to the previous week, and adjusted the onboard chems inventory to match. While Kerzanna was still resting, he found a dusty cargo bag under a desk and took it to the supply cabinet and allowed Jess-the-medic to shop for useful medical supplies so he could continue field treatment for her.

A faint smile played on her face as she watched him without comment. He enjoyed the unexpected freedom of not having to hide his quirky self behind the layered façade of a flat zero personality. It had kept him safe over the years from intrusive therapists and invasive telepathic minders, and sharp and suspicious CPS handlers and investigators, but brought few friends and only one lover, the woman in front of him, who had somehow seen through it.

"Ready?" he asked.

She stood and slung the straps of both her bags over her shoulder. "Green go."

They exited the clinic and checked that the door sealed tight, then walked the two blocks to where he'd left his ground hauler. She matched his long-legged stride. A phantom memory of walking with her, hand in hand, on a rare sunny day in the perpetually dank city of Ridderth made a bid for his attention, but he relegated it to the periphery of his mind, just like he did with other distracting fragments.

She slowed at the end, exhausted but trying not to show it. Rapid-healing procedures depleted stamina, and he'd interrupted her treatment because Jess-the-bomber said trouble was already on its way, and Jess-the-man agreed.

He helped her web into the wide passenger seat and handed her a blanket to use for a pillow. In the cabin, he stowed the medical bag and programmed the onboard map for Omicono City. His old hauler was capable of making the trip in an hour if he pushed it, but ninety minutes would do, and wouldn't attract attention.

As he passed the pile of rocks that marked the unofficial town perimeter, it occurred to him he'd completely forgotten the CPS meeting he'd made the special trip into town for. Something about a post-exit longitudinal study of Kameleon Corps operative veterans. He'd have to reschedule after this was over, or they'd use less polite methods. It had been phrased as an invitation, but one way or the other, the CPS always got what it wanted.

CHAPTER 4

RAVILORI GOSSANDORILAIKA, OR Vahan, as she preferred to be called professionally, added "taking privacy to extremes" to her long mental list of "Reasons Branimir Should Be Planet-Poisoned."

A brisk springtime breeze swirled dust in patterns across the Markalan Crossing public flitter pad. She busied her fingers with sealing her protective vest to hide her annoyance with the truculent beetle of a man in front of her. "If I gave you the ID number, could you at least confirm whether or not the crashed flitter is ours?"

She'd spun him a tale about having been hired by a mythical air service to track a stolen flitter with valuable cargo. She was ninety-percent sure the flitter was her target, because the Branimir traffic system had coughed up the record when she'd prodded it with CPS auth codes, but the middle-of-nowhere location was unexpected. It was hundreds of kilometers off course from where Nevarr's known meeting with a rare-mineral mine customer was to take place in the Sinroth Mountains.

The man crossed his spindly arms, evidently enjoying his petty power. "Like I said, ask the constable." His German accent suggested he was a Branimir native. He wouldn't even give her the constable's personal ping ref, but he grudgingly described how to get to the office.

"Thank you for your time," she said politely, imagining his painful, fiery demise as she did so. She nodded her head toward her hired heavy mercenary to get her to follow, then took off toward the center of town. Cracks and wavy sections in the walkway made it obvious the tiny town had never bothered finishing its original foundation glass. She'd be surprised if the street's solar collectors still worked.

From what she'd been able to pry out of the sparse official traffic control records, the flitter had crashed, as expected, but the pilot had made a miracle landing instead of a kilometer-long smear of slagged parts in some farm field. Vahan had delayed Nevarr's trip long enough to avoid the big "accident" at the mine, but had found out too late that it had been a secondary, follow-up plan, and that the primary attack plan had been to rig the flitter to explode when it dropped below a certain altitude. The orders Vahan had been given were clear: prevent the kill attempt altogether, or make sure it succeeded.

From the moment her new boss, Dixon Davidro, had departed Branimir with his monstrous menagerie of "pets," as he called his long-time contractors, leaving Vahan to clean up the mess that Senga Si'in Lai, his "special project," had made, not one single thing had gone right. Vahan was not a goddamn housekeeper. She was a CPS Academy-trained shielder, with the talent to contain telepathic and telekinetic minders, and protect her non-minder boss's thoughts from being read, twisted, or cleaned. She was a good, fast fighter and knew how to spot threats before they materialized. But he was her boss, which meant she had to smile like she respected him and put up with his warps, whims, and delusional bullshit. He should have had his top monster and enforcer, Renner, put Senga Si'in Lai down hard or permanently, not rewarded the vindictive slagger with a second chance by taking her to a lush destination resort.

Vahan was also not a goddamn therapist. Davidro's former employee, Neirra Varemba, was weirder than the rest of his pets, combined, and Vahan was supposed to be "evaluating" Varemba to make sure she wasn't faking her illness. Vahan snorted. The woman willingly chose to spend what few weeks or months she had left to live in a rotting ship at the Branimir spaceport. If yesterday's visit was anything to go by, Varemba was also a few dozen parsecs away from anything resembling sane, so how the hell was Vahan supposed to tell—ask her if she thought too much interstellar space travel turned people into minders?

By the time Vahan was done hiking through the misbegotten town, discovering that both the constable's office and the only medical clinic were deserted and sealed tight, she was ready to personally terminate Kerzanna Nevarr on sight, just to work off her frustration, instead of letting the hired help earn their keep. It wasn't personal. The Jumper hadn't done anything except be in the wrong group at the wrong time, but now that she knew someone had tried to kill her, any questions she asked might be a threat to Davidro's special CPS project, so she had to go.

Vahan climbed back into her rented flitter to consider her options, leaving the armored merc standing outside looking armed and dangerous to deter the asshole port manager from hassling her about moving.

She had to assume Nevarr recognized the threat and would take steps to protect herself. If she were in Nevarr's boots, she'd take the opportunity to leave the miserable excuse for a planet, but maybe Nevarr liked the stinking place.

Vahan's bracelet-style percomp interrupted her musing with the results of a priority records request, telling her a medevac capsule had transported a patient from the Markalan Crossing flitter pad to the regional medical center. She quickly programmed the center's coordinates into the flitter's console. Finally, her luck had turned.

She tapped her lips thoughtfully, then sent an order through to the mercenary company. She and her hired merc companion could take care of Nevarr at the medical center, which likely had multiple penetration points and laughably bad security. However, if the medical center didn't pan out, she wanted Branimir's only spaceport and shuttle services covered, since Branimir was too tightfisted to have its own space station. Just to be thorough, she authorized a squad of six for adequate coverage to make sure Kerzanna Nevarr didn't leave before Vahan got there. She knew Davidro would want her to handle the final termination herself. Mercs lacked subtlety.

She still needed to do something about the wrecked flitter. If Nevarr had survived, so had evidence of the explosives that downed the flitter. Eventually, even lazy town constables who couldn't bother to show up for work, or smarter insurance investigators, would see the evidence and dutifully report it. Maybe she could entice the rental company that owned it with a short-fuse offer of a premium salvage price. Otherwise, well, accidents had been known to happen in poorly maintained small-town storage units.

She allowed herself a predator's smile, imagining Davidro's howl about the expenses she was racking up. It served him right for abandoning her on mind-numbing, no-redeeming-features-whatsoever Branimir while everyone else was off in the new paradise with Si'in Lai.

CHAPTER 5

KERZANNA WOKE TO the vibration that had lulled her to sleep. Jess's vehicle looked to be in good shape, but the glass roadway wasn't. Branimir wasn't big on spending money on infrastructure. Or anything else, for that matter.

The hauler's passenger seat wasn't designed for someone of her height. She'd slept in a lot less comfortable places in the service, but she'd come to appreciate civilian comforts. She sat up and awkwardly stretched her legs diagonally as she looked out the cab's window. She massaged her sore neck to work some of the stiffness out of it.

They were at the edge of what had to be Omicono City. The subtle change in sound from flat farming country to unprepossessing, block-formed buildings was probably what had awakened her. Her former captain had called it shark brain. Probably why she'd lived through eighteen years of the difficult, dangerous, and downright impossible missions that were stock in trade for the CPS Jumper Corps.

"How long to the flitter port?" Her mouth tasted of drug residue and dust. She surreptitiously wiped the window she'd been leaning against with a corner of the blanket, in case she'd been drooling.

"Twelve minutes." Jess apparently trusted the ground hauler's onboard comp and the city's traffic control system, because his eyes were on her, not on the road. "Want to borrow my jacket, or need a slap patch for the pain?" He pointed to holdfasts on the hauler's side panel where the cargo bag of medical supplies and a tan coat were hanging.

She shook her head. "Not unless those patches you took are Jumper rated." She snorted. "And if they are, you'll have to carry my dead weight to the flitter." She winced at the dryness in her throat. "I would take something to drink if you have it."

He paused a moment, then fished around in the storage bin between them and found a pouch, which he handed to her. "Mixed vegetable juice."

"That'll do." She activated its cold pack, unsealed it, and took several long swigs of the salty liquid, which helped quiet her complaining stomach for the moment. The thought of solid food nauseated her. Her chest was numb from the bone knitter, but the pain in her head and neck clamored for attention. The juice tasted off, and she felt detached from her twitchy body.

She flicked her left eye to access her cybernetic stats. The controller's readout indicated impaired reaction times and anomalous control responses, which was confirmation of the blindingly obvious. Gods of chaos, but she deeply detested autodocs. Even some big-city CPS clinics barely knew how to treat ex-Jumpers; small-town, outdated autodoc treatments were sometimes worse than the injury.

She focused on Jess, because he looked like he was wanting to talk to her. Odd how she remembered the little things about him. Or maybe not so odd, since she'd only ever known the little things. He'd never talked about anything in his past or his Kameleon career. At the time, she'd consoled herself with the fact that he'd chosen silence over lying to her.

"Are you safe to fly a flitter for five or six hours?"

She pursed her lips. "Are you any better a pilot than you used to be?"

The corner of his mouth twitched with humor. "Depends on the metric. I won't kill us."

She sighed. "Sad to say, but I probably would." She held up her hand flat and watched her fingers and wrist spasm randomly. Happytime drugs, autodoc rapid-heal protocols, Jumper metabolism, cybernetic controllers, and waster's disease were a chaotic mix from hell, making her unfit until her systems settled down. Even her not-exactly-legal emergency capabilities would likely fail. She slumped in the seat and closed her eyes. "Goddamn autodocs."

Kerzanna didn't know whether to be peeved or pleased that Jess chose the most expensive high-low flitter available. After buying out her dead partner's heirs in their mining transport business, she'd worked hard to replenish her financial reserves, but high-end flitter rentals and full-price interstellar trips would put a noticeable dent in them. On the other hand, the flitter was spacious, and the navigator seat, complete with backup flying controls, fit her long legs and felt as comfortable as a sleep pod. Plus, the flitter was fast, meaning they'd get to the spaceport in four and a half hours or less.

Jess handled the takeoff well enough, and the sync to the local traffic system. She sipped the blessedly rich hot chocolate he'd bought for her and watched as he inserted a wirejack from his clunky-looking percomp into the flitter's console, then promptly set about hijacking the flitter's systems. She suspected he could take over a military dreadnought in a couple of hours, so ordinary civilian transports didn't stand a chance.

He patted the console and gave her a small smile. "It thinks we're going to Wunderschön Inseln. When the local traffic system hands us off to the planetary system, I'll drop us off the grid and pick it up when we hit Branko."

The "Wonderful Islands" was a good choice. Branimir's only luxury resort destination got a lot of traffic from all over the planet. She didn't trust her own memories any more, but she trusted him, or at least, she wanted to.

Now that she was comparatively safe and comfortable, she allowed herself to ponder the dozens of questions that her busy little brain had been bothering her with ever since she woke up. She'd have to prioritize them, or she'd miss something important.

He beat her to the first question. "Why were you going to Markalan Crossing?" He finished entering something on his percomp and checked the coordinates readout on the console.

"I had a meeting." She frowned. "I can't remember why or with who, though. I don't have any customers in farm country. I could check my calendar… No, that's not safe right now." Like most service businesses, her booking schedule was public, meaning nosy people could easily monitor net traffic to it. She shook her head, but it just made her neck complain. "I remember the time, thirteen hundred, and that it was room six in the public flitter port, and that's it." Her head injury could mean the memory was lost forever.

Jess swore, something he rarely did.

"Problem?"

"Yesterday, a CPS representative pinged an 'invitation' for a meeting today at thirteen hundred in room six of the public port. That's why I was in town." His jaw tensed.

She knew without asking that he'd have verified the sender as legitimate. Which suggested her meeting had been with the CPS, too. A cold knot formed in her stomach. "The CPS discovered one or both of us is still alive and wants to change that."

"I don't think so." Jess engaged the autopilot controls and swiveled his seat to look at her, so she turned hers to face him. "Much easier to kill us separately." He drummed his long fingers on the plushly padded armrest. "Someone went to a lot of trouble to bring us together again."

"So the flitter sabotage was to *stop* us from getting together?" She couldn't imagine why.

He shrugged, and his right eye twitched once. "Maybe whoever is after you found out about me through our shared history." The Nordic accent clipped his consonants. Most people didn't notice the minute changes, but she'd learned to be hypersensitive to them, since he tanked at telling her what was going on with him.

Of all the voices in his head, she disliked the paranoid one the most, though she grudgingly appreciated that its devious turn of mind had probably saved her. Like most Jumpers, her usual solution to problems was to stomp all over them with a planet-fall mech suit until they went away. She'd learned discretion while on the run from the CPS, but she'd never make a good spider, setting up webs of intrigue to catch her prey.

She shook her head. "You already said it. If they found you, it would be easier to kill us separately."

Jess frowned and drummed his fingers again. "Business rival, or someone looking to corner the market?" His right eye stayed still, and he was back to flat Standard English.

"I have a few competitors, but transporting ores and minerals to and from mines and refineries is a niche business with a low profit margin." She shrugged. "It suits me because I get to fly. When my partner died, his family was grateful when I bought out his share. They needed the funds, and no one else was offering."

She swallowed the last of her chocolate and folded the cup for the recycler. Mysteries made her tense, and unrelieved tension was bad for her health. She counted three breaths as she willed her body to stand down. Thank the stars that Jess had prevented the town medic from giving her oxy-stim. She'd have needed days to recover.

She caught Jess's gaze again. "How did you know about my waster's disease, and how to work around it? The CPS is jealous of its security secrets." The confidentiality section in all Jumper contracts included serious consequences for disclosure even to family or civilian medics, and the CPS regularly made public examples of violators.

He blinked, and she knew she'd startled him with her question. He never talked about his past, so she'd had to piece it together from observations and little things he'd let slip. Maybe she'd get a straight answer, for once.

He turned his seat forward again.

Or not. "Never mind." Pain was making her irritable and impatient. "I appreciate you stopping the chemmed medic from malpracticing on me."

She wanted to ask him a dozen questions about his life, from what happened to him that day four years ago after they'd split up to avoid the detain-and-restrain order, to what he did for a living now, to who he thought had meddled in their lives back then and why, but they all formed a logjam in her throat. He'd barely shared anything when they'd been intoxicated with passion and love. He'd have considerably fewer reasons to trust her now.

She swiveled her seat forward and stared at the clouds, relaxing into the moment, letting her imagination free-associate while she reached for the serenity she needed to stay alive. She smiled briefly. If her method could help her deal with meeting her surprise-he's-not-dead lover and running from possible killers, or just his paranoia, it could handle anything. She let the smile slip away as she breathed and counted heartbeats. Since the day she'd been told she had no hope for a future, she'd made a vow to herself to enjoy each moment of body feedback while she still could.

His voice almost startled her. "I always knew about the waster's. Well, part of me did. I studied it whenever I could. The CPS isn't as careful with their data as they like to think."

She glanced at him, but he kept his face forward. It was as close as he'd ever come to talking about what went on in his head. The least she could do was give him honesty in return.

"I'm in Stage Three, with an impairment percentage of thirty-eight, as of yesterday's test. Stage Four officially starts at forty-two percent, with noticeably degraded reaction times. The CPS clinic will issue a testing unit so I can check the percentage and track the disease's progression. By fifty percent, I'll experience intermittent motor intention paralysis, and by sixty percent, if I live that long, I'll probably be in an end-stage sensory-deprivation coma, with my delusional mind locked in a paralyzed body. I have seven or eight years with quality of life, if I'm lucky. The official CPS line is that only half of us have it, but I've never met a single Jumper veteran who *doesn't* have it, and I've met a lot of us and chatted with more. No one I've run into has ever met the waster's-free Jumpers the CPS trots out for the media. Neither the CPS nor the pharmas have even found a way to slow it down, despite seventy-plus years of research." She smiled humorlessly. "Medical treatment may be a foundation right for all CGC citizens, but it's no help if there's no cure."

"Why are you telling me?" Implied in his question was, *why now?*

"You always wanted to know. Back when we were in Ridderth, I was still in my high orbit about ideals and the oath I signed. I thought the CPS had good, valid reasons for the secrecy." She'd been incredibly naïve and stubbornly thick skulled about a lot of things. "I lost what was left of my faith in the CPS when they chased me across the galaxy after your…" She took a deep breath, and willed the adrenaline to subside, but her temper was winning. "The fact that you're alive means some farkin' CPS minder telepath twisted my memory, made me think you were a police informant, passing on information you learned from me about Minder Veterans Advocates. Some of that day is a blur, but I have an indelible memory of a CPS Minder Corps field agent forcing you to kneel on the walkway and executing you in broad daylight. Your brains decorated the wall behind you like a splash of curdled paint."

The memory used to be her worst, the one that sucker-punched her each time and left her shivering, but every moment she spent now with a living, breathing Jess was diluting it into a vivid scene from a bad horror holo.

Unlike some of her more binary-thinker squad mates, she'd never hated minders, but she'd been queasy around telepaths, especially twisters, with the power to warp memories into believable lies, or cleaners, with the power to erase memories altogether, leaving anything from neatly excised bits, to gaping holes, to blank-slated zombies. The CPS Minder Corps recruited the most powerful minders in all classes—telepath, telekinetic, patterner—and subcategories, and used them without compunction. They also gave telepath and telekinetic categories powerful enhancement drugs with usually debilitating side effects.

When she'd volunteered for the Minder Veterans Advocates and worked with all the CPS veterans, she'd come to realize that minders had it worse than Jumpers. She had the data to prove it. And that nasty drug addictions and waster's disease were an easy-glide ride compared to whatever the CPS had done to Jess. The supreme irony was, they'd all volunteered for it, minders, Jumpers, and Kameleons alike, in the name of keeping the galactic peace.

"Thank you." His face was turned away from her, so she couldn't watch for telltales.

On impulse, she asked, "Who's thanking me? The just-Jess part of you, or the medically-trained part of you that speaks classical French, likes ancient pre-flight jazz, and is a workaholic?" She smiled in soft amusement. "The one who pilfered medical supplies from the town clinic?"

He stared at her, blinking rapidly a couple of times. "What else do you know?" His tone was more cautious than accusatory. He dropped his eyes, and a visible tremor went through his body.

Dammit, she should have known better than to step into this minefield. When they'd been together, rare conversations like this had ended with him in near-catatonic withdrawal.

"I'm sorry, Jess." It was cruel to push for answers just to satisfy her curiosity. She owed him kindness for getting him involved, both four years ago and now, and for saving her both times. He owed her nothing.

Numb with empty, creeping cold, she wrapped her arms around herself and focused on the ever-changing, never-changing clouds.

Chapter 6

JESS GRITTED HIS teeth against the fire that danced on his skin. He knew it was an illusion, but it still hurt. He'd figured out how to neutralize the self-preservation routines in the various overlays, but clever Kerzanna had taken him by surprise and had unwittingly triggered the fire feedback loop that was the default warning built into the neural net hardware they'd implanted deep in his cortex. The bioware alert was supposed to have been purged by the CPS when he'd retired, but he couldn't very well complain without them asking how he knew it hadn't been.

The fire subsided, and he wanted to explain, or maybe apologize. He hadn't been able to tell her anything four years ago, and he knew it hurt her feelings. He could talk more now, but he didn't know where to start.

When he'd officially retired, his CPS handler, the military-to-civilian transition coordinators, and the CPS Minder Corps counselors observed, evaluated, and monitored him for a full year. Ironically, the very things they'd been looking for, the inadvertent residual personalities known as "bleedovers," had helped him hide the truth, or the CPS would have brought in a trusted Minder Corps cleaner to blank-slate him the day he left active duty. He was a walking security breach.

Since then, he'd used trial and error—mostly error, at first—to develop internal controls for the remnants of the personality overlays in his head. The complex Kameleon procedures and technologies supposedly prevented the bleedovers, and he'd been tested after each mission, but either the tests weren't effective, or the CPS ignored the results. Few Kams retired after career time in service like he had. Most left on disability, either because the overlays couldn't take full control any more, or because they were leaving too many residual memories and knowledge in "unmonitored" areas of the brain, which was code for the organic, not the bioware.

The existence of the CPS's Kameleon program was an official secret, so there was little accountability for it. In the rare, cautious discussions he'd had with the few other Kams he'd met between assignments, he'd concluded that in his case, his CPS handlers had played fast and loose with the protocols that were supposed to prevent using the same overlay too many times, not purging his onboard record storage unit often enough, and not giving him enough downtime between missions. There'd been no accountability for that, either.

He glanced at Kerzanna, but she'd turned away. "I try not to use the… other parts of me if there's no need." Tension gathered in his left temple.

Silence stretched between them. He ignored the temptation to open his percomp, which he recognized as a subtle push from the bleedovers to end the conversation.

"What do you call them? I mean, do they have names?"

"Not really. Just jobs, like 'medic' and 'spaceship engineer.'"

"I occasionally heard stories about Kameleons and the Kam Corps from Minder Corps veterans, but mostly after a lot of drinks or chems." She snorted softly. "Until I met you, I thought they were a confabulated myth, like Ayorinn's Legacy."

"There aren't that many of us, and we're made for stealth, so it's easy for the CPS to pretend we don't exist." He gave her a sardonic smile. "I'll bet they wish the Legacy was as easy to control."

She laughed. "Can't send in the Jumpers to stomp a meme."

"Can't erase history, either." The safer conversational ground soothed his incipient headache.

She nodded agreement. "Not unless they clean the memories of everyone who was living in the city of Ridderth at the time. Hell, Ayorinn's forecast was the talk of my blink-and-you'll-miss-it town, thirty years ago. Not that it's sparked transformation of anything, like it was supposed to." She rubbed her palms on her thighs. "I don't suppose you or the medic happened to stuff anything to eat in that bag, did you? My stomach has suddenly woken up to the fact that I missed breakfast and lunch."

"Sorry, not even nutrient concentrates." He should have thought of it. He'd grown selfish in his solitude on the farm, not having to think of others. A memory fluttered of when Kerzanna had been teaching him how to fly, something about flitters throughout the galaxy still having supplies for a crash landing, a holdover from frontier planet days. "We could raid the emergency stores."

"Yeah, I think I'm going to have to." She released her seat web and stood. "Make sure to add the rental company's up-charge to your invoice to me."

She came back with three mealpacks stacked on top of one another. "Water?"

"In the bag, short side, closest to me."

She kneeled to fumble with the bag. "Want one?"

"Sure."

By the time he had opened the water pouch and taken a sip, she'd already triggered the top mealpack's heater, and began using the included spoon to efficiently shovel food into her mouth as fast as she could chew and swallow. She only slowed down about halfway through the second mealpack. "That's better," she said between mouthfuls. "Autodoc happytime drugs mess with my feedback."

Guilt flashed through him. "Emergency wake-ups probably don't help."

She glanced at the flitter console readouts and the sky periodically as she ate. He doubted she was even aware she did it. The few former squad mates he'd ever met of hers said she'd been a legendary pilot, both atmosphere and interstellar, and he believed it.

His clunky-looking but highly customized percomp pinged with an incoming message from his neighbor, Bhalodia. He read it while Kerzanna folded up the two empty mealpacks for recycling. Bhalodia reported that the port manager, Bhalodia's poker buddy, said two mercs had been nosing about for information on the flitter crash and seemed uncommonly interested in the pilot, who they somehow knew was female and a Jumper. Bhalodia ended the message with a warning that Castro would probably be happy to sacrifice the flitter pilot to draw attention away from Pitt.

He showed Kerzanna the entire message, without comment. She was smart, and he doubted she'd be in the mood for Jess-the-bomber's "told you so" attitude. He wasn't, either.

He braced himself for an argument about changing the plan, but instead, she took a deep breath and held it, then let it out slowly.

That was the second time she hadn't lost her temper. It dawned on him that she'd probably had to train herself to stay calm to control her waster's disease symptoms, the way he'd had to train himself to control the bleedover fragments, or fracture permanently. He intended to ask her about her methods, once they were in the safe seclusion of an interstellar ship's stateroom.

He quieted his thoughts and embraced the silence as he watched the sky and the console readouts.

"Did you ever buy that farm you wanted?"

"Yes." He'd have told anyone else to mind their own business, but he'd never been able to resist the low, velvety tone she reserved for people she cared about. Something about her attracted the people who needed her, and she compassionately let them in. "It's small, only about two square kilometers. The previous owner depleted the soil with monoculture fiber plants. I rotated in some grains and have a greenhouse full of new seed starts for biofuel crops ready for planting this week." He gave her a crooked smile. "Mostly, though, I repair the pest repellers, irrigators, and the sensor arrays."

She chuckled. "I sync that. I spend more hours on flitter and shuttle upkeep than flying them. That's why I rented..." Her voice trailed off and she frowned. She caught his eye. "Could you crack my business domain and leave no trace? It's a standard commercial perimeter, nothing special."

He shrugged. "Probably. Why, do you think it's been cracked?"

"No, I want you to crack it so I can change my entire fleet's status to 'down for maintenance.'" She flattened her palms against her thighs. "I don't want any of my contract pilots going near anything until someone checks every one of them for sabotage."

In his mind, Jess-the-bomber sent him a rare wave of approval for Kerzanna's new prudence, even though Jess himself thought she was more worried about her pilots' safety than her own personal security. "Give me your company ping ref and ten minutes."

He passed control of the flitter to her, remembering her opinion that autopilots were programmed by amateurs. He used his percomp to bounce a set of code fragments through a few hundred entry points before letting them assemble and slither through Drasmilik al Haq Mining Transport Service's layered security. He took the opportunity to copy the financial account IDs she'd probably use to transfer funds to him later, so he'd know to let the transaction through. She'd hunt him down if he didn't.

"I'm in. Do you want to wirejack into my percomp, or do it manually?"

"Manual," she said, holding out her hand, palm up. "No offense, but I don't jack into strange percomps." She gave him a sly grin. "I bet yours is stranger than most."

He nodded and handed her his unit. He liked that she respected his skills, but he wished she trusted him. That would take time. Considering the twisted memory of him in her head, it was a wonder she was still speaking to him.

She passed flitter control back to him and turned her attention to the percomp. In the meantime, he used the flitter console's side net to check for traffic in the area, but prevented it from uploading any data to the artificial intelligence that ran the planetary traffic control system. The AI would alert a live person if it noticed their present vector was perpendicular to their claimed destination.

"Done." She rubbed her neck and leaned her head back with a wince. "While I'm in, can I do anything to stop intruders?"

"Not with your setup. Branimir business security services are a cut above most planets, but they're not state-of-the-art." He tilted his head toward the percomp in her hand. "I could customize something for you."

She glanced at him then looked away, her face scrunched in thought. "Maybe later." She focused on the interface for a few more moments. "Okay, so here's another question. Can you tell if someone else has been here before us?" Her grim expression belied her calm tone. "Because my calendar for the week is as blank as my memory." She showed him the display with no entries.

He had the absurd impulse to pat her shoulder or hug her, anything to comfort her, but he knew the timing was bad. "Sorry. I'd need an hour or two for a forensic deep dive."

She sighed and handed him the percomp. "I assume you need to sign off."

He repaired the holes he'd made and exited her system, then put his percomp back on his wrist.

She laced her fingers together in her lap, took a deep breath and let it out slowly, then did it again. "I keep looking at my internal chrono because I have no frelling idea what time it is." She pointed her chin toward the flitter's console. "The local readout says we're five hours from the Islands, but I know the spaceport is maybe three hours away." She drew up one leg to put her foot on the seat and rest her elbow on her knee. "My last clear memory is waiting for the rental company to get me a new flitter, because they couldn't find the one I'd reserved. That was a little after eight in the morning. Now it's nearly fifteen hundred hours, and it feels like two days have gone by." She shook her head and turned her seat to face him. "How's your headache?"

He must not have hidden it as well as he thought. "Gone." He shrugged. "I don't usually get them any more. Farm life is peaceful, and I don't get many visitors, except Bhalodia's lunatic family, who have boundary issues." He twitched a small smile at her. "Today has been exceptionally challenging."

She smiled back. "That it has." Her smile faded and she turned away from him.

The silence felt less comfortable than it had before, but he didn't know what to do about it. She deserved time to sleep and heal before they tackled the big issues between them, like what the hell had really happened four years ago, and if it was connected to who was manipulating them now, and why. Not to mention figuring out who wanted her dead.

"Could I borrow your jacket?" She pointed her thumb over her shoulder toward the bins.

"Sure." He should have thought to ask if she was comfortable. He really needed to learn to think of other people again. She'd been good for him, though he hadn't appreciated how much at the time.

She swung out of her seat and headed toward the fresher, which was little more than a shallow cabinet for short people, but got the job done.

Jess resolutely trained his eyes on the console, the sky, or his percomp, to keep from staring at her, wondering how much else had changed.

She returned to her seat carrying a blanket with the rental company's logo and wearing his jacket. She webbed herself in, then pulled the blanket over her and muttered something about a nap.

To ward off the deluge of memories, he passed the time sending a ping to Bhalodia to hire him and his family to watch the farm and handle the spring planting. Bhalodia had managed the farm before Jess had moved to Branimir, so it would be in good hands. And even though he knew it would torque Kerzanna's jets to overload when she found out, he created an interplanet escrow account in her name that only needed her biometrics and a challenge response she'd know for her to receive it. He owed her a lot more than a fluxed bank balance, but it was a start.

At forty minutes out from the spaceport, he nudged her awake.

"I'm connecting with the Branko traffic system in about five minutes." He pointed to the foldout platform, where he'd put the unopened mealpack and another water pouch. "That might be better than anything we can find at the spaceport." Branimir's only spaceport, owned by the planetary government, was infamous for outrageous prices and horrible food.

She triggered the mealpack's heater. "What about you?"

He shook his head. "Not now."

She snorted. "Still think mealpacks taste like cardboard, huh?"

He lifted his chin superciliously and affected a prissy tone. "Jumpers have no standards."

She tossed him a cheeky grin. "Civilian."

She unsealed the mealpack and ate all of it, even the beige lumps that purported to be spinach dumplings.

The traffic system connected to the flitter without complaint, meaning he'd successfully mimicked the planetary system's transfer sequence.

Another twenty minutes had them in the queue for one of the dozens of spaceport flitter stackers. They were old and slow, and looked like giant tractor treads, with lifts for humans to ride down to ground level. Branimir's miserly planetary government rarely upgraded anything unless it broke. As he took control of the flitter and landed it on the stacker's pad, Kerzanna carried their trash to the recycler, put the borrowed blanket back in its bin, and moved her bags up front.

"I'll put your coat in with the medical supplies."

"Thanks." He waited for the stacker forks to grab the flitter so he could make note of the stacker slot number. He'd paid for a ten-day rental, but he could ping the rental company with the flitter's location if it turned out they'd be gone longer.

He started to remove the wirejack from the console, then belatedly remembered he needed to remove all evidence that he'd been tinkering around with the flitter's control systems. That kind of sloppiness wasn't like him.

"Jess…" Her voice trailed off. She was kneeling right behind his seat, so he couldn't see her face.

"What?" He started tracing the redundant system logs, to make sure they weren't stealthily recording things he didn't want them remembering.

"Forgive me," she whispered, then pressed something cold and clammy to the exposed back of his neck.

He jerked in surprise as the overlays in his head fought viciously to take control and respond to the perceived threat. He twitched spasmodically as he fumbled with the seat web, even though Jess-the-medic told him not to bother, because two dormo patches at once were already swamping his synapses and sending him to twilight.

Her face appeared in his line of sight. Her expression was raw pain, regret, and determination as she palmed his cheek.

"You don't deserve to have your life go chaotic again because of me. Four years ago, you said separating would keep us alive." She caressed his rapidly numbing cheek with her thumb. "I didn't believe you then, but here we are, alive. You were right."

"Wasn't…" His fingers found the seat web release. "Not… safe…"

She gently pushed his flailing hands into his lap. "I'll be careful. I've learned a lot. You taught me well." She covered him with his jacket and tucked it under his chin.

His peripheral vision narrowed. She leaned forward to kiss him gently on the forehead. "You deserve peace."

Jess was reaping the whirlwind for which he himself had sown the seeds when he'd abandoned her four years ago instead of combining their strengths. Although he'd given up his beliefs long ago, he suspected that somewhere, the relentless, judgmental god of Fate, the one that ruled the childhood he'd barely survived, was savoring the delayed justice.

He lost his battle with shadowed fog and surrendered to oblivion.

CHAPTER 7

KERZANNA'S FIRST STOP in the spaceport was to use one of the ubiquitous net kiosks to fund an anonymous cashflow chip, then use it to buy an overpriced, disposable percomp. She sealed herself in a fresher stall and queried interstellar ship departures.

A lot of people must have wanted off Branimir that evening, because regular berths were booked solid. Wincing at the cost, she booked the last business-class slot on a passenger liner that left in three hours. She was tempted to look into ship staff positions, but it wasn't smart. While she could hide in the crowd of a big liner's manifest of tens of thousands, she'd stand out as a pilot. For the first time since moving to Branimir, she regretted leaving her alter ego, Malory Solis, behind, because Solis's bartender license would have been an effective cover.

She looked at herself critically in the mirror. Her bruised and swollen face looked like she'd been in a fight, meaning she'd be memorable. She could hide her Jumper tattoos with her hair if she kept it loose. She was glad she hadn't gotten around to going to the body parlor to have it cut. She wished she had some temporary color for her hair and eyes, and dermaskin to cover her tattoos, but quick-change cosmetics were another thing she'd left behind with Malory Solis.

Kerzanna wasn't presentable enough to wait in the passenger lounge area for an uplift shuttle, but she couldn't stay in the fresher for hours, either. The port police were attuned to undesirable persons loitering in the paying passenger facilities. They'd ask pointed questions and run an ID check, meaning she may as well announce her presence to the entire city. The safest place for her, although safe was a relative word, was in Branimir's dirty little secret, the slums below.

The spaceport was built on a geological anomaly, a series of caves and a massive cavern of a volcano that blew its top millions of years before humans discovered and terraformed the planet. The original settlement company promised to build it out as an interstellar ship dock, but never finished it. Smugglers and squatters moved in and illegally carved out more nooks and crannies, and the slums were born. She only knew about them because she'd lived in them the first two months she'd been on Branimir, until she could reestablish her real identity and get funds transferred into usable accounts.

Central Galactic Concordance foundation law said people were free to move to or from any member planet, but it didn't say the planets had to make it easy for people to take up residence. Branimir went out of its way to discourage immigration and prevent non-citizens from buying property or businesses. Flat rentals in Branko, the capital city that sprawled around the spaceport, were highly regulated and expensive. People without money, jobs, or friends on Branimir mostly ended up in the "transient layover district," as spaceport officials called it. Residents called it *untenboden*, or the downbelow. Port police called it the shithole.

She lifted her faded green top to look at the portable bone regenerator still adhered to her sternum. Jess had said six hours, so she didn't need it any longer, but it was easier to leave it than figure out how to make this model retract and not leave holes. Luckily, her breasts were compact, with smallish nipples, so they wouldn't be jiggling around, drawing the eye of people who liked such things. Even so, she fished her hooded orange jacket out of her luggage and pulled it on. The frayed hem of her top hung well below it, giving her a scruffy, indigent look. Her pants would have to go, because despite the rips and stains, the fabric was good, and they fit too perfectly. She swapped them out for her baggy blue workout pants, but kept her work boots on. They were good protection, and ten minutes walking through dusty subterranean hallways would make them look old and worn.

She pulled the hood up, pulled her hair forward to cover her skulljack and tattoos, and slouched like a woman who didn't want to be tall. When coupled with downcast eyes, occasional jerkiness, and mumbling that suggested she was chemmed, it was a surprisingly effective disguise. She'd learned it from watching Jess, especially when the paranoid part of him was in charge. He preferred corners and shadows, and somehow made people overlook the even taller, very handsome man.

No more thinking about Jess until she was done with her priority list and safely away, luring whoever was after her away from him. It had been too frelling hard to leave him in the flitter. Two dormo patches would keep him down for four hours or more, and then he could go home and be safe.

Her chest felt like someone had hollowed it out with a jagged rock.

She slung the straps of both her bag and her case over one shoulder and eased out of the fresher. She wandered seemingly aimlessly until she ended up by the north bank of storage lockers. In a lull between other customers, she stashed her equipment case quickly, paid for four weeks' rental, and keyed it to her biometric and a passcode. The case was distinctive, and she doubted she'd need to test mineral composition anytime soon. She shouldered her bag and slunk away, keeping to the edges of crowds and less convenient hallways, where the always-murmuring, full-wall advertisements that responded to human movement sometimes froze or blacked out.

Next on her list was a weapon, because she needed an equalizer. She was no longer a healthy woman with ramped reflexes and a hundred more years of life ahead of her, she was an ex-Jumper slowed by the waster's disease that was killing her, and she wanted every precious day she had left. She'd have preferred a hand beamer or a small railgun, but that kind of firepower was expensive and drew too much attention, and needlers were fussy and too indiscriminate to use in crowds. Her compromise choice was a shockstick, a strong, flexible baton that stunned, and was good for close-in physical combat. If she was lucky, the same stall was still selling them in Level S-4 by the giant northeast solar reflector tube.

The narrow-eyed gaze of a blue-uniformed port police officer told her that her cover of anonymity was fraying. She drifted to the nearest stairs. Lifts and escalators were for the paying customers.

Four flights down put her at the first of the transition floors between the commercial transport levels and the carved-out caves of the slums below. They also served as the unofficial marketplace for micro businesses and purveyors of less-than-legal goods and services.

She re-slung her bag across her so it protected her abdomen, then sat on a bench—the hulk of a burned-out gravcart—to disguise her height while she got the lay of the land. As usual, unaffiliated mercs hung around in clumps, nodding hopefully at well-dressed corporate types and staring daggers at the competition. The density of the makeshift stalls seemed thinner, and she didn't recognize anyone.

After scoping out the area, she got up from the bench, assumed her slouch and mumbled her way through the maze of stalls, listening for news and keeping a wary eye out for opportunists who mistook her for easy prey.

"...seventeen is my final offer..."

"…judge zeroed her accounts and sent her to the penal system for restitution…"

"…*dumkopf* got himself killed in the popper raid over nothing worth dying for, and now his kid's being sent off-planet to some…"

The slum dwellers called the port police "poppers," who in turn called the slum dwellers a colorful variety of less pleasant names, starting with "subbies," for "subhumans," a formerly common and still rude epithet for minders. It was no farkin' wonder some minders chose to hide their talents from their friends or the CPS Testing Centers. She sure as hell would have, if she'd had any, since the CPS would have immediately forced her out of the Jumper Corps and into the Minder Corps.

She narrowly avoided a running child and an angry adult pursuer, and ordered herself to quit daydreaming and find the shockstick vendor. Unfortunately, the stalls near the solar collector had been reduced to shards of debris, and the locals avoided the area like it was radioactive. It had probably been a casualty of the recent police raid.

The internal chrono built into her Jumper systems said she still had two hours before liftoff, and a sensation of being watched had her shuffling her feet faster to disappear into the crowd. She'd learned the hard way to pay attention to the subtle cues that her subconscious noticed while her mind was wandering. She slipped through the crowd toward the south stairway, but regretted it the closer she got. Burn marks and shiny beamer scars said the area had been a battleground within the last week. Eventually, scavengers would clean out the piles of slagged metal and glass, but until they did, only a narrow cleared path led to the stairs.

She turned away and caught furtive movement to her left. *Merc*, said her subconscious, *ducking behind a scorched pillar*. She snapped her fingers as if she'd remembered something and moved right, only to catch a glimpse of another merc, a wide-hipped woman in the same dull orange uniform tunic, turn toward a vendor stall.

Kerzanna spun quickly and headed briskly toward the stairs. The moment she rounded a ruined stall, she poured on the speed and bolted down the stairs three at a time, using the handrail to help control her descent. She pushed off the landing wall with her feet to manage the turn and pounded down the rest of the stairs.

More, taller piles of debris indicated the raid had been bigger than she thought. Spotty lighting over the deserted area made it hard to tell how to hide without boxing herself in. A noise from above sparked her into action.

She dropped her bag and covered it with a pile of ruined sheeting, then glided quietly behind a collapsed booth, where she slowly, quietly freed a fifty-centimeter length of stiff ceramic pipe from its connectors. She checked to make sure no reflections gave away her position, then twitched her left eye to access her cybernetic readouts and got ready to activate the hidden switch.

The CPS modified Jumper bodies with built-in systems to increase their speed and strength, among other things, but when Jumpers retired, the CPS deliberately ramped them down to normal human capabilities. Fortunately, there were ways around it, for a price. As soon as she'd escaped the Mabingion Purge, she'd found a shady body shop on a shadier outlier planet to give her a controllable ramp-up. It was a rough ride and didn't play well with her cybernetic hip and thigh, but it was better than dying.

She pushed back her hood so she could hear better and took three, long, calming breaths to quell her emotions. She needed the speed and clarity that relaxation brought, not the mind-numbing tension of adrenalin.

She got a glimpse of boots and brown uniform pants as the male and female mercs descended the stairs.

They were professional enough not to give themselves away by talking, but one of them wheezed and the other carried something that jangled softly, so she knew when they arrived at the bottom and that they were splitting up to search.

The jangling merc came her way. Instinct told her to move left.

A man's voice muttered in a language she didn't know. He was a few steps away from discovering her.

"*Down*," a telepathic voice said in her mind, and she went down on one knee even as she questioned why she did.

The merc's boot crunched on something that cracked loudly, drawing a startled oath from him.

"*Now.*" The mental word came with a clear overhead image of exactly where the merc was. Kerzanna rose up into his space and smashed the side of his head with her pipe. He cried out and stumbled back. She wasn't fast enough to avoid his flailing hand, the one that held a phaseknife. Burning pain exploded in her forearm as he fell to his hands and knees.

She snap-kicked his pointed chin with her hard boot, and he collapsed. She bent quickly to relieve him of the phaseknife, a holstered beamer, and a neurowhip, then moved to retreat behind the ruined booth, but the voice in her head had other ideas.

"*Right, behind the green.*" An image came with it.

Kerzanna stuffed the weapons in her pockets as she stepped carefully to the right, looking for the slagged green booth. Too bad the beamer had a biometric safety that prevented her from using it. She ignored the pain and tried to control the adrenalin threatening to shut down her higher thinking. Survive now, she told herself. Ask questions later.

A light flickered to her left. She oozed into the shadows and stilled, listening intently. A soft groan from somewhere behind her said the male merc was on his way to regaining consciousness.

A quiet wheeze and a footstep was all the warning she had that the female merc had found her, but it was enough. She turned into the woman's strike at her shoulder, blunting its power, and rammed her elbow into the woman's midsection. The flexin armor under the orange uniform absorbed some of the blow, but it still distracted her long enough for Kerzanna to engage her internal ramp-up. Power surged through her, along with the expected excruciating pain in her spine and right knee where the cybernetics interfaced with her flesh. It never got any easier.

The merc went for a fast controlling headlock, but Kerzanna ducked under, then up, using her superior height to put her head and neck out of reach. The merc dodged Kerzanna's flashy jab to her jaw but grunted when the pipe's strike on her unprotected thigh hit home. Kerzanna stepped back into the open area. If she could get to the stairs…

The merc launched a flurry of kicks to cover herself as she pulled a needler from her belt holster. Kerzanna snaked a quick shot with her pipe to force the woman to raise that arm to defend, then struck the woman's hand. The needler dropped.

The woman snarled as she connected a sweeping side kick to Kerzanna's right knee with a sickening crunch, sending Kerzanna stumbling sideways past a pile of scorched fabric. She fell onto the injured knee, and it froze. Damage warnings popped into her cybernetic display. So much for a quick escape up the stairs. The merc pulled a sonarc out of a cargo pocket and powered it.

Kerzanna reached for the serenity she desperately needed to ease the tension in her leg so it would work with the cybernetic interface instead of fighting it.

"You're zeroed. Stay down," said the merc in German-accented English, suggesting she was a Branimir native. "It's only a detain order unless you escalate." She shook her bruised hand and winced.

"Who wants me?" Kerzanna took a deep breath and let it out slowly, willing all her tension to drain. The ramp-up power crackled like prickly static electricity along her nerves. Her hands shook.

The merc shrugged. "Outlander." To the proudly insular people of Branimir, that could mean anything, from someone just off the shuttle to someone who'd been around for ten years. Without taking her eyes off Kerzanna, the merc opened a pouch pocket on her belt and pulled out a loop restraint. "Wrists." The merc's toss landed the loop near her foot.

"Make her come closer to you," said the voice in Kerzanna's head. She covered her surprise by dropping her head as she bent down for the loop.

The woman took one step closer. "Slow," she warned.

"More," said the voice. Kerzanna hated feeling vulnerable, but her knee was still frozen and the voice had helped her disable the other merc. She deliberately fumbled the loop so it popped out of her grasp and landed a few dozen centimeters away.

"Jumpers." The merc woman's tone held an abundance of exasperation as she stepped closer and pointed the sonarc's barrel at Kerzanna's ribs. The focused sonic wave would leave a massive bruise, and break bones if left on long enough. Kerzanna clenched her teeth against the pain she knew was coming.

Suddenly, the scorched pile of fabric moved, and a skeletal hand shot out and grabbed the merc's calf. The merc barely had time to look dismayed before she collapsed like someone had tripped her off-switch.

The hand belonged to a bone-thin black woman with shock-white hair and a face that looked older than the volcanic cavern. She struggled to her feet, apparently hampered by a stiff torso and stooped shoulders. Her elbows and ankles looked oversized because the rest of her was so thin. Her shapeless, lumpy dress was only slightly less stained and tattered than the ruined fabric at her filthy feet.

The woman motioned impatiently at Kerzanna. "Up. No time. We walk fast."

"Give me a few seconds." Kerzanna dropped her pipe to massage her synthskin thigh, just above the knee on the floor, but it was like squeezing a sandbag, with zero neurofeedback from her cybernetic processor.

The woman hobbled to where the male merc was stirring and put her filthy bare foot on his leg. "Quiet, noisy fish." He went inert.

The woman turned back to Kerzanna and tilted her head sharply sideways, like a crow. "Ramp down, *pa thidi.*" The accent to her broken English was odd and unidentifiable, and the last words sounded like Mandarin but weren't.

Kerzanna hesitated, then nodded. She didn't trust the woman, but she didn't distrust her, either. Questions could wait. She stiffened her back to force herself to stay upright during the wooziness and momentary tunnel vision that always happened when her system returned to normal operation. It didn't deplete her new, long-lasting cybernetic power source like it used to, but she'd need food and downtime soon. The knee stayed stubbornly frozen. She pivoted on her dead knee so she could reach a length of plasteel to use as a temporary crutch.

The old woman frowned, then hobbled close enough to touch Kerzanna's left knee. She was barely taller when standing than Kerzanna was on her knees. Soothing energy flooded through her. The frozen knee unlocked, and the red warning notice in her cybernetic controls blinked out. Kerzanna stood cautiously, but the knee operated perfectly. She could feel the neurofeedback from her cybernetic thigh again.

What in chaos was a top-level minder healer doing in the slums?

"Come." A crafty look crossed the woman's face. "I hire you." She pointed up to Kerzanna and down to herself. "Guard."

She stepped back and turned to hobble into the wreckage of the destroyed stalls. She slowed to stroke bony fingers down a bedraggled length of rainbow-colored bunting and pull a piece of it to caress her face, then looked up and whistled a distinctive pattern. A flying spy eye floated down into view. It explained the overhead images the woman had sent. Kerzanna didn't see the matching viewer, but the cloud of hair and shapeless clothing could be hiding anything. The woman snatched the camera out of the air like it was a pesky insect and started off again.

Kerzanna considered her options. Stay and find out who hired the mercs, assuming they knew, or hide and hope they didn't have merc friends. Or she could follow the woman who was obviously a telepath as well as a healer. Who had felled a healthy merc in two seconds. Who might be an escapee from a mind shop.

Who had saved her ass.

Curiosity would probably be the death of her one day, but she had a soft spot for fractured people. Besides, an old, crippled woman would be easy pickings in the slums. Maybe Kerzanna's presence would scare away an opportunist or two.

She crossed to the pile where she'd hidden her bag, marveling at how comfortable her knee felt. She stopped at the female merc's unconscious body long enough to take the needler, another beamer, the sonarc, and the restraint loop. She stuffed the collected armament into her bag, then slung it across her body. The beamers and the sonarc had biometric safeties that made them useless to her, but at least the downed mercs would have to go back to their armory for more before resuming the hunt. After a moment's consideration, she slid the neurowhip she'd taken from the other merc into her jacket pocket. She was out of practice using one, but it was better than nothing.

With her longer stride, she easily caught up with the short, gaunt woman who might be her new employer. Kerzanna pulled up her hood and stayed several steps behind, partly out of respect, and partly because the woman exuded a nose-numbing stench of sweat, urine, and decay. She muttered in what sounded like Mandarin but wasn't, and jerked her head and shoulders like she was dodging things only she could see.

Kerzanna tried to remember the layout of this level of the slum market, but she'd had little reason to visit it when she'd lived below. She had no need for illegal chems, freelance sex workers, or down-and-out mercs who couldn't hack regular gigs, and no interest in the numerous informal fighting events. All she could do was follow the birdlike woman through the tangle of aisles, alleys, and ancient storage containers that served as dusty stores and makeshift offices. She slouched and hunched her shoulders a little, so as not to look so much like a Jumper or offer an unspoken challenge to people looking to catch the eye of talent scouts for the fight promoters.

Kerzanna began to doubt her companion's need for a guard. Despite the woman's disability and obvious vulnerability, sellers and locals studiously looked away from her or stepped out of the way. Kerzanna ignored the covert inquisitive glances at her and watched for trouble.

It came in the form of a shark-faced man in a cheap flash suit and the entitled swagger of someone much richer and prettier. He'd been leaning indolently against a shop counter until his eyes lit on her charge. He glanced at Kerzanna, but obviously dismissed her as a non-player. At the right moment, he thrust himself directly into her companion's path and sneered. "Crazy Maisie."

Kerzanna kept her head down as she slid the neurowhip out of her pocket and let its barbed end fall to the side of her leg.

The woman he'd called Maisie started to step around him, but he blocked her again. "Ya'hudeh is looking for you. Your dues are *way* past due." He gave her a toothy grin as he opened his vest to show her a lethal-looking high-res beamer in a quick-release holster.

Maisie spat on his glowing red shoe, causing it to short out.

Kerzanna switched on the neurowhip and checked the thinning crowd for more trouble or the port police.

The man snarled and grabbed Maisie's thin, naked arm with a vice-like grip, spinning her sideways.

Astonishingly, Maisie gave him a wide grin. "Thank you."

The man went rigid and his eyes glazed over with naked terror. Maisie reached up with her free hand and patted his cheek like he was a child. "Dream, little bottom feeder, and remember."

His body and expression lost tension, but he stood, frozen. After about ten seconds, Maisie peeled his fingers off her upper arm, then posed him, forming his fingers in a rude gesture and inserting his middle finger up his nose. She reached into the man's vest to pull the beamer out and handed it to Kerzanna like it was a dead sewer rat.

Bemused, Kerzanna added it to the collection in her bag as she glanced around. The few people still in the area had found the ceiling or their feet suddenly fascinating.

Maisie started off again, and Kerzanna followed as she switched off the neurowhip and put it back in her pocket. The stasis box into which she'd shoved all her questions was bursting at the seams.

At last, they came to a wide set of doors that led into the interstellar ship dock section. Maisie waved a hand over a battered but sturdy biometric reader, and the doors opened without hesitation.

Kerzanna knew the area well and felt the tension in her shoulders ease once they stepped over the threshold. Maisie appeared to be headed to the dry dock, where the original architects had taken advantage of the humongous cavern with its open roof to create a cliff-dweller design. The builders had roughed in twenty levels and hundreds of berths, but only finished about a third of them with platforms, airlocks, and hallway access. They rode a clear freight lift down to the bottom level, the widest part of the cavern, mostly used for hangar-queen ships that would never fly again.

They crossed paths with a few technicians and ship crew, who avoided making eye contact with either her or Maisie. The farther from the lifts they got, the more debris and ash-gray volcanic dust lined the hallway, and the more sporadic the lighting. At a scarred, unmarked airlock that was intended for cargo handling bots instead of humans, Maisie glanced furtively both ways, then lifted the corner of a rotting crate to reveal a biometric reader. She placed her bare left foot on it, then entered a sequence into the holo display that appeared. The airlock door slid open slowly but silently.

The short woman ducked through and beckoned. "Come."

Kerzanna hesitated. For some reason, she trusted the birdlike woman, and it bothered her that she did. Her options, however, were few, and she needed a place to stay out of sight for a while.

She bent over at the waist to enter into what turned out to be the common room of an ancient interstellar ship. The airlock door closed behind her. Her host crossed to rummage in a dented crate.

Kerzanna had never been in a ship this old, but she'd seen history holos. Two hundred years had worn off the shiny details, leaving ghostly images of the luxurious appointments that had once graced the interior. Its current decor was trash treasures.

Maisie grabbed Kerzanna's wrist and put a small tech suppressor in her hand. "Hold." The tech suppressor blinked as the woman produced a modern tech scanner. She visibly relaxed after a few moments and turned the scanner off.

She took the suppressor back and looked up at Kerzanna, then pointed to a fold-down bench with gutted padding. "Sit. You're make my neck hurt." The smooth, unaccented Standard English was unexpected.

Kerzanna tested the bench with part of her weight before sitting on the edge. She pulled her bag around to her lap. Her arm burned like fire from the phaseknife wound, and the hole in her jacket sleeve was wet with blood. Her right knee was sore and swelling, but at least it was mobile.

The close quarters of the once-elegant ship's common room made the stench from her host unavoidable. Kerzanna tried to keep her breaths shallow as the woman dug through another crate of what looked like light-drive engine parts. She was back to muttering in her non-Mandarin.

Kerzanna's curiosity made her speak. "What should I call you?"

The woman straightened with a wince and turned to face Kerzanna. "Neirra. Are you squeamish?"

"Not usually."

"Good. I hate wearing this." Neirra pulled her dress off over her head and dropped it on the floor. She was naked underneath, except for battered and patched bracelet-style percomp and a nasty-looking bag stuck to her belly. She pulled it off and dropped it into a larger bag, which she sealed. Some of the stench in the room dissipated. The malodorous bag was certainly an effective incentive for people to keep their distance.

Neirra's starved, bony body looked older than her face, with flattened, drooping breasts and wrinkled, sagging skin. All of it was fixable, and for free if she went to a public body shop, because it was considered normal health maintenance for all citizens. Then she turned around and walked toward a rack with clothes, and Kerzanna swallowed hard.

All along Neirra's spine, starting just below the shoulder line and ending at her tailbone, a chunky, articulated silver armature rode the flesh and bone of her back. It was a cruel external version of a reinforced cybernetic spine, and where it plunged into skin, muscle, and bone, small pools of sluggish pus oozed from putrid and blackened tissue. Her entire back was puffy, dull red under the brown skin.

"What the frelling hell is that?" She didn't realize she'd it out loud until Neirra answered.

"My leash." She pulled on a loose, kimono-styled robe and turned to stare at Kerzanna speculatively.

Kerzanna shoved her horror aside with difficulty. Some minders she'd worked with back in Ridderth shared dark rumors of the methods the CPS used to tightly control top-level minder talents, but she hadn't believed them. It was wrong on so many levels. Whatever they'd done to Neirra prevented her from healing herself, or seeking conventional medical care, and it was killing her. It made waster's disease practically genteel by comparison.

Kerzanna drew breath to ask the first of her million questions, but Neirra held up a hand. "I'll answer three questions. You need healing."

Kerzanna shook her head. "Any medic can fix me with a burn patch and microjet flushes for the bruises. You should save your energy." It was probably taking most of Neirra's considerable healer talent to stay alive for another day. "Why are you helping me?"

Neirra smiled enigmatically. "You're one of my children."

"Really?" Kerzanna raised her eyebrows. "My parents will be relieved to hear it. They swear I was switched at birth."

Neirra snorted. "Kept the humor, I see."

Kerzanna started to ask if they'd met before, because Neirra would be impossible to forget, except that Kerzanna's memory had recently proved to be untrustworthy. "I'll ask again: Why are you helping me?"

Neirra closed her eyes for a long moment. Kerzanna couldn't tell if she was thinking or sleeping. Finally she opened her eyes. "I'm righting a wrong."

Neirra was being deliberately cagey, and Kerzanna's interrogation skills lacked finesse. She tried another tack. "How did you happen to be in the right place at the right time today?"

"All the local wolves forget about ears and eyes." Neirra tapped a bony finger above her heart, then pointed at Kerzanna. "I always know where my children are, when they're in range."

Kerzanna barely suppressed rolling her eyes at the non-answer. Neirra might be more coherent than she'd been before, but she still had one foot in crazy town.

Neirra shook her head. "You're asking the wrong questions."

"So I gather." Kerzanna's internal chrono said she still had an hour before she had to be in the passenger area, but she'd rather take her chances somewhere else. Now that she was in the dock area, she should be able to slip into the crowds. She got to her feet, ignoring everything that hurt. "Thank you for your hospitality, but I have a shuttle to catch."

Neirra pursed her lips and narrowed her eyes. "Kept the impatience, too." She waved casually.

Kerzanna's body sat back down without her having anything to say about it. Icy claustrophobia threatened to overwhelm her, but she clung to a thread of reason. Survival first. She knew from bitter experience that she had no defense against a powerful telepath, other than clearing her mind and pretending that whatever happened to her body wasn't her. She took a breath and exhaled slowly.

"I'm sorry to have resurrected that memory," said Neirra softly. "I've lost my subtlety." She stepped closer and put her surprisingly hot fingers on Kersanna's neck. "The question you should have asked is, 'will you heal my waster's disease?'"

Neirra put her other hand on Kerzanna's shoulder. "And the answer is, 'yes.'"

And the price? Kerzanna asked in her mind, knowing Neirra would hear it. Nothing was ever free. Curiosity was her besetting sin, and was about to get her killed.

The answer was a long time coming, and held a complex mix of rage, regret, and despair. *Carry a message for me to Tuzan the Janitor in*

Ridderth.

Hire a courier, Kerzanna thought snappishly. Goading her attacker was stupid, but it was the only weapon left to her. She called up her dream memory of Jess and told him he'd been right all along, and said goodbye.

I can't. You are *the message.*

And between one moment and the next, the world went black.

CHAPTER 8

JESS-THE-MAN chose to watch the crowds of passengers from the shadow of a pillar, partly to stop Jess-the-bomber from trying to take over and make him, and partly because he appreciated the stability of the pillar. He still reeled from the double dose of dormo and the improvised counter-agents he'd administered to himself once he'd awakened. Luckily, Kerzanna hadn't known that dormo and similar chems didn't work on him well or for long, or she'd have chosen a different method. The stims he'd bought from one of the spaceport's several chems and alterants shops needed a little longer to kick in.

He glanced at his percomp again, wanting to read the strange message one more time, though it never changed.

> Reunion of hai pai pa sunsia moved to gate CL1617-D46R. Hurry or you will miss our sadiq qadim. Purple yesterday, blue today, opal tomorrow. P.S. Don't let the bright blues or dark oranges bring you down.

His percomp said *hai pai pa sunsia* was "lost little fish" in Lao, one of the dying relic languages, and he knew the Arabic *sadiq qadim* meant "old friend," which made the message even more nonsensical. The spaceport passenger kiosk didn't recognize the gate ID. The message ostensibly originated from a prepaid percomp from within the spaceport, but had been sent to his local ping ref, which few people knew. The breezy tone and language mix was so unlike Kerzanna that he'd immediately discounted it as coming from her, but now he had second thoughts. It might be code, or her way to warn him of a trap. Something in the message struck a deep chord in his mind, reminiscent of a bleedover remnant, but more like he'd forgotten to do something, or *déjà vu*. Unsurprisingly, Jess-the-bomber didn't like it.

His head throbbed. He'd screwed things up badly with Kerzanna, or she wouldn't have felt the need to drug him to get away. Hard not to think of it as rejection, but her parting words made it clear she thought she was protecting him. He understood that, since it had motivated him from the moment he'd suspected she was in danger, and made him drag his sorry self into the spaceport instead of succumbing to sleep in the rented flitter. He pulled the cargo bag's strap to a more comfortable place on his shoulder.

"Are you all right?" An average height, muscular woman wearing a blue port police uniform stood in front of him. Her look was half concern, half suspicion. Her hand hovered ever-so-casually near her holstered stunner.

"*Ja*, just a headache," he said with a touch of a German accent, as if he'd been born and raised on Branimir. He gave her a hopeful look. "I'm lost, actually. I'm looking for gate C1415-D46." He assumed the slightly bewildered expression of a yokel who'd never been in a spaceport.

She took in his rural clothing at a glance. "You're in the wrong terminal. You need to go to the cargo dome." She gave him directions and accepted his thanks with courtesy, but watched him closely as he headed toward the wide blue archway that would take him to the commercial shipping lobby.

Keeping with the farmer-in-the-big-city guise, he went to one of the spaceport's kiosks and called up a map. He had no idea the spaceport was so large and complex, including a surprising number of numbered subterranean levels cryptically marked "TLD" under the passenger wing. He figured out the commercial gate numbering system without having to leave a record of his interest in the specific ID from the message. It wasn't lost on him that the port police wore bright blue uniforms.

To give the stims more time to kick in, he took several flights of stairs down, then briefly locked himself in a fresher to make a half-assed defensive weapon by using a tiny medical laser from his bag to amp up the all-purpose wirekey he'd bought from a luggage shop. He didn't want any real weapons purchases showing up on his official records, and didn't have time to wake up one of his private, dormant alternate identities and transfer funds to it.

He rode a lift down to the bottom level. His anxiety level ratcheted up slowly as he neared his destination. The port locks looked increasingly dark and disused, like their doors hadn't opened in years. He cross-slung his bag and let it rest across his back, freeing his hands and arms. He hadn't seen or heard anyone in the last five minutes. The plascrete floor seemed clean enough, probably because cleaning bots kept it that way, but they apparently ignored the dusty stacks of debris along the rough-carved walls. He stopped at a port lock and made a show of referring to his percomp while he eyed his target. The final "R" designation in the gate ID apparently meant it was for automated carts, because humans would have to crawl to use it. The lighting was too conveniently dim in that part of the corridor. Just as he turned to leave what was obviously a trap, the wide, low doorway opened almost silently, and a tiny, white-haired black woman in a faded robe stepped into the corridor.

"Where you go?" She cocked her head sideways and squinted at him. "No *pa thum fuwai*, not party." She made herding motions toward the open door. "Quick, quick!"

Jess backed up, suppressing Jess-the-bomber's desire to take emergency action. "Sorry, wrong gate." He pivoted fast and took two steps away before he heard another voice.

"Jess, please stay."

He slowed to a stop and turned. Next to the woman stood Kerzanna, her expression neutral, her body language relaxed.

Her plea reverberated in his mind, dredging up echoes of their last day together. He ignored them as he tried to imagine scenarios that fit the facts, but came up empty. His eyes caught on a new burn mark on the sleeve of Kerzanna's jacket. "Who hurt you?"

"Mercs in orange with a detain order." She tilted her head minutely toward the tiny, dark-skinned woman beside her. "She fixed me." Kerzanna had never lied to him.

"Jabber stop now," hissed the woman, her accent reminding him of his neighbor. She pointed to the open doorway. "Inside no little eyes, little ears."

It made no sense, but Jess trusted the woman. Even Jess-the-bomber wanted to trust her, though he was unhappy about it. He nodded once and met Kerzanna's gaze. "After you."

A corner of her mouth twitched in what may have been a smile. She ducked low and disappeared through the doorway. Jess approached cautiously, skirting around a precarious pile of trash, then crouched and crab-walked into the hold of an old interstellar ship. In the background of his mind, Jess-the-engineer stirred, telling Jess the ship had once been a pleasure yacht but obviously converted to a blockade-runner around the last days of the Central League, some two hundred years ago. Jess-the-engineer wanted a look at the engines, as usual.

The white-haired woman ducked in, palming a biometric plate to close the door behind her. She crossed to the far side of what was once the common room to increase the light levels, then turned to face him with a tech scanner in her hand. She raised an eyebrow. "Nice trick with the wirekey." Her voice sounded somehow familiar, and she'd lost her Thai accent. She turned the scanner off. "I see you kept the height and the pretty mahogany skin. I told Dixon you would."

Apparently, Jess had reached his limit on being surprised, because recognition of who she was didn't stun him as much as he'd have thought. "Neirra Varemba." Dixon Davidro's once-favorite independent contractor.

Now that he was seeing her in good light, he forgave himself for not recognizing her sooner. Either she'd had body mods to make her look almost as old as the ship, or she'd contracted an unknown, premature aging disease that even her extraordinary healing talent couldn't fix. He waved a hand to indicate the cluttered space. "Not exactly Davidro's style."

She smiled lopsidedly. "Kind of the point." Her unaccented Standard English sounded like he remembered.

"Is he on Branimir?"

"Not any more, but one of his contractors still is." Neirra twitched a shoulder. "He moved the circus to Tajidin Farkani."

"He let you stay here? Alone?" Jess remembered that Davidro had zealously kept his most valuable "pets," as he insultingly called them, close at all times.

"Not alone, exactly." She opened her robe and turned her back to him. The intricate, articulated metal appliance that attached to her back looked like a parasite that ate spinal fluid. Even Jess-the-medic had never seen one of the CPS biometal leashes, though he recognized it and knew it was designed to prevent her from healing herself. She was losing the battle with the ever-evolving poison it injected to keep her talent busy. She pulled her robe back up and turned around again. "I'd love to have a reunion over tea, but we have more important things to discuss."

The word triggered an idea. "You sent the message, didn't you?"

Kerzanna spoke for the first time. "Message?"

He glanced at her, but kept his focus on Neirra. "She lured me here with a nonsensical message, something about a reunion of lost fish and old friends, and avoiding the port police."

Neirra interrupted. "Yes, yes, you have a lot to talk about, but later." She pointed to Kerzanna. "She needs to get to Ridderth, and you need to go with her."

"Not part of the deal," said Kerzanna, crossing her arms. "He can't trust me, and I'm not getting him killed again."

"You didn't get me killed," he said testily.

Neirra put her hands on her hips. "Both of you, sit! You make my neck hurt." She glared when neither he nor Kerzanna complied. "Don't make me make you."

Kerzanna put her hands up in surrender and perched on a fold-down bench. Jess sat on the edge of a dented packing crate, belatedly remembering Neirra was also a high-level telepath. Just the kind of skills the CPS Minder Corps loved.

"Kerzanna's mind has a message packet that must get to Tuzan the Janitor in Ridderth." She stabbed a finger toward him. "I'm giving you the key so you'll fucking stay together this time." Her body jolted, like she'd been shocked, and she shouted a vicious curse in Arabic. Her eyes fluttered closed for a long moment, then snapped open. She stalked over to Jess to stand in front of him. "Out of time." She raised a hand but didn't touch him.

She spoke to him in his mind. *Do this, and you'll shatter Dixon Davidro permanently, like he deserves.*

Jess glanced at her hand and met her eyes. In that long moment, he understood they both deserved justice, and she was trusting him to get it for her. "Yes."

Her hand gripped his shoulder. In his mind, a wave of calm washed over him, followed by a sensation that felt like when he visualized hypercubes of data, just before cracking them. He panicked when he couldn't feel any trace of the bleedovers in his mind, but they returned when the calming wave receded. He wasn't always fond of the bleedovers, but he'd be less than whole without them.

She's important. What she's carrying is important. Talk to her. Don't lose her. Steely emphasis accompanied Neirra's thoughts.

Jess nodded. *I won't.*

Neirra withdrew from his mind as she marched over to Kerzanna. "You owe him for four years ago as much as he owes you." She gently pushed a stray lock of Kerzanna's hair back almost tenderly, and Kerzanna let her do it. "The headache will go away after you sleep." She leaned in and whispered something that made Kerzanna glance at Jess and snort with amusement.

Neirra backed away, then reached over to a table and picked up a portable bone regenerator. "This is pretty. I'll trade you a shockstick for it."

Kerzanna looked to Jess, asking tacit permission. He realized it was the unit he'd applied to Kerzanna's injured sternum that morning. It seemed a lot longer than six hours ago. "Sure."

Neirra dug in one of the crates and quickly unearthed a short, fat cylinder, which she tossed to Kerzanna.

As Neirra started to turn, her body jolted again. "You have to go now."

The urgency in her tone made Jess stand up at once. He visualized the map he'd seen. "Is the only way out through the hall?" He tilted his head toward the ship's portal door and the corridor.

"Yes, until you get to the intersection. Left to the air, right to a dead end, straight to trouble."

"Air, meaning the cavern?" asked Kerzanna as she grabbed her bag from the bench.

"Yes, yes, airspace." Neirra crossed to the portal door and palmed it open. "Go, go, go, or be caught by the *pa hak*."

"Will you be all right?" asked Jess.

"Crazy Maisie. Orange tasty," she said in her exaggerated sing-song accent as she pushed him toward Kerzanna, who was already ducking under the doorway. "Dixon is bad with details and thinks you're a zero-witted flatliner. Use your friends." She tapped her temple.

Jess wanted to stay, but logic and the bleedovers all screamed at him to follow Kerzanna and avoid being contained in a no-exit corridor. He crouched and ducked under the low portal.

The portal door closed quietly behind him as he stood and broke into a trot to catch up to Kerzanna. He matched her graceful, distance-eating stride.

"Airspace has ship gantries and maintenance ladders, but it's windy," she said, adjusting the straps on her bag to make a backpack as they walked. "I don't know what has Neirra spooked, but she knows the spaceport and the slums like you know data systems." She slid her arms into the straps and pulled the last two straps around her waist.

"Slums?"

She glanced at him. "Later. What does your Nordic pal say—hide in the dead end, or freeze our asses off outside?"

He blinked with the realization she meant Jess-the-bomber, who of course had an opinion. "Airspace has options. Dead end doesn't."

She nodded. "Good, we agree. Are you okay to go faster?"

"Yes." It seemed that for now, she'd decided not to leave him again, but since he didn't know why she'd left the first time, he couldn't count on it holding.

They sped up to a fast trot and turned left. It looked no different from the main hallway, except it had no portal doors on the walls, and dust seemed to hang in the air. A quick glance behind showed faintly visible footsteps where they'd been. Couldn't be helped.

The corridor ended at doublewide doors that had once been clear permaglass, but had been etched by visible swirls of dust. Kerzanna ignored the biometric reader and instead punched a long sequence into the keypad. At Jess's questioning look, she tapped her temple. "Gift from Neirra. I have a map, too."

She punched the bright blue bar, and the glass doors rose. A cloud of dust blew in and buffeted their pant legs. "We're at the bottom level, but still about twenty meters from the bottom of the cavern. It's a big oval. Left takes us back toward Neirra's ship, right takes us toward the repair shops. Commercial transport hangars start about six levels up, and passenger terminals are at the top."

"We can't blend in with passengers," said Jess.

"You mean *I* can't." She sealed her jacket and frowned at that burned and stained sleeve. "You could pass for a frontier homesteader. I look like a chemmer coming down from a three-day glide." She stepped out into the wind. "The lower repair levels are more storage than shop. Maybe we can find a safe place to figure out how the hell we're going to get off this planet, since according to my chrono, my paid ride just left orbit."

CHAPTER 9

VAHAN CHECKED HER appearance one more time before keying the sequence to make the connection to the highly secure, highly expensive real-time conference with Dixon Davidro on Tajidin Farkani. Her unadorned black and red suit complemented her short black hair and walnut-brown skin. Serious, calm, and professional delivery of bad news usually blunted the blame game and made it easier to focus on solutions.

"You're looking *formidable, Femme G.*" The holo image of Davidro showed him in a swirl-patterned, gauzy caftan, lounging in what looked like the plush adaptive chair of a luxury spa. Renner had undoubtedly ensured that the endpoint connection was encrypted, but he couldn't enforce endpoint privacy if Davidro didn't cooperate.

"Thank you, Mr. Davidro." She ignored his empty flattery and attempt to irritate or ingratiate her with yet another nickname in badly pronounced French. The man had absolute zero abilities with languages beyond Standard English and barely adequate Mandarin. "I have two pieces of bad news."

"Nobody calls interstellar real-time with good news," he said dryly. "Go."

"First, Subcaptain Nevarr is in the wind. It seems *someone* ordered a backup plan involving explosives on a flitter, a purchase she neglected to mention when you caught her." *Someone* being Davidro's special protégé, Senga Si'in Lai. Whatever secret procedures the CPS had done to the woman as part of the ultra-secret Charisma project gave her a magnetic personality, made her highly sexual, and gave her an uncanny understanding of political dynamics. However, she was also fracturing like a slow-motion maglev train wreck, and becoming increasingly jealous and vengeful over nonsensical things. The Branko Regional Council's transgression had been withdrawing their endorsement of Si'in Lai's candidacy for regional governor. Si'in Lai's warped response had been to arrange the murders of everyone on the council. Nevarr apparently got special attention because she'd cast the deciding vote.

Vahan laced her fingers. "I paid the kill fee on the other two contracts, and I delayed Nevarr so she missed the mine accident, but I didn't find out about the flitter sabotage until too late. The only reason she survived was because instead of being over the water, she crash-landed in a small farm town, hundreds of kilometers off her known itinerary. She evidently had help from a local farm owner, who I believe is a retired CPS quartermaster named Jessperin Orowitz. He's the only one in the area I can't account for. She was injured, but she didn't go to the medical center, she went from the local town clinic straight to the spaceport and vanished."

Davidro, who'd been looking merely irritated, frowned deeper and set his luminescent drink out of view. "Are you sure about Orowitz's involvement?"

Vahan shrugged. "As sure as I can be, without personal contact. Nevarr is smart enough to know a termination attempt when she survives one. I'm guessing here, because the locals won't talk to strangers and Branimir's records are sparse, but I think Nevarr somehow convinced Orowitz to rent a flitter and take her to the spaceport. Nevarr transferred business funds to a cashflow chip, bought a last-minute slot on an interstellar liner, but didn't show, probably as a false trail. She could still be on Branimir, but smart money says she's off-planet. Maybe he is, too. For some reason, I can't get a line on his finances."

Davidro looked to his left and spoke louder. "Mr. Renner, get Georgie and Lamis in here." He leaned forward to rest an elbow on his knee and put two fingers to his chin in thought. "I wonder what drew Orowitz out of his shell."

"Sir?" asked Vahan.

"He was one of my Kams for a few years, right before he retired. He's a loner. I'd completely forgotten he was on Branimir until Neirra decided she wanted to retire there, of all places, and Lamis reminded me." His tone said he couldn't imagine why anyone would want to live on Branimir, and Vahan had to agree.

Vahan tilted her head. "Orowitz was in the Kameleon Corps? Does that make him dangerous?" Davidro mentioned the Corps occasionally, but had been uncharacteristically cagey about details. Usually the man was happy to over-share, or at least boast.

"Dangerous? More like zero-witted. The best Kam candidates are personality flatliners, and he was no exception. Kams are well paid, and he got a full-tour retirement bonus, too. He could've bought a fully furnished estate anywhere, but he holed up on a tiny farm on one of the most boring planets in the galaxy."

Vahan made a mental note to find out more about Kameleons. Maybe retired, wealthy veterans needed personal security managers.

A sound on Davidro's end had him looking up and to his right. "Lamis, do I have an official record of anyone named Kerzanna Nevarr?"

Lamis bel Doro, Davidro's only official CPS employee, was a minder of the general filer variety, with an eidetic memory for everything. She had a love-hate relationship with all the independent contractors, but especially with Georgie, Davidro's brilliant but flawed, childlike forecaster, mostly because bel Doro got stuck with babysitting him most of the time. No one loved Renner, Davidro's angry enforcer.

After a long moment, bel Doro's voice said, *"A 'Nevarr, K' is on the initial Ridderth police action casualty list dated GDAT 3238.082. A list dated 3238.085 superseded it, and the name isn't on it."*

Davidro rolled his eyes. "As I recall, half the city was on that first list. What about our records? Any connection between her and Jessperin Orowitz? Friends? Known sex partners?"

"Orowitz's record lists none of either." Davidro relied on bel Doro for detailed information because details bored him and his official records were deliberately vague and full of holes. He kept personal journals, too, but rarely referred to them in Vahan's presence. She sometimes wondered how he ensured bel Doro's loyalty, but wasn't sure she wanted to know.

Davidro's fingers drummed along the fashionable glowing studs highlighting his cheekbone. "I suppose it's possible they met in Ridderth, but it's more likely they met on Branimir." He leaned forward and focused on Vahan again. "Send me whatever local records you can extract on Orowitz and Nevarr, and I'll ask sweet Georgie Pie to work his magic on them both." He said the last with a loving smile and a blown kiss directed off-camera. Georgie, the often-drugged savant forecaster who was an idiot in everything else, fell for it every time.

Vahan cleared her throat. "I have an idea on how to complete the Nevarr assignment if I act fast, but it will cost extra to stay anonymous, and Orowitz might be a casualty if he's with her."

He pursed his lips and laced his fingers. "I'll make the budget work. Do it."

Vahan hid her disdain that he cared more about money than his former special ops employee. No wonder Davidro had to make his contractors act like they were his friends; it was the only way he'd have any.

"What's the other bad news?"

Vahan drew a deep breath. "Neirra Varemba is dead."

Davidro gasped in shock. "How?"

"After Nevarr vanished at the spaceport, I figured I may as well check on Varemba again since I was there. I took one of the hired mercs with me, in case we spotted Nevarr along the way. Varemba took one look at the uniform and started screaming about an 'orange fish of death.' I'd have just left her alone to sleep off the bad chems, but she pulled a high-res beamer out of one of her crates of crap and pointed it at the merc. Before I could get to her, the merc hit her with a neurowhip. We didn't know her back had that… appliance." Davidro didn't seem surprised, meaning he'd known about it. Probably installed it himself. Vahan's mouth went dry. "Made her jitter like she'd been struck by lightning. Set the back of her dress on fire, and nearly took the ship interior down, too, until air filters and suppressor foam kicked in."

The horrific image haunted her thoughts, making the rest of her memory of what had happened seem vague by comparison. She suppressed a shudder and continued. "The merc and I, uhm, agreed that the age of her ship and the clutter she collected caused an unfortunate accident, and chose not to notify the authorities, rather than be detained for questioning."

"My beautiful, sweet Neirra." Unexpectedly, tears welled in Davidro's eyes. "She was the best pet I ever had. She deserved better." One tear fell. "A peaceful death, surrounded by the people who cared for her."

Most of Davidro's emotional displays seemed calculated, but this looked genuine. Her momentary sympathy was tempered by the suspicion that he meant he should have quietly killed Varemba instead of letting her retire. "I could have her remains made into a memory diamond, if you'd like." She knew of a couple of no-questions-asked cremation services, but she'd have to ship Varemba's body to them.

He wiped at his tear with the back of his hand. "It's a kind thought." He sighed a little raggedly. "But her cover story there was as a fractured loner, and making family-style arrangements for her would draw too much attention." He shook his head. "We'll have to be satisfied with the fiery destruction of that junker ship of hers." He gave her a sharp look. "See to it yourself. I don't want any more mercs involved."

Vahan nodded. "Of course, sir." She clamped her jaw to stop herself from testily reminding him she was a professional. If she aggravated him, he might make her stay on the stinking sinkhole of Branimir even longer. Time to focus on the positive.

"So, here's my idea for handling Nevarr…"

CHAPTER 10

* Interstellar: "Faraón Azul" Ship Day 03 * GDAT: 3242.006 *

KERZANNA SMOOTHED THE front of the burgundy and silver uniform jacket over her stomach and hips and pulled the silver shiplink on the undertunic's collar into position. Even though the ship's fifty-one passengers would never see her and the commercial shipping company knew she was a temporary fill-in, the ship captain's standing orders required all crew, regardless of position or status, to wear the company uniform. The ship's part-time logistics officer grumbled about having to autotailor hers because the set sizes he had in supply wouldn't fit, but she gathered he enjoyed complaining. She was pleased with the crown of variegated pale braids she'd fashioned for herself with some hastily added hair extenders. They kept her hair out of her way while hiding her skulljack nicely, and the opaque permaderm coating on her skin hid her Jumper tattoos. She straightened the nametag that proclaimed her to be Stellar Navigator Laraunte Kane.

She stepped out of the cramped fresher and into the cramped quarters with the foldaway everything. She closed her bag and stowed it, then sent a quick message to "Cadroy"—Jess—that the room was all his.

In the nav pod, situated in the upper center of the ship, she listened to the shift turnover briefing from Ritanjali Bhatta, a Commercial Class 3 navigator and the only other navigator on the ship, not counting the pilots. So far, the trip had been routine, but she only had two previous shifts to judge by.

"The captain wants to make up some of the wait-time we lost on Branimir by making ultra-short packet drops from here on out," said Bhatta, her English softly accented by her primary language of Hindi. "I preset the next plot and left it in the queue."

"Thanks," Kerzanna said, trying to mean it. Class 1 navigators should be grateful when better trained and more experienced navigators handled challenging tasks, even though it left the Class 1 navigator with nothing to do for most of her upcoming shift.

Bhatta stood and stretched. She was a round-faced, brown-skinned woman with narrow shoulders, dark wavy hair, and sparkling eyes. "I hope they've found us another navigator on Win-Prox. These long shifts are giving me a fat ass."

Kerzanna smiled sympathetically as she sat and manually adjusted the seat for her longer legs. As a Jumper, she'd worked a lot longer shifts, but they'd been a lot less dull, and rarely involved sitting. Her waster's disease made it much easier to sit still for long periods, but she paid a price in all around stiffness later if she didn't stretch and take a brisk walk during each of the allowed hourly breaks, and visit the utilitarian crew gym daily.

Bhatta removed the wire from her skulljack and put it in a drawer that had several boxes of them, then sealed it with her biometric. For safety and security, pilot/nav wires were segregated from general ship jackwires. Instead of leaving, Bhatta sidled closer and spoke quietly. "Maybe it's none of my business, but Cadroy spent your last sleep shift glued to his percomp and the public shipcomps. He was pretty intense about it."

Kerzanna rolled her eyes. "Probably working on a new algo to beat the house. This year, he thinks he's a gambler." She heaved an aggrieved sigh. "If my idiot fourth cousin spent half as much time and energy on a real job, he could buy his own casino and try out all the algorithms he could dream up."

Bhatta laughed. "Sounds like my uncle. Ran from work, but never ran into an avoid-work scheme he wouldn't try." She touched the side of her head in a mock Space Div salute. "See you in twelve."

Kerzanna was glad she and Jess had taken the time to come up with a layered story for their presence on the ship. Little details like that made it work.

She formally checked in with Malámselah, the third-shift pilot on duty. He was a kindly older man with a potbelly, an infectious laugh, and a slight Arabic accent to his English. She liked him better than the second-shift pilot Liao, a supercilious, dark-skinned woman who liked to pretend she owned the nav pod unless the captain was present. Kerzanna only knew first-shift pilot Kreutz as a name and holo image on the crew roster.

The *Faraón Azul,* a mid-sized, sphere-shaped passenger-freighter ship, ordinarily operated with a crew of twenty, but they'd lost two navigators, an engine tech, and two ship stewards on the last two planetary space station stops, for unrelated reasons. This segment of the scheduled run called for the ship's modular interior to be configured for more cargo than passengers, but that would change once they hit the Mabingion Space Station. She felt mildly guilty that she and Jess would be disappearing there, meaning the shipping company would be needing yet another new navigator.

Transport Estrellita company policy said she had to mostly stay in her seat in the nav pod, even though commercial navigators had few duties while the ship was in interstellar transit other than being another pair of eyes on transit space performance and logs. To keep busy, she ran a status check on all the ship's systems she had access to and familiarized herself with the star charts for the upcoming packet drop that would happen toward the end of her shift. Ships in transit couldn't send or receive communications, so they regularly dropped into real-time space at one of the millions of comm-and-position-reference buoys deployed throughout the explored galaxy to send and receive communications packets. If someone ever developed an interstellar comm system that worked from ship to ship in transit, or ship in transit to realspace, they could buy their own solar system with the first month's profits.

Keeping herself occupied with the navcomp was also good cover for exchanging messages with Jess, a.k.a. Cadroy Joffalk, her disgraced, flatline broke distant cousin who was shift-sharing her crew quarters on the trip back to their family's home planet of Osapan. Back on Branimir, he'd created cover identities for them on the fly, using only his percomp and a hijacked hypercube in a ship repair company's unattended office. He'd added a basic Class 1 commercial nav cert to her "Laraunte Kane" ID when she'd found a crew opening on a ship that had Mabingion on its itinerary. Luckily, the *Faraón* had been stuck at Branimir's space station until they could find a second navigator, so they'd rushed through the background and credential checks, and sweetened the deal with the "family rides free" benefit. They hadn't even run her or Jess through the security scanners, saving her from explaining away her cybernetic femur and hip. Civilians got vat-grown cloned replacements, not biometal.

Once on board, Jess had unsurprisingly cracked the *Faraón's* main shipcomp within an hour, and soon thereafter, owned every other onboard comp, code, and data hypercube. Once he controlled the ship's communication systems, he sent her instructions on how to use the stolen, wiped, and customized percomp he'd given her to send private messages to him that wouldn't be recorded or traceable.

More surprising was Jess's ability to convince the crew he was a sociable, mercurial gambler with a colorful past and the attention span of a hummingbird. He was already on a first-name basis with everyone, even the grumpy logistics officer, and his memorable antics gave the crew something to gossip about and drew attention away from her. Once she'd figured out what he was doing, she made every effort to be as unremarkable as possible.

When "Cadroy" pinged a quick message to "Laraunte" that he was going to use the room, she waited ten minutes, then sent Jess a private message.

> K: Captain ordered fast packet drops from here on out. Navigator Bhatta says you've been intensely busy. What are you working on?

So she'd look legitimately occupied, she called up a chart for the star system that had Winnogralix Proxima, their next planetary port of call, where they'd take on more cargo at its space station.

> J: Packets of code seeds to strengthen our IDs and collect data. I'll explain sometime. Made more IDs, just in case. They'll go out at each stop. What does Bhatta think I'm doing?
>
> K: I told her I suspected another new gambling system.
>
> J: Good. Hoping for query results on the janitor. Not holding my breath.

All they had from Neirra Varemba was the name "Tuzan the Janitor." Old, rotten Ridderth had twenty million residents, and that didn't count the military bases or the transient body-shop customers. People who wanted to get lost could usually stay that way. Jess's long-distance data queries to Mabingion's planetary net were a shot in the dark.

He knew about her skirmish with the mercs and how she'd met Neirra. When Kerzanna had awakened after whatever the healer had done to her, Neirra had again apologized for her methods, repeated the strongly worded request to find Tuzan, and told her the reunion would start soon. Neirra had insisted that Kerzanna wait for Jess, even if it meant giving up the expensive passenger liner berth. Neirra had also claimed Jess was another of her "children," whatever that meant.

Although Neirra had healed Kerzanna's other injuries, and maybe even repaired the interface between her "aftermarket" ramp-up and her cybernetic systems, it was highly unlikely that Neirra healed the waster's disease. The CPS hadn't yet solved the problem with platoons of minder healers and seventy years of research. On the other hand, even under the constant assault of the horrifically cruel leash on her back, Neirra had formidable talents. Kerzanna had been treated by top Jumper Corps healers during her years of service, and Neirra's deft skills rivaled the best of them.

J: Can I ask a question?

It was his way of bringing up a delicate issue. They'd had no time to talk about personal matters in the mad scramble to get off Branimir under the noses of the vigilant and irritated orange-uniformed mercs, and zero face-to-face privacy since boarding the *Faraón*, since they supposedly disliked one another. She appreciated the effort he was making to communicate, so if he found it easier to handle using only words through a percomp, she'd take it. If she was honest, it was easier for her, too. She was far too aware of him as the tall, sexy, handsome man she'd once loved, and her hormones and remembered feelings got in the way of rational thinking. The powerful intimacy of sex would make it too easy to fall back into old, bad patterns.

She glanced casually around the nav pod. Captain Tanniffer was out in the passenger dining hall for dinner, and Chief Drive Engineer Yarsulic rarely ventured out of the engine pod if he could help it, so that left only the pilot in the nav pod. Malámselah's distracted expression said he was jacked into multiple ship systems, as usual. She didn't blame him. It was more interesting than playing "count the stars," and much more ethical than using the ship's emergency comm system as a private entertainment channel, as some pilots did. Speaking for herself, she'd rather tag the precise coordinates of an entire nebula's worth of the space objects than listen to people complain about politics, the food, or each other. And she'd much rather have sex with someone than listen to others having all the fun.

K: Sure, go ahead.

J: How do you feel?

She knew he meant her waster's disease, not the massive headache she'd still had when boarding. Jess was more susceptible to the hope that Neirra's extraordinary claim was true, but then again, he could afford to be. He wasn't the one dying.

K: No better, but no worse. No more twitchy after-effects from the autodoc, thank the gods of chaos. Has your medic noticed anything different?

J: No. We need a PTVS test meter and the baseline percentages from your medical records.

"Kane."

Kerzanna turned to face the pilot. "Orders?"

Malámselah grinned at her. "Sure you're not military?"

Damn, but that automatic response was a hard habit to break. "No, sir. Just worked with a lot of pilots who were." Kerzanna gave a slightly embarrassed shrug. "Combat makes me queasy."

"Ping me if something drastic happens." He tapped his earwire. His order was a formality, since Laraunte Kane wasn't a pilot. He was still jacked in and would know about any problems a lot sooner than she would. "I need to go drain the lizard."

She assumed that meant urinate. He seemed to delight in collecting colorful metaphors in various languages and peppering his conversation with them whenever he got the chance. "Yes, sir."

He strode out the door toward the freshers. Luckily, none of the nav pod staff were military, much less ex-Jumpers, or she'd have probably given herself away the first day.

Now that she was alone in the nav pod, she made herself write Jess one of the questions she'd been avoiding, because it brought her hard up against the false memory of his death. She *knew* it was false, but it still packed one hell of an emotional punch.

   K: On our last day in Ridderth, what did you do after you left?

Rather than obsess about Jess's possible answer, she opened a copy of Bhatta's navigation solution for the in-and-out bounce for the packet drop. The transition from transit to realspace was always tricky. The Central Galactic Concordance government maintained and updated current maps of all comm buoy locations, but speedy re-entry impaired a ship's ability to avoid new or transient obstacles. On the other hand, it also made the ship a less inviting target for any lurking interstellar thieves, such as jackers or pirate clan, looking for an easy slice-and-haul.

She spot-checked a few of Bhatta's calculations and verified the solution used the most current realspace data, all confirming the plot was solid. Which, according to her internal chrono, left seven hours to kill for this shift before the drop. Dutiful Laraunte Kane had already read two years of logs and the ops manual for the nav system. Her navcomp was blocked from reading the newstrends or playing games, and she couldn't go poking around the pilot logs or engine specs without drawing undue attention. Maybe she'd ask Jess for stealthy access.

Needing to curb her impatience, she began sketching in a packet-drop solution that assumed a couple of jackers were waiting for them at the packet drop. The star charts said the comm buoy was in the middle of a small void, with no convenient places to hide, so the jackers would have to play dead in the dark until the unsuspecting victim exited transit, wait until after their victim's routine scans and the first packet pull, then power up and pounce.

Kerzanna first added spin to the exit, which would cause the ship to emerge into realspace at an unexpected angle. In case the new vector happened to put them in the jaws of the two-prong trap, she added a pre-calculated two-step, stop-and-turn vector change option. It would save the *Faraón*'s flux for…

A ping from Jess interrupted her.

> J: After I left our flat, I stole a case of percomps and put our names on them, then gave them to some Canals kids and told them to scatter. Took a shuttle to the space station, but got caught by a biometric scanner. Nearly got detained and restrained, but Dixon Davidro intervened and kept me safely iced until the police contained most of the riots. He asked me about missing data hypercubes for Minder Veterans Advocates and had Neirra Varemba show me the holos of CPS people killed in the riots to see if I recognized any of them. Your holos were the last. My Nordic friend kept me functional until I could get away from Davidro and company. I bought farming property on Branimir and moved there after the CPS released me from the observation period.

The dry facts didn't tell her what he'd been thinking or feeling, but she'd seen how even talking about the holos of her supposed death had jolted him. She still didn't like the cynical, paranoid part of Jess, but she was glad it had been there to save him.

> K: Why did Davidro protect you?

She'd never met the man who had been Jess's supervisor for the final years of his Kameleon Corps service. She'd heard enough about him through Jess to make her think Davidro was ambitious and considered Jess and the other Kams he handled to be tedious obligations at best.

> J: Guessing, but he tanked at following safety procedures when I was active, hence my "friends." My detainment or death would have triggered a detailed review of my service records, and caused him trouble. He had a new special project that he thought would flux his career.

She was deeply curious about what an active Kameleon did, but it wasn't as important as figuring out who was chasing them now. Chasing *her,* with Jess as collateral damage. She didn't know the new, more confident Jess, but she respected the hell out of him for finding a way to make use of the "friends" in his head. She still felt guilty about unwittingly dragging him into her problems, but he'd willingly helped her without hesitation. Which made her feel guilty for having left him behind in the Branimir spaceport to lead the trouble away from him, though she thought he'd have done something similar if he'd suspected he was endangering her. Which brought up another question.

> K: *Any new ideas on why Neirra went to all that trouble for our reunion?*

In their working theory, Neirra had sent the CPS message to get Jess to the meeting at Markalan Crossing, and tampered with Kerzanna's calendar to insert the fake meeting. Kerzanna had never met Neirra, but Jess had interacted with her dozens of times during his service years. He said she'd been quiet and distant.

> J: *No. I still think it's what she told you, righting a wrong, but no clue what. Maybe Tuzan will know?*

Kerzanna heard Malámselah's voice coming from the corridor.

> K: *Company's coming. Later.*

She signed off the private channel and brought up the navigation solution she'd been creating.

Malámselah wandered over to her. "That the packet-drop solution?"

Kerzanna shook her head. "No, sir, Bhatta already plotted and queued that." She hunched her shoulders and tried to sound diffident. "I'm just fooling around."

"Show me." Evidently Malámselah was bored, too.

She made the navcomp display the holo, then play the visual simulation. He had her play it again.

"That's pretty clever. Going for a higher cert?"

She shook her head. "No, sir, I won't have the cumulative hours for a few years yet." She hoped that was true, because she hadn't memorized that data. She'd never make a very good spy.

"Your solution is good against jackers. They think superior ships always win. If I was pirate clan, though, I'd have a gunship or two about right here"—Malámselah pointed his finger in a location in the holo map—"in case the welcoming committee missed." He gave her a challenging smile. "Come up with a way around that, and I'll play lion pride to your gazelle."

Besides giving her something productive to do, working on her solution also gave her a good excuse to ask for access to the ship and engine specs. She'd feel better knowing what the ship could handle, even if she couldn't be the pilot.

"I'll do my best, sir." She appreciated Malámselah's impulse to mentor and encourage Laraunte Kane's interest. She'd have to make sure the initial solution was suitably conventional, maybe even timid, and let him improve it.

CHAPTER II

JESS GAZED UP at the unfamiliar simulated stars in the sky as seen during summer from Cadroy Joffalk's supposed hometown on the planet Osapan. The *Faraón*'s advertised "observation deck" was a small, re-purposed storage room near the engine pod. It was hard to find and offered no other multimedia features, which probably explained why the other passengers avoided it. He'd found it the second day and made it his refuge when the bleedover headaches flared. He liked the darkness and whisper-quiet thrumming of the flux drive that the engineer part of him wanted to get a look at, and the chance to sprawl his long limbs wide on the deeply padded floor instead of hanging over the edges of the fold-down sleeping platform in the crew quarters he shared with his "cousin." One of the ship's cats, a long-bodied, yellow-striped creature with broad shoulders and a raspy voice, liked the room, too, or maybe just the warmth of Jess's chest. He'd never been around enough cats to know.

The incoming comm packets they'd picked up at their stop at Winnogralix Proxima brought troubling news. His code snippets gleaned all incoming data for subjects of interest, in case he needed to do damage control. He'd toyed with waiting to tell Kerzanna until she was off duty, but he was trying to be better about not hoarding information. He subvocalized a text message to ping to her, knowing the code he'd inserted into the shipcomp's communications module gave it immediate amnesia regarding any private conversations between him and Kerzanna. In recompense, he was untangling the snarly mess several previous, woefully incompetent comms techs had left. Once he relinquished control, the *Faraón*'s comm system would work faster than it had in years.

J: Packet has two pieces of bad news. Now, or later?

She responded almost immediately, meaning she was probably alone in the nav pod at the moment. The jump to transit from the Win-Prox system must have gone smoothly, or he and the passengers would have noticed. He hadn't traveled enough to feel the subtle transition from realspace to faster-than-light transit space the way Kerzanna and the crew could.

K: Now, please. Wondering is worse than knowing.

J: My neighbor says the flitter port hangar building burned to the ground, with your sabotaged flitter wreckage inside. Neirra Varemba died from a fire on her ship, with heat intense enough to reduce the interior to biomass char. They only found her yesterday.

This response was slower in coming.

K: Frelling hell.

He wished he had comfort for her, or new ideas, but he'd already told her he thought she'd seen something or knew something that she didn't recognize as important. Jess-the-bomber grumbled that she might be lying about not knowing, but couldn't explain how that fit with her trying to leave him at the spaceport. Kerzanna's inclination to look out for others, even strangers, went bone deep. She'd gone to the trouble of releasing her business's contract pilots for a couple of weeks while she was "dealing with personal issues," and giving up scheduled runs to competitors so her customers wouldn't be inconvenienced. For people she cared about, she'd do a lot more.

J: Only you and I know the two events aren't random. Constables won't unless we tell them.

He knew he didn't have to tell her it would be a bad idea to involve law enforcement until they had more facts.

K: Someone likes fire.

J: Agreed. When is the next packet drop?

K: In 10.2 hours. Pilot Malámselah plans to surprise Kane by using her spin-exit nav solution. He likes teaching. After that, Felterholdt for cargo and flux, in 2.7 days. Bhatta invited Kane to a joyhouse there she knows. Loriray Mejo in 6.1 days. Mabingion in 8.2 days. Comm drops every two ship days, but might skip some if running late.

Jess's mouth quirked in amusement. Kerzanna couldn't help but make friends, even when she was supposed to be in hiding. Flamboyant, flighty Cadroy Joffalk amused the crew and provided warmth to cats, but they'd remember Laraunte Kane long after Cadroy was forgotten.

J: We'll have new IDs on Mabingion.

K: Okay.

Jess wished she was there in the room with him, so he could maybe tell if she agreed with his caution or thought he was being paranoid. That was just an excuse, though. He missed her. He'd only realized it once they'd boarded the *Faraón* and couldn't talk to her, much less feel the warmth of her presence or see how she was holding up. Just one day of being with her again had already changed his life, just like it had when he'd first met her five years ago.

K: Ridderth will be different.

J: Yes.

He both anticipated and dreaded what they'd find in the city that held so many memories. Once they delivered the packet in her mind with the key from his, would she want to leave him again? Could he survive losing her again if she did? And that didn't even take her deteriorating health into account. Even if she stayed, they might only have a few more years together, if Neirra's miracle cure didn't pan out. The cat on his chest meowed quietly. He rubbed behind the cat's ear, which it seemed to like.

K: What can you tell me about Kams?

He'd been expecting the question a lot sooner, but considering how fractured he'd been four years ago, maybe she'd been afraid to ask. Even now, her phrasing gave him latitude to provide safe answers. He'd like to tell her he'd gotten better, though he wasn't sure that was true.

J: Newstrend version, or in depth?

K: I have five hours till dinner and ten hours until the next drop. Malámselah wants Kane to study an introductory transit physics text and an ancient, pre-flight Japanese text on the art of war. What do you think?

He smiled. It sounded just like something she'd say, probably with a touch of asperity. She'd always hated inactivity.

J: Kams are spies the CPS tailors for each mission with body mods and personality overlays that take over the conscious mind for the duration. The tech and procedures are black-hole secrets. The CPS recruits people with a flexible mind and tolerance for the brain hardware and multiple chimera implants. After each mission, they're supposed to download the memories and remove the overlay, and give us downtime to recover. Dixon Davidro only followed procedure when it suited him.

He subvocalized the words carefully, in case the subject triggered the fiery protective subroutine in his neural net, but it didn't even twitch. Jess-the-medic suggested that the forbidden subject plus a strong emotional shock would be needed. Otherwise, an innocent casual conversation could fracture a whole mission.

K: Do all Kam vets have "friends"?

J: Maybe? I only talked to a few. Not something to admit to the CPS if we wanted to retire with any memories at all. Most Kams are decommissioned early on disability. Probably should have happened with me, had Davidro been paying attention.

K: What happened to your consciousness while the overlay was in the pilot's seat?

J: Deep sleep. Wake up, and suddenly it's four, six, or eight months later, different room, modified body, constant flashes of déjà vu for no reason. Downtime intervals were like a series of holovid vignettes. I kept a secret journal, for continuity. Not sure it helped.

After he'd left active duty, he couldn't bring himself to destroy the journal like he should have. Not counting his savings and the fictional service record, it was his only souvenir of his years of actual service.

He gently lifted the muscular cat off his chest and sat up. The cat started licking its hind leg with remarkable flexibility, inspiring Jess to lean forward, stretching his fingertips toward his toes, then spread his legs wide and doing the same, repeating the sequence several more times. The cat made it look easy, but his muscles felt heavy and stiff. Cadroy needed to spend more time in the ship's passenger gym, since Jess didn't have farm work to keep himself in shape. Left to his own devices, he'd rather play with all the shipcomps and create code, so farm labor—or gym exercise— was good for him. It helped with the bleedover headaches, too.

K: Modified body? Gender, too?

J: Don't know about other Kams, but they always kept me in the male-to-neutral range. Sometimes drastic mods, like thirty centimeters shorter, skinny, Asian features, and embossed, light-up body art. Usually just skin color, hair, height. My final exit body mod is as close to unaltered me as I could guess. I wasn't fully grown when I enlisted.

K: Even your mismatched eyes?

He'd almost forgotten about his eyes until Kerzanna had reminded him back in Branimir's spaceport. For Cadroy, he'd used drops to temporarily color his green left eye to match the brown in his right.

J: Both should be brown, but body shop missed it. I let it go. Kam body shops hurt.

K: Sync that. Jumper medics think pain builds fortitude. Healers are good, though. Another question: Major body mods are expensive. Why doesn't Kam Corps just hire more spies?

Before he could answer, she sent another ping about company, meaning she was no longer free to chat. How she tolerated being cooped up in the small, featureless nav pod for long hours was a mystery to him, considering her claustrophobia. Parts of him liked ships and the bustle of urban environments, but Jess-the-man preferred wide-open spaces and the smell of fresh air.

He got to his feet and brushed off his chest and the back of his pants as he watched the cat saunter out of the room, tail confidently high. He made a deal with himself that if he spent thirty minutes with the gravity weights and thirty on the treadmill, he'd take a shower with real hot water instead of using the usual sonic dry-chem. He smiled briefly. It would be just like Cadroy to charge it to his cousin's tab, too.

He'd given a lot of thought over the years as to why the CPS didn't hire more spies, especially on the days the bleedovers left him paralyzed with pain, or he'd had to work around some new quirk of the bioware in his brain so he could function as Jess-the-man. He'd decided against doing a cost-benefit analysis because it wouldn't change anything. Considering what CPS drugs and leashes did to minders and what CPS service mods did to Jumpers, he'd concluded the CPS's unofficial motto was that the ends justified the means. All willing recruits believed the CPS knew what the right ends were. He didn't think he did any more.

The small, brightly lit dining hall buzzed with background music and the pleasant hum of conversation, punctuated by the sound of clinking glassware. Jess's formerly empty table was filling up as more passengers arrived for the ship's first meal. He used the last bite of flatcake to mop up the sweet-and-sour syrup before popping it into his mouth. The *Faraón's* buffet-style cuisine wouldn't win any prizes, but it was edible and plentiful, and the ship's hydroponics section supplied a good variety. He folded a few bits of mild sausage into a napkin to offer to the ship's—or more specifically, the captain's—yellow cat, who he'd been told was called LZ. The smaller, sleeker, ebony-colored cat, called Igandea, after the heroine of a popular fantasy serial, preferred orange melon, and stole chunks from the buffet if it was left unguarded.

Jess plowed through a full plate, but Hunter Solano, the gregarious, athletic woman seated next to him in a dusty purple lounge suit, only drank coffee. She said she only came for the company. He thought she might be a minder of some sort, maybe an empath, though he couldn't have said how he knew. Remnant knowledge from a bleedover, probably.

Across the round table from them was a thick-bodied, impeccably groomed woman who'd introduced herself as Henrietta Lily Dowyer, seated next to a pinch-faced teenager she'd introduced as Hollandia, her daughter. Jess hadn't met them before, despite five days on the small ship together. Hollandia laughed with a loose-limbed young man named Pandrus, two chairs over, about a new trendy song that poked fun at the equally trendy Ayorinn's Legacy that resurged in popularity every few years.

"That song," announced Dowyer loudly to the whole table, "should be outlawed and purged. Ayorinn's Legacy is dangerous. It riles up the minders so they riot." Dowyer stabbed her spoon toward Hollandia. "When the minders take over the Concordance High Council, you'll have to get permission to have children if you aren't one of them." Dowyer's punctilious English diction made her statements sound all the more ridiculous. Her tone made it clear she disdained minders as subhuman or worse.

"Oh, hell, here we go again," muttered Hunter.

Hollandia flushed and rolled her eyes. "Careful, Mother, your conspiracy theories are showing again." Her tone was sharp and bitter.

Dowyer continued as if she hadn't heard. "After that, they'll make slaves of the nulls. That's what they call non-minders like us. There will be no *natural* people left." She sipped delicately from her teacup. Her body language said she unequivocally believed what she was saying.

An unreadable expression crossed Hollandia's face, and her lips thinned. The other passenger at the table, an older, gender-neutral person named Ameya, hunched and looked down as they shredded a sweet roll.

Cadroy, or more precisely, the overlay remnant of a gambler that made Cadroy's personality believable, wanted to leap to the defense of the minders at the table, which likely included everyone except himself and the hateful Dowyer, but Jess-the-man knew it was a lost cause. A hypercube's worth of facts only strengthened a true believer's shield of faith.

Dowyer, apparently dissatisfied with their responses, sniffed. "If you don't believe me, just ask the survivors of Rashad Tarana."

Jess was used to the horrific events of thirty-eight years ago being invoked for all sorts of inappropriate comparisons, but hearing that it had been caused by a legendary minder forecaster was new.

"Let me get this straight," said Hunter, sans her usual geniality. "You think Ayorinn's poetic predictions about the future of civilization work *backward* in time? That he somehow caused a messianic, murderous psychopath to invent an apocalyptic religion and recruit followers, spend twenty years conquering the whole planet under the noses of the galactic government, and kill millions through war, torture, and starvation to enact his vision of the road to spiritual paradise?"

"Not at all," responded Dowyer, blithely waving dismissive fingers at the atrocity. "Those so-called Rashad Tarana 'victims' are all rich, you know. I met one once. She seemed perfectly fine to me." Dowyer dabbed at the corners of her mouth with her napkin. "No, Maisie Ntombi was executed on galactic simulcast because she was a scapegoat. She knew the real truth."

Everyone at the table, Jess included, stared at her, slack-jawed.

Hunter recovered the fastest. "What truth is that?"

"That criminal, militant minders had taken control of the planet and were about to take over the entire Concordance and destroy the galactic peace forever. The so-called 'religion' was a fiction for the gullible masses." She folded her napkin into a thin triangle. "Besides, statistically speaking, not nearly that many people could possibly have died that fast when the planet got accidentally poisoned."

As everyone who'd watched the very public, live-broadcast trial knew, Subgeneral Ntombi's unleashing of the planet-poisoning scatter array had been the opposite of accidental. She'd done it to hide the seventy-percent casualty rate she and the Space Div fleet she commanded had carelessly caused when implementing High Council orders to forcibly remove and replace the murderous Rashad Tarana dictatorship. The horror that was Rashad Tarana had been the unlucky convergence of insanity, greed, egregious bureaucratic negligence, arrogance, incompetence, and malfeasance. It was a shared cultural memory across the Concordance, and no Rashad Tarana survivor over the age of two would ever forget it unless cleaned of the memories.

"R-i-i-i-ight," said Hunter sarcastically. "Tell me, what's it like in whatever galaxy you're from? The one where they make up shit as they go along?"

Dowyer ignored Hunter's sarcastic question. Hollandia stood up, looking miserably embarrassed. She mumbled something about going to her room and left. After a long moment, Pandrus abandoned his nearly full plate and left as well. If it bothered Dowyer that she'd offended everyone at the table, she hid it well as she continued to cut her slice of ham into precise cubes.

Hunter shook her head and muttered about history teachers needing to improve their game if they were going to counter the crazies of the universe.

Jess gave up trying to pretend his head didn't hurt from the bleedover and finished his meal quickly. He needed to check in with Kerzanna, but maybe after that, he'd have the shipcomp "accidentally" send information to Hollandia about how to declare her independence from her deeply warped mother the day she turned seventeen.

Chapter 12

"TRANSIT WARNING. TEN minutes to transit exit. Transit warning. Ten minutes to transit exit."

The ship's artificial voice sounded in the nav pod and over the navcomp earwire Kerzanna wore while on duty. The crew got similar alerts through their shipcomp earwires.

Malámselah grinned at her. "Are you excited?" He liked to move around, so he usually waited to the last minute to web himself into the pilot's seat.

Kerzanna nodded, smiling at his enthusiasm. He probably played with the birthday toys more than his twin boys did. For the sake of her cover story, she added, "I just hope it works right."

"We'll be fine." His eyes glazed a little as he interacted with one of the ship's systems via his skulljack.

Kerzanna thought so, too, but just in case, she'd readied a few contingency solutions and tagged them as "exercises," as if they'd come from one of the dozen textbooks he'd forwarded to her. The ship's faster-than-light drive was an older, reliable KUSP, but the BEQram system drive had a history of extra visits to the repair dock.

She sent Jess the ping she'd readied to tell him the packet drop was imminent. He'd tried to explain what he was doing with the code fragments and insertion thingies, but she got lost about thirty seconds into it. All she knew was that he needed the packet drops, so she told him about them. After the drop, she planned to tell him about her idea for using his methods for another purpose.

At the two-minute warning, she brought up the holo map, her plot simulation, and a copy of the pilot's real-time holo display, and added a calculation algo she could adjust on the fly. Malámselah nodded his approval and webbed into his pilot's seat, but pushed the manual console out of his way.

The exit from transit was slick as newly formed road glass, and the spin only decreased their realspace speed by a few points, just as Malámselah had promised Captain Tanniffer when he'd asked permission for the maneuver.

Kerzanna noted the comms packet exchange started the moment the automated systems detected realspace and locked onto the buoy's broadcast link. She checked the realspace active and passive scan results, even though doing so was technically the pilot's job. All were nominal except a significantly high value for flux residue.

To hell with it being above her pay grade. "Pilot, sir, flux trace in—"

Malámselah had already noticed, and pressed a control on the manual interface. "Chief Yarsulic, are the engines leaking?"

"*My engines don't leak,*" came Yarsulic's testy reply.

"Kane, boost the active object scan by one hundred percent and execute when ready, then repeat in two minutes and compare."

Kerzanna complied. Flux trace meant another ship had been in the area in the last five or six realspace hours. The drop was well trafficked, and Malámselah's body language said he was alert but unconcerned. Kerzanna the Jumper pilot would have readied weapons and flux-punched back into transit, with or without all the comm packets, but all Class 1 Navigator Kane could do was look worried.

Malámselah eyed her consideringly. "Kane, give me a solution for a random two-angle vector change, with maximum system burn on the last segment and prep for transit."

"Yes, sir." If Kerzanna jacked into the navcomp, she could do it in seconds, but Kane could only use the manual interface, which is why she'd created and saved the various "exercises" in Kane's private data space. Out of boredom, she'd done the same for the next five stops, too. She brought up a relevant nav plot, adjusted it with Malámselah's specifications, and sent it to his data space.

"Thank yo… *shit!*" Malámselah stood up.

The reason for his curse became apparent when the navcomp displayed the results of the sequential active scan comparisons. Three ship-sized objects were vectoring straight for them. Malámselah tagged them MO-1, MO-2, and MO-3 in the real-time holo display.

"*Multiple active scans detected. Projectile firing solution achievable by MO-1.*"

She hoped the ship's warning announcement only sounded in the nav and engine pods, or the passengers would panic.

"Kane, get the captain online, even if you have to personally drag her out of the shower."

"Firing solution achievable MO-3."

"Yes, sir." She brought up the emergency monitoring system, which told her Tanniffer—or at least her shiplink—was in the passenger lounge, which she seemed to prefer over her office. She pinged Tanniffer with an attention-getting tone and briefly described the situation. Tanniffer sent a crew-only announcement ordering them to emergency response stations. Another automated announcement with a calm and pleasant synth voice told the passengers to return to their staterooms for their safety owing to "realspace turbulence."

"Firing solution achievable MO-2."

Kerzanna quickly calculated the amount of time before contact, assuming the MOs wanted the *Faraón*'s contents more or less intact. Only three ships meant they were likely jackers. They relied on superior technology, rather than relying on small, fast swarms the way the pirate clan did. This comm buoy was popular and regularly patrolled by Space Div, so the jackers were either hungry or thought something in the cargo was worth the risk. The scans identified the jack ships as big corvettes, which they usually outfitted with shield generators and multiple weapons. Projectiles covered the longest distances, but even with variable propulsion and targeting AIs, they often missed when victims didn't obligingly sit still. The closest jackers were still twenty minutes out from being able to use energy cutters to slice open the cargo bays.

Kerzanna knew the *Faraón* had a three-layer incalloy hull and fair armor, but it wouldn't hold up against a sustained assault. She wasn't supposed to know the *Faraón* also had illegal weapons it wasn't admitting to in the official ship configuration. Most commercial shipping companies chose to risk paying fines over losing the cargo or the whole ship.

As fast as she could with the manual interface, she updated and sent her other "get out of trouble" nav solutions to Malámselah's data space. She'd cover her ass later if he asked.

Captain Tanniffer arrived at a brisk walk, accompanied by Pilot Liao. Tanniffer pointed to Kane. "You're relieved. Liao volunteered to take over nav until we can get Bhatta in here."

Kerzanna hurriedly vacated the seat, swallowing her frustration at knowing they could use her expertise. They wouldn't believe her now, even if she offered.

Liao pulled one of the nav wires out of the drawer and adjusted the seat for her short legs while giving Kerzanna a thinly disguised look of disdain. "Why don't you make yourself useful and go find out what's keeping Bhatta."

Malámselah gave Liao a sour look, then swiveled his seat toward Tanniffer, who was webbing herself into her captain's seat and jacking in. "We need help with defense."

Tanniffer nodded and looked at Kerzanna. "Report to Yarsulic in Engineering. He'll tell you what he needs."

"Yes, sir," Kerzanna replied, and only barely stopped herself from saluting. She hunched her shoulders and ducked her head until she was in the hallway and out of view, then took off at a fast jog to the crew-only lift that would take her straight to the engine pod. She keyed her private percomp and pinged Jess urgently, subvocalizing her message as she stepped in.

> K: Trouble. Three jacker corvettes, probably want to slice the hull and haul our cargo."

The response came quickly.

> J: One of the stewards ordered me to our quarters. I'm on my way now.

Crew and passenger quarters should be relatively safe, even if the jackers managed to slice open all seven of the cargo holds.

> K: Monitor nav pod comms so you know what's happening. I'll ping when I can.

She wanted to tell him what to expect, but the lift doors opened to reveal the engineering pod, and she was no longer alone.

Yarsulic was a short, muscular man whose Russian accent thickened when he got excited. "Kane, good." He pointed to an even shorter young man with pointy, shock-orange hair. "He is Engine Tech Moon." He pointed her to a section of curved wall that was unfolded to reveal a compact weapons station. "You have guns experience?"

She scrunched her face but nodded. "Some." Kerzanna had plenty, but she wasn't sure what Kane would plausibly know.

"Good. Moon can't hit broad side of moon. Take earwire, listen to pilot and captain. Shoot when they tell you." He handed her the earwire and gently pushed her toward the station. "Don't shoot us."

"Yes, sir." She turned and ducked her head to cover her amusement as she pressed the earwire to the left side of her face and hooked it into her ear. She hoped she could keep it straight from the hidden one on her right side that allowed her to subvocalize to Jess.

She strapped herself into the foldout seat, then checked the consoles. She recognized most of the controls, and paired the rest with the inventory in her head. Fortunately, the conscientious Yarsulic had kept the power storage at max capacity. The console featured a sophisticated built-in AI, which made sense when weapons officers were usually part-timers with more experience handling cargo than combat.

Her internal chrono said they had sixteen minutes before estimated contact, and right on schedule, the system engine surged audibly with the first vector curve in the nav plot she'd sent Malámselah. Unless the distributed, redundant gravity compensators failed, the passengers wouldn't feel it.

The engine pod was three-fourths of a donut, wrapped around the central engine core that held both the system and light drives. The nav pod controlled use of the eight propulsion spokes that made the ceiling of the engine pod look like the underside of a giant octopus.

"Kane, weapons status," demanded Liao through her earwire.

Before Kerzanna could answer, Malámselah interrupted. *"Liao, if you can't stick to the nav job, why don't you make yourself useful and go get Bhatta."*

Kerzanna rolled her eyes as Liao and Malámselah traded barbed comments about who had more experience, forcing Tanniffer to tell them both to chill their jets. Pilots could be such farking drama queens. She waited a moment, then reported.

"Captain, debris lasers, energy torps, stingray, and nets are all online and ready." Except for the powerful stingray, the weapons were typical for a commercial ship, and they all seemed to be good quality. They must have gotten a good deal on displacement nets, because they had nearly a hundred.

"Acknowledged," said Tanniffer. *"Pilot Malámselah will give you orders."*

"Yes, sir," subvocalized Kerzanna.

Yarsulic came up behind her and looked over her shoulder. "Good, you find Boris." He pointed to indicate the glowing, friendly-faced icon for the AI assistant. "Don't let him take insurance shots. He thinks power charge grows in ship's hydroponics section."

"Yes, sir." She turned to look at Yarsulic. "Will Moon be at the other console?" She pointed to the darkened icon that indicated another weapons control station.

Yarsulic frowned. "No. Broke again yesterday. Waiting for 'system drive repair' at Felterholdt." He made air quotes with his fingers. That explained the lengthy repair record, and made her feel better about the coil drive. Some people still preferred the old-style fuel drives, fearing the radiation from fractured coils, but as her old subcommander used to say, die fast from radiation, or die slow from zero fuel.

Kerzanna frowned. "Does Boris run both consoles, then?"

"Yah. You have three-sixty sphere control for stingray." He patted her on the shoulder as a uniformed crew member entered and shouted his name. "Do good job." He took off around the engine shaft, neatly dodging a dangling fiber cable.

She brought up a copy of the pilot's holo display, just to be looking at something besides the countdown on her internal chrono. She started to ping Jess to make sure he'd made it to their quarters.

"*Kane,*" said Malámselah through her earwire, "*Ready all torps, please. I think we can get enough velocity to go transit before our playmates arrive, but let's be prepared. The stingray burns flux, so we'll save it for another day. The debris lasers have three times the normal range, but they're still a last resort. A displacement net might fool one ship, but not all three.*"

"Yes, sir." She twitched a smile when she realized Malámselah was trying to keep her focused instead of worrying, since combat supposedly nauseated Kane. "Thank you, sir."

The engines surged with the stop-and-turn maneuver, and stayed loud. Their new vector and velocity change took the closing ships by surprise, but not for long, and the active scans said the MO-1 corvette was faster than the *Faraón.*

A chorus of vile oaths erupted from her earwire, and after a moment, the holo display showed her the reason: a fourth unknown ship appeared.

The *Faraón* was outclassed and out-gunned.

Tanniffer spoke to the whole crew via their earwires. "*Three corvettes and an unknown are closing in on us. We're preparing for transit. If that fails, cargo is replaceable. Lives are not. We will follow standard procedure for passenger safe... one moment.*"

The comms went silent.

From behind her in the engine pod, Kerzanna heard Yarsulic yelling at Technician Moon about putting tools back where they belonged. She opened the holo display as large as it would go, then rotated it. The fourth ship, MO-4, was labeled as a medium warlighter, a popular model with jackers. Boris, the AI, helpfully showed her targeting solutions using each of the *Faraón*'s weapons, apparently unaware that solo warlighters were typically shielded to the max. Considering its aggressive action, it was probably armed to the max, too.

Yarsulic stepped up behind her just as she realized MO-4's trajectory put it on an intercept course for the lead MO-1 corvette. Yarsulic saw it as well.

"Wolf packs fight, prey slips away." He sounded more hopeful than certain. He turned and strode away, shouting for Moon to prep a wide flux-line connector because the nav pod was about to ask for maximum speed. Most private ships only used flux to power system drives if needed, whereas the military, with its priority access to flux resupply, could afford to burn flux in system whenever they wanted.

If she were in the pilot's seat, she'd stutter the side jets and bend the vector to avoid any hobbling measures from the jackers, then burn flux like a supernova and punch into transit. The *Faraón*'s spherical hull should take the stress in stride, and they could load more flux at the next station. However, since she was only the provisional weapons officer, all she could focus on was her job. She rotated the display again to show the two slower corvettes, both of which were still headed straight for the *Faraón*, then asked Boris for targeting solutions.

Tanniffer came back online to the crew. *"Our situation is fluid. A fourth ship may be engaging our fastest pursuer. Cargo Master, get ready to space Cargo One and Two on my order. Logistics, issue exosuits on the double. I'll notify the passengers."*

Kerzanna knew Jess was listening to the ship's comm chatter, but she pinged him anyway.

> K: If you're in our quarters, ping Logistics about a tall exosuit. They might forget you otherwise. Passenger berths all have multiple exosuits, but crew quarters only have one.
> J: Do cats get exosuits?
> K: What?
> J: No one was looking out for the captain's two cats, so I took them with me.

She wouldn't have pegged Jess as a cat lover, although perhaps he preferred them to some of the passengers he'd told her about.

> K: Ask Logistics.

"*Kane*," said Malámselah through the earwire, "*target MO-2 and MO-3 main propulsion signatures with energy torps, two-second pulse, on my mark. We'll stop and zag to forty negative ten right after, so be prepared.*"

"Yes, sir. Max fire power, or save some for later?"

Malámselah paused, then replied, "*Fifty percent.*"

A distraction, then, to cover the course change. She quickly gave Boris the instructions, then gave the AI the data from the other nav solutions she'd provided to Malámselah. If he disliked Liao as much as he seemed to, he might choose to use one of Kerzanna's over anything Liao suggested, and Kerzanna wanted weapons to be synced.

She reported torpedo readiness to Malámselah. Six minutes to weapons-range contact with MO-2 and MO-3.

Waiting was always the hardest part of space combat, because stress and adrenaline demanded immediate action and narrowed focus, and made it hard to keep the big picture in mind. She took two centering breaths and distracted herself by picturing Jess carrying two unhappy cats all the way to the crew area. Good thing crew quarters had first-aid kits. It made her wonder if he had any pets on his farm, and if they'd be…

Malámselah interrupted her thoughts. "*Kane, Liao wants to know if you have any Jumpers in your family.*"

"Uh, no, sir." No one else in her family had been tall enough—or naively idealistic enough—to enlist. "Why?"

"*She says your nav solutions are typical Jumper tactics. I told her they're exercises from the texts I recommended.*"

Subvocalization flattened tone, so she couldn't tell if he was warning her that Liao was suspicious, or needling Liao that even a Class 1 Navigator did a better job than Liao.

"They're exercises, sir," she said earnestly. "The Myrian and Etibar text has a whole section on military tactics." Kerzanna hoped Liao didn't have time to track down and read the book, because Myrian and Etibar were academicians who'd never spent a single hour in actual combat, and didn't know their ass from a black hole in space.

Yarsulic tapped her on the shoulder. "Exosuit. Now." He pointed to an open storage closet she hadn't noticed before that had six or seven exosuits on hooks.

Yarsulic and Moon already had theirs on. Fortunately, the largest one was rated for her height, so she shimmied into it fast and returned to the weapons console. Equally fortunately, the shipping company didn't skimp on exosuit quality, at least for the engine pod, meaning the excellent tactile transmission of the gloves allowed her to accurately work holo interfaces.

She strapped herself in and checked that Boris was still locked onto the targets, and that the other two jack ships were still intent on each other.

"*Standby, weapons,*" Malámselah warned.

"Copy," Kerzanna replied, then realized that was another military response. She was rotten at undercover work.

"*Countdown. Three, two, one, launch.*"

Kerzanna keyed the command right as Malámselah said the last word, and heard the roar of the system engine as it strained to effect the ship's flux-burning full-speed vector change. The gravity compensators held steady, so the passengers wouldn't be panicking.

Fifty seconds later, Boris reported that both torps hit their targets. The next active scan said MO-3 wavered and slowed, but MO-2 was still barreling toward them, having already adjusted to the new vector.

The engine pod shook with several seconds of vibration. The passengers would definitely feel that.

"*Alert. Hull compromised. Cargo Three pressure loss. Seal not possible. Cargo Three gravity seventy percent.*"

The growl of the engines made it hard to hear the shipcomp's synthetic voice repeating the announcement.

"*Cargo Master, jettison Cargo Three now,*" ordered the captain.

Kerzanna didn't hear the reply. If their power storage held, they had enough for ten, maybe eleven full-power torp shots, if they wanted to save some power for the amped-up debris lasers. She directed Boris to analyze the MO-2 jack ship for vulnerabilities and propose single-shot solutions.

The engine pod vibrated again, stronger than before, enough to rattle things off shelves.

"*Alert. Hull compromised. Cargo Four pressure loss. Cargo Four gravity zero percent.*"

Liao's angry voice came over the earwire. "*Kane, what are you waiting for? Shoot the jack-bastards now!*"

"*Cancel that!*" yelled Malámselah.

Tanniffer sternly ordered Liao to calm down.

The engines ramped up even louder than before, meaning they were making the final sprint to transit… except the velocity was dropping, meaning they were making another manual vector change instead. Kerzanna rotated the holo to see.

"*Captain,*" Malámselah growled, "*get this asshole out of my nav pod. She just cost us… What the hell?*" She heard an inarticulate sound of pain. The comms went silent. The vector change put them on course directly toward the MO-2 ship, with weapons intercept in seventeen minutes.

CHAPTER 13

KERZANNA SURREPTITIOUSLY SUBVOCALIZED a message to Jess, hoping he was online.

> K: *Is Liao booting everyone out of the shipcomp's command module?*
> J: *Yes.*

So much for hope that the trouble in the nav pod had been a simple mishap.

> K: *Stop her and isolate her jack and comms—nothing in or out. Physically lock her in the nav pod if you can. I think she sold the ship's schedule and cargo to one of the jack crews.*

Seconds dragged by.

> J: *Done. Do you want control?*

Relief shot through her. She hunched over her console to hide her reaction.

> K: *No, I'd need a pilot's wirejack. Have the shipcomp order Pilot Kreutz to take the helm, emergency protocol. He should be able to do it from wherever he is. Tell him to stay away from the nav pod. Liao will probably shoot anyone who comes in. Get Bhatta online, too, if you can find her. Check her records for pilot experience.*
> J: *You're not in the nav pod?*

She realized she'd forgotten to tell him where she'd gone.

> K: *Engineering. Weapons control.*
> J: *Emergency monitoring system says Kreutz's shiplink isn't on board. Bhatta is in her quarters.*
> K: *Frelling hell. Either he's eating hard space, or he's in on Liao's plot. Let Bhatta—*

Through her earwire, she heard Kane's private ping tone and her name being whispered. "*Kane, can you hear me?*" It sounded like Malámselah. "*Liao has... beamer... killed... captain. I'm hurt. Don't let Yarsulic seal... pod. Engine rigged to fail.*"

"Copy." She unlatched the seat strap and walked fast to the other side of the engine core. She found Yarsulic at the engine control console and pulled him backward and away from it. "Don't seal off the engine pod." She had to shout in his ear to be heard over the tortured system engine as she explained. She added the fact that Kreutz wasn't responding, letting Yarsulic think that information came from Malámselah as well.

Moon finished opening a panel and put the access plate and the multidriver on the counter. Yarsulic voiced a string of colorful oaths, then stomped over to Moon, and unexpectedly delivered a roundhouse punch to the jaw, knocking Moon to the ground. "How much did she pay you?"

The man curled up as he fell, covering his head. "Nothing! Who? What are you talking about?"

Yarsulic leaned in. "Maybe it was evil clone Moon who let Pilot Liao in system drive access tube two days ago?"

The man hunched tighter. "She said there was a problem with the controller," he whined. "She said you asked her to take a look."

"Brainless idiot. Your job and engineering career ends at next station." Yarsulic made a disgusted sound. "Pilots know nothing about engines." He turned away from Moon to look at Kerzanna. "Go back to weapons. I look for trouble with my *nalozhnitsy*."

Only an engineer would refer to his engines as his mistresses. Moon clambered slowly to his feet, mumbling.

"Yes, sir." She started to turn, but something about Moon's movements caught her eye. He was fumbling for something in his tool belt, and his expression had morphed into rage focused on Yarsulic. She launched herself toward Yarsulic, but even as she did, Moon stabbed at Yarsulic's back. Her height and momentum carried her and Yarsulic to the floor a meter away. Yarsulic grunted as she rolled off him to use her leg to sweep Moon's out from under him.

Moon cried out as he fell to his knees and stabbed at her thigh with what looked like a phaseknife, but he missed, and the motion threw him forward, exposing his torso to another kick from her. The impact sent him toppling sideways. He rolled away, but got tangled up in Yarsulic's feet and lost the phaseknife, giving Kerzanna enough time to scramble to a crouch and tackle Moon.

He drove fists into her ribs and snapped teeth at her ear. She slammed his forehead with hers and stunned him long enough to roll him onto his stomach and pull his wrists up hard behind his back. She cast about for something to secure his limbs, but the only thing in view was the dangling strap to one of the engine pod's gravcarts. She hooked her foot around the cart's railing and pulled it closer, then wrapped and tightened the strap around Moon's wrists.

She picked up the phaseknife and powered it down, then left it on the console counter while she pawed through the engine room drawers until she found a long enough scrap of fiber cable to hobble Moon's limbs, like he was a sheep ready for shearing. He moaned and began squirming away, so she grounded the cart and locked the controls. She pulled off his shipcomp earwire, a second one she found hidden behind his ear, and the silver shiplink from his collar, then put them in her pocket.

Yarsulic hadn't moved from where she'd tackled him, and blood pooled on the floor, but his carotid pulse said he was still alive. He might survive if she could get him to an autodoc, but she needed to figure out how to neutralize Liao and anyone else in on the treachery, regain control of the ship, and keep the jackers from killing them all. Just an ordinary outing for a single active Jumper with resources, but she wasn't one any more and needed help. She pinged the one person on the ship she trusted.

K: Jess, I need your help in the engine pod.

She quickly returned to the patiently waiting weapons console.

J: Coming. Liao tried to escape. I sealed nav pod under emergency protocol. Are you okay?

Boris, the trigger-happy AI, showed nine minutes until weapons-range contact with the MO-2 corvette at present vector and velocity, and multiple weapons solutions. The pilot's holo showed the MO-3 corvette hanging back, suggesting she'd gotten lucky with her earlier shot. The MO-1 corvette was now on an elliptic that was taking it toward the aggressive MO-4 warlighter.

K: Yes. Yarsulic needs an autodoc.

J: What about Bhatta? She says she's locked in her quarters. Shipcomp says the door is open, so it's mechanical, or she's lying.

Either she was an obstacle to Liao and Moon's plot, or they were simply betraying a fellow thief for a bigger share of the proceeds.

K: Ask your paranoid friend. We need Bhatta on our side. She has the only nav pod skulljack wire that isn't sealed in with Liao, unless Kreutz is still on the ship.

Kerzanna adjusted the firing solution for the energy torps to give the MO-2 corvette a one-two punch in the larger weapons port. She'd have liked to target the engines, but that shot had a much lower probability of success.

"*Captain,*" said the cargo master through her shipcomp earwire, "*should I go ahead and jet Cargo Four? It's the organics, and it'll make a godawful mess if it stays. It's already a total loss.*"

Apparently, the crew hadn't heard any of the nav pod drama. She wracked her brain for some excuse as to why a lowly temporary navigator would be telling the cargo master what to do.

> J: *If you subvocalize into the shipcomp earwire, the crew will think it's from Tanniffer.*

Thank the universe for Jess's extraordinary skills.

"Cargo Master, we'll jettison Cargo Four on my mark." After a three-second delay, she heard her words repeated in Tanniffer's higher-pitched voice and slightly Germanic accent.

She was about to ping Jess, when the man himself walked in the main engine pod door. Damn, but he made even an exosuit look sexy. He carried a large, bulky orange cargo bag and wore the straps of both their personal bags across his shoulder. It felt ridiculously good to see him in person, but there wasn't time to pursue it. She pointed to the big engine core. "Yarsulic is on the other side, by the lift. Technician Moon is tied to a gravcart. He let Liao into the drive access tube two days ago to tamper with the engine. When Yarsulic figured it out, Moon stabbed him in the back with a phaseknife. We need Yarsulic." She pointed to the holo display of the ships in space. "We'll be in long-distance combat in four minutes."

Jess nodded as he dropped off the bags in one corner, then opened his. "How's your head?" He touched his own forehead in the same location that she undoubtedly was sporting the start of a bruised lump on hers.

She gave him a smartass grin. "Biometal skull beats ordinary bone every time." She tilted her head toward the weapons console. "I'll help you once I get this set." She quickly checked the display and started Boris on the countdown, stifling an impulse to second-guess herself about the target choice.

She raced around the engine core to find Jess kneeling, scanner in hand, over Yarsulic.

Nearby, Moon tugged ineffectually against the cable binding his wrists and snarled at her. "Stupid cow! I hope the jackers fraggin' slag you all!"

Kerzanna ignored him and crouched by Jess.

"Vertebrae compromised, but the spinal cord is intact." Jess's French accent was back. His left eye subtly twitched. "Liver and lung damage."

"Nearest autodoc is down the main corridor to the left about twenty meters. Carry him or cart him?" She tilted her head toward the grounded gravcart Moon was still tied to.

"Let's strap him to that cover plate, and I'll carry him. Give me the phaseknife, and I'll cut the exosuit open once I get there." He pulled the access plate off the counter and quickly slid it under Yarsulic. She pulled universal sealer tape out of the drawer and measured off a long length to hand to Jess, who wrapped it around Yarsulic's chest and activated the bond. He did the same with another length of tape around Yarsulic's hips. Kerzanna helped Jess lift the man's body so Jess could carry him in his arms, then put the phaseknife in Jess's exosuit chest pocket.

Jess gave her a pointed look. "We need to talk to Moon."

She kept her face straight. "Okay, I won't kill him until after you get back." She spoke loud enough for Moon to hear.

Jess's mouth twitched as he turned toward the engine pod door, and she turned to the engine console. To her relief, she found the *Faraon's* builders had integrated limited emergency nav control from the engine pod. She brought up the same pilot's view of the real-time holo, then copied in the local nav solutions she'd sent to Malámselah.

"Shui Li will kill you if you kill me!" shouted Moon over the din of the engines.

Standard tactics called for a vector or velocity change as soon as they fired the energy torps, to evade the jacker's similar salvos, but getting the hell out of realspace was their best hope of survival, so they couldn't afford the momentum loss. She took a deep breath and poured every erg of energy from the reactor coils into the system drive. If they could get the flux line going, and she timed it right, the *Faraón* would go transit just inside the MO-2 jacker's laser-cutter range.

Jess returned just as Boris fired the one-two punch of energy torps, which showed up as bright blue lines on the holo. He put a hand on her shoulder and leaned close enough to talk without Moon overhearing. "Autodoc says Yarsulic needs four hours before we can talk to him."

The ship vibrated.

"*Alert. Hull compromised. Cargo Two pressure loss. Seal commencing. Cargo Two gravity ninety percent.*"

Kerzanna subvocalized for her shipcomp's earwire, trusting she still sounded like the captain. "Cargo Master, jettison Cargo Four now." With luck, the move would make the jackers underestimate the *Faraon's* spaceworthiness and quit taking potshots at them.

She turned to Jess to speak into his ear, and made herself ignore the increasing desire to wrap her arms around him and take comfort in his solid strength, if only for a moment. "Moon thinks Liao will avenge his death. I want to use the flux line to augment the system drive, but he could have sabotaged it, if he was brazen enough to do it under Yarsulic's nose."

Through the shipcomp's earwire, she heard the cargo master's confirmation that the damaged cargo was away.

The ship vibrated again, but no synth voice announcement followed, meaning the hull held against the second shot. The jackers had to use care not to damage the cargo, if they wanted their payday. The *Faraón* was free to kill them if it could.

The ship's announcement system came to life. *"If anyone can hear me, this is Pilot Liao. Someone's taken over the engine pod and is–"*

Jess swore viciously as his fingers danced over his percomp interface, Liao's urgent voice cut off. "I'm a null-brain. I forgot about the emergency comm system. Everyone heard that."

Kerzanna quickly subvocalized into the shipcomp earwire. "Please ignore Pilot Liao's announcement. She's overstressed. We're relieving her of her duty for time being." The delayed announcement played through her earwire in Tanniffer's voice. She'd have to deal with the passengers later.

She glanced at Moon, who was glaring at both her and Jess, deep suspicion on his face. She pulled Moon's earwires and shiplink out of her pocket and handed them to Jess.

"These are Moon's." She pointed her chin toward the blood on the floor and Moon. "Despite what the 'captain' said, someone might come to check anyway. Can you sound like Yarsulic, in case we need it?"

"Give me a minute," he said, frowning in concentration as he worked his percomp.

Through her earwire, she heard a woman's voice without a tone identifier. *"Kane, if you can hear me, don't let on."* The voice was quiet, as if whispering, but clearly Liao's. *"Subvocalize and tell me where you are."*

Jess looked up. "She's using the analog wired system to access the nav pod secure net. I can hear it, but I can't stop it. She thinks you're a pawn." He gave her back Moon's earwire. "Use this when I tell you. Bhatta will hear, if she's listening."

Kerzanna nodded and pulled off the earwire that made her sound like the captain and put Moon's in its place. When Jess finished with his percomp, he pointed to her.

"Liao? I'm at the weapons console." she subvocalized. "Why?"

"The captain sold us out. She spaced Kreutz out the crew airlock and killed Malámselah. She sent someone to take over engineering. You have to seal the pod now, or we're all dead."

So much for hoping Kreutz was alive. Kerzanna decided Laraunte Kane wouldn't be comfortable bucking authority. "I'll tell Mr. Yarsulic–"

"Don't do that! He's in on it. He turned us right into the jacker's path." Liao sounded panicked.

Kerzanna let the moment stretch before she answered, trying to sound very earnest. "I'm sorry, but I'm not following. If Yarsulic is in on it, why does the captain need someone to take over engineering?"

"Goddammit, stop arguing and seal the engine pod now! Or tell Tech Moon, and he'll do it. I'll explain later."

Jess touched her arm. "She's been trying to ping Moon for the last ten minutes." He held up Moon's other earwire. "A note in the captain's private data space says Moon and Liao are cousins."

Behind Jess, Moon tried unsuccessfully to flop himself like a seal up onto the gravcart's platform.

"Yarsulic's coming," Kerzanna hurriedly subvocalized to Liao. "I have to go." She stripped off the earwire.

She grabbed a spare strip of red cable tie and wrapped it around the earwire, so she could tell it apart from the one that let her impersonate the captain. "I say we keep her completely bottled up, unless you or anyone else has any better ideas." She tapped her temple to mean the voices in his head.

Jess's left eye twitched. She'd stupidly forgotten that he paid a painful price for involving his "friends." She'd spare him this, if she could.

Her remorse must have shown on her face, because his expression softened. "I'm here by choice." He brushed the side of her cheek with his knuckle. She only barely stopped herself from capturing his hand to hold against the side of her face. He stepped back. "I'll take care of Moon and get Bhatta in here. You get us out of trouble." He turned and headed toward Moon.

Kerzanna glanced at the holo to check the status of the jack ships, but not much had changed. Despite advanced propulsion technology, space was vast, and it took time for things to unfold.

An idea formed, and she sped around the engine core to the weapons console.

CHAPTER 14

RITANJALI BHATTA LIKED to think she had an adventurous spirit, but she didn't appreciate the God of the Gaps rubbing her nose in it.

The engine pod hummed with constant vibration, and smelled of lubricant and metal, which couldn't be good. She looked back and forth between Laraunte Kane, standing beside the engine console station, and her cousin, Cadroy Joffalk, standing on a stepladder and doing something with a big line connector. Their dissimilar skin color and looks testified to early divergence of their direct family tree lines, but they certainly shared the height genes. And the craziness.

"I've piloted some for the family business, but I'm not rated for interstellar flight," she said, crossing her arms protectively. The alert had woken her from a dead sleep, and her exosuit wouldn't warm her in the chilly engine pod unless she powered it. "Besides, we don't have full control from here."

"I'll give you captain's rights and reroute as many systems to you as I can." Cadroy pointed to the large holo display of realspace, where the four jack ships glowed in threatening red. "I'd rather take my chances with you than with them."

Ritanjali half wished Cadroy hadn't pried open the stuck door to her quarters and walked her to the engine pod while telling her what the snotty Liao and her whiny cousin Moon had done. She shivered. "Okay, I guess. Don't come back to haunt me if I kill us."

She sat in the foldout seat and strapped herself in. Using the navwire in her skulljack, she accessed the unfamiliar pilot system, then yelped. "What was Liao thinking? We're accelerating straight toward the jacker!"

"Don't change course," said Kane urgently. "Our only hope is to go transit before they can catch us."

Ritanjali stared up at Kane. "*You* did this? How? Why?" Ritanjali made the shipcomp give her a countdown to laser-cutter contact range. Nineteen minutes at present velocity.

Kane sighed and hooked her thumbs in the tool belt around her hips. "I used to be a military pilot." She tilted her head toward Cadroy. "My cousin here isn't just flatline broke, he owes a lot to some powerful cashflow sharks. If I used my military credentials, they'd trace us through me. Liao sent us toward the jackers. I maxed the velocity because it's our only hope to outrun them. They've been using skip scans, so I'm betting they won't think we'd be crazy enough to speed up. We'll pour on the flux as soon as he finishes checking that Moon didn't sabotage the line."

Ritanjali blinked. "What does a gambler know about ship engines?" They were absolutely screwed.

"He went to engineering school, after giving up on being a flatland farmer, but before emergency medical technician training and computer school." Kane snorted. "When Career Day rolled around, he was standing in the line for shiny objects. I've got to check the weapons." She stepped aside and gave Ritanjali a military salute, then a short, respectful bow before turning away.

Ritanjali shook her head. "I am definitely coming back to haunt you if you kill us." She carefully extended her connection into the pilot space, to get a feel for the engine interface and the familiar nav space. Except it wasn't so familiar.

"Uhm, Kane? We have another problem." She had to raise her voice to be heard over the engine noise.

Kane stopped and turned. "What?"

"The entire nav data hypercube is gone. If we go transit, we have no way of knowing how to get out." Ritanjali shivered again. "We're crippled. Why would Liao do that?"

Cadroy dropped his multitool and started communing with his percomp, both subvocalizing and gesturing. In that moment, he looked a lot more formidable than the charming troublemaker she'd pegged him for.

Kane swore in what sounded like some variant of French. "She's desperate. I think it's just her and Moon left on the deal, and Moon's not answering. The jackers are her only hope of getting away with two murders. Must be one hell of a hot cargo."

Cadroy shook his head. "Main and archives are zeroed. She must have used the wired analog system." Cadroy frowned. "I'll scour the slack space, but that'll take time. I wish we could keep an eye on her. She's too damn clever."

"Why don't you use the emergency monitors?" Ritanjali pointed to the face-shaped control icon on the holo display, eyes and mouth currently closed to indicate the cameras and microphones throughout the ship were off.

Cadroy shook his head. "The system is either on or off. If we turn it on, Liao can see what we're doing, too. The less she knows, the better."

Ritanjali shook her head. "I won't enter transit without knowing where we're going. Going into transit blind is much more likely to kill us than a few jackers." Despair at the equally bad choices made her shoulders slump.

Kane snapped her fingers. "Cadroy, copy my official dataspace to Bhatta's. I got bored and did transit solutions for all the planned stops between here and Mabingion. It limits our choices to those six, but better than waiting for the local lions to eat us." She spun and walked fast around the core and out of sight, presumably headed for the weapons console.

Ritanjali spared a few seconds to glance at the solutions as they appeared in her dataspace. They looked streamlined and complete, which made sense now that she knew Kane was military, not just a wet-behind-the-ears Class 1 commercial navigator.

The ship earwire she'd almost forgotten she was wearing played a priority tone. *"Captain, could someone tell us what's going on? The passengers are starting to get antsy."* The Logistics master sounded more peeved than alarmed. If he only knew.

Ritanjali nearly fell out of her seat in shock when the captain answered. The very *dead* captain, according to both Cadroy and the shipcomp's life-signs monitor for key personnel.

"My apologies," said Captain Tanniffer. *"We're making a run for transit. It's better odds than waiting to see which pride of lions catches us first. Please remind the passengers about emergency transit entrance procedures."*

The voice may have been Tanniffer's, but the phrasing sounded a lot more like Kane. Ritanjali spared a glance up at the too-handsome-for-his-own-good Cadroy, but he was just getting off the ladder. She hadn't noticed earlier, but he seemed tired as he collapsed the ladder and put it in the holdfast on the wall.

A pilot system alert caught her attention. She voiced a private ping to Kane. "Whatever you shot at MO-2 made a splash, but no secondaries."

"Copy. I'm going to launch some displacement nets into our vector."

"Okay, I'll bite. Why? They're supposed to decoy scanners and projectile AIs, not lead them to us."

"If we wear those nets, it'll look like shields to routine scans. I'm hoping it'll make the MO-2 corvette hold off with their cutters until they can get close enough to punch through our shields. By which time, I hope we're gone."

Ritanjali had never heard of that trick, but she guessed it wouldn't hurt. She liked Kane, and she trusted her new confidence. "As long as they don't muddy our sensors."

"The nets will burn off by the time we go transit."

"Uhm, okay, then."

Cadroy's voice came online. *"Flux line is clean and green go."* Smart of him not to try to yell over the engine noise. The vagaries of the *Faraón*'s glitchy communications system gave him an almost Arabic accent. The company really needed to get the system fixed.

"Bhatta," said Kane, *"as soon as we hit the displacement nets, ramp-up fast to max velocity and hold this vector. I hope it fools the jacker. It's tricky judging the speed of an oncoming object."*

"Acknowledged," Ritanjali replied. The incoming data from the pilot systems was starting to make sense, and now she could see the holes. They'd lost some sensors with the hull damage, but that didn't worry her nearly as much as the complete lack of control over the external docking and positioning jets that gave them maneuverability in realspace.

The moment she felt the displacement nets hit the *Faraón*'s hull, she gave the acceleration command, and felt the ship respond. The engine noise raised in pitch. No wonder Yarsulic had to periodically be treated for hearing loss.

The pilot training manual said she should be forward scanning every two minutes before transit, but training manuals didn't cover scenarios that involved playing "made you blink" with an oncoming jacker corvette that wanted the ship's cargo and probably didn't care if the crew lived or died. Besides, the standard scans would tell the corvette they were headed for transit, and all they'd tell her was that a big corvette was in her path.

She felt the launch of more displacement nets, this time to the side, toward the slower MO-3 corvette that was staying out of it for now. Something tickled one of the ship's systems, but she couldn't trace it. "Cadroy," she subvocalized in a private ping to him and Kane, "I think Liao is up to something with the analog systems, but I can't tell what. It feels like something to do with comms." A large burst of data nearly swamped her. How the hell did Malámselah and Kreutz handle all this input and have time to joke with her when they were on duty?

"Bhatta, is that you piloting?"

It was Liao's voice, but with no tone indicator, meaning she was on the analog system. Ritanjali waved to get Cadroy's attention and pointed to her earwire. She mouthed Liao's name. He nodded quickly and pointed to his own earwire, which she took to mean he heard Liao, too.

"Bhatta, I know you can hear me, and I know you're in the engine pod. It's just you and me left. You're in way over your head. Yarsulic is no pilot, and Kane is barely out of nav school. You're going to get us all killed."

"Not all of us," Ritanjali snapped. "You already took care of Tanniffer, Kreutz, and Malámselah."

"Kreutz reneged on our deal. You can have his share if you keep us in realspace for our payoff. I'll even..."

The engine pod vibrated. Ritanjali frantically buffered Liao's comms and checked the data streams. She private-pinged Kane and Cadroy. "Liao launched an emergency comm buoy. I can't tell what she programmed it to say or do."

"How many does the ship have?" asked Kane.

"Five more," replied Ritanjali. "They're independent, like the analog wired systems, in case we get boarded by jackers." The black humor of the situation made her roll her eyes. She checked the countdown. Their velocity, still increasing, put them at transit entrance in nine minutes, which was plenty of time for Liao to wreak havoc. "Liao is right. I'm in over my head."

"She wishes," said Kane. *"You're good. Let the shipcomp track the data stream, so you can watch the anomalies. Stall Liao. We'll see what we can do about the buoys and her access."*

Ritanjali unpaused Liao's comms and listened to the buffered recording of the rest of what she had to say, something about giving her a cut of Moon's share, since he'd dropped off the net.

"I'm listening," was all Ritanjali could think of to reply. More politic than "eat hot death."

It was all well and good for Kane to tell her to watch for anomalies, but how was she supposed to know what was unusual and what wasn't? And she still needed to queue up the nav solution for wherever they were going once they made transit. Not another packet drop, which left the three space stations.

"Bhatta, tell me what you need to make our deal happen. I don't want

the passengers and crew to be casualties of your lack of experience. Training simulators are nothing like the real thing."

Now Liao's uncharacteristic sociability at dinner yesterday made sense, especially her interest in Ritanjali's career goals and piloting experience. She'd been evaluating threats to her plan.

Ritanjali felt another analog system twitch, and another displacement net launch. The shipcomp reported success on sealing the damaged cargo hold. She accessed the data on the hull damage. The ship had incalloy infrastructure in the hold areas, meaning it could go transit even with a few holes. "For a start, you could guarantee you won't kill me like you did Kreutz."

"I won't, as long as you keep to our deal. Is Yarsulic watching you?"

"Sometimes," Ritanjali answered, happy to let Liao continue to think Yarsulic was in charge of their mad scheme.

Updated scans said the two competing jackers made the first pass at one another, but no indication on whether or not either took a hit.

"Okay, here's what you do. Trip the transit sensor diagnostic routine." Like Cadroy said, Liao was clever. It would look like a rookie mistake and delay the entrance to transit until the routine was done.

Ritanjali felt another analog tickle. "Why did you launch an emergency comm buoy?" she asked suspiciously, and hoped Liao would think she hadn't noticed the first one.

"Insurance. If this all goes chaotic, I wanted Space Div to know what happened and exactly who was responsible."

Ah, the teeth in Liao's deal. Ritanjali would bet half her company profit share that Liao's fictional version of events featured prominently in the emergency message, with the names Bhatta and Kane added as co-conspirators in the captain's supposed plot.

Cadroy pinged her privately. *"I can send a regular comm packet with the truth."*

"God, no," said Ritanjali hastily. "I'll get arrested for piloting, or at least terminated. If we live through this, we can set the record straight then. I can't stall her for much longer, though. She's chattering to distract me from noticing she's meddling with other analog systems. Five minutes to transit, and uh, the captain should warn the crew and passengers."

"Copy," said Kane. *"I think our best destination is Mabingion. Longer transit time from here, but the heavy military presence should deter any new players."*

Ritanjali felt the weapons AI release a double-shot energy torpedo toward the sidelined MO-3 ship, presumably as a distraction. "It'll piss off the passen… oh farkin' ark, Liao is triggering the nav pod emergency eject sequence!" Ritanjali frantically sent a flood of cancel and counter commands, but too many analog systems ignored her, even though she had captain's authority. "It'll rip the ship apart!"

The engine pod shuddered and shrieked. Ritanjali powered on her exosuit, even as she told Kane and Cadroy to do the same. No time for protocol. She switched on the all-ship comms. "This is Navigator Bhatta. Seal your exosuits now. This is not an exercise. Strap yourself into the emergency jump seats in your quarters, or whatever you can find. Do it now. It's going to be a bumpy ride." She told the shipcomp to repeat the message and play the obnoxious alert tones until she told it to stop. Out of the corner of her eye, she saw Cadroy race toward the pile of bags along one wall and grab the large orange one, then take off around the engine core in Kane's direction.

Sealing the headpiece of her exosuit brought blessed silence to her ears, but now she knew what a chew toy felt like when a dog shook it back and forth. She grabbed the Mabingion nav solution and gave it to the shipcomp, with an extra encryption key that would make it harder for Liao to erase. Every ship alert flooded her input. She felt the ship's bones cracking when the nav pod fired up one of its docking jets, and all she could do was hope it didn't take out the adjacent engine pod. "Ninety seconds to transit. Engaging transit drive," she announced to the whole ship. She hoped she didn't sound as scared shitless as she felt.

Ritanjali felt the nav pod tear through passenger berths and Cargo Seven, but the docking jet sputtered out right as the nav pod reached the hull. The ship's transit engines burned flux and created the field that slid them into transit space. She shut down to the system drive and transit enveloped them. The engine pod vibration subsided to almost unnoticeable. She drew a ragged breath.

According to the shipcomp monitors, they'd probably lost half the passengers and two thirds of the crew. They had barely enough flux left to make it to Mabingion, and five interstellar days for the weirdness that was transit space to eat at the non-incalloy parts of the ship's interior. And that didn't count the extra problem of having a rogue nav pod infesting the ship like a burrowing parasite.

Her stomach was about ten seconds from rebellion at the thought of how many had died. *Be the ship*, her great uncle used to tell her. *Be human later.* She rode the inputs. The ship and crew were completely and royally screwed, but they were alive.

"*Bhatta, how are you holding up?*" asked Kane. Her warm and caring voice helped Ritanjali focus on the moment. One hornet's nest at a time, as her great uncle used to say.

"I'm good," Ritanjali said, pleased that her voice didn't crack. "I just wish I was wearing more than an exosuit and pajamas."

CHAPTER 15

JESS STUMBLED, ALMOST dizzy with exhaustion, into the little observation deck that he'd commandeered as executive sleep quarters. He'd forgotten what it felt like not to have a bleedover headache. If he wasn't playing Cadroy Joffalk, the gambler-slash-computer-wizard, he was Jess-the-engineer, trying to keep the *Faraon's* damaged engines going, with advice and direction from the too-stubborn-to-die Yarsulic. Or he was Jess-the-medic, making hard choices about who should have priority for an autodoc. Jess-the-bomber had strong opinions about his and Kerzanna's security, and begrudgingly, the rest of the ship.

The ship's main engine core survived Liao's desperate escape attempt, but flux had leaked out via one of the compromised cargo holds until they'd found and patched the hole. He and the remaining crew had rigged a few makeshift connections to the rogue nav pod's systems to check its status, but Liao hadn't once responded. Moon died because he'd been tied up and couldn't seal his exosuit when the supply closet they'd locked him in ripped open to the void in the entrance to transit. He might have died anyway, but Kerzanna blamed herself for his death. What was left of the cargo hold monitors said the waves of transit space were eroding any non-incalloy materials. Jess-the-engineer suspected this was the last voyage of the *Faraón Azul*.

Counting Bhatta, Kerzanna, and Yarsulic, nine crew were functional, and they were as exhausted as he was. The three working autodocs were running out of supplies to treat the injured. They'd crammed twenty-one surviving passengers into the twelve intact staterooms, and the crew slept wherever they could. They'd converted Cargo Seven, the smallest of the holds, into a morgue for the bodies they could find. Jess mourned the tragic loss on the second day of practical, genial Hunter with a high-level empath talent and a gift for calm, who'd been trying to stop the hateful Dowyer woman from pushing her teenage daughter out an airlock for the unforgivable sin of using her healing talent to help another passenger, thereby exposing herself as a minder. None of them survived, and the breached airlock devastated the hydroponics section.

Focusing on the smaller miracles made the disheartening losses easier to swallow. For reasons known only to Liao, she'd shoved Malámselah's and Tanniffer's bodies out into the hall before Jess had sealed her in the nav pod. Tanniffer was dead, but Malámselah still clung to a thread of life in one of the autodocs. Two crew members and seven passengers had holed up in the passenger gym and thereby avoided the obliteration of their quarters by the nav pod jet. Several of the passengers and crew with minder talents put them to good use, healing the injured, or using telekinetic skills to help with temporary repairs. Navigator Bhatta rose to every challenge thrown at her, and if the ordeal didn't put her off interstellar travel for good, she'd make an excellent captain some day soon.

Another smaller miracle, or more accurately, two of them, woke and meowed a greeting to him as he kneeled next to one of the three sleeping pads he'd dragged in. He'd carried the cats' bulky orange habitat bag into the room, but they preferred sleeping with him, Kerzanna, or Bhatta when they could. Saving the cats had been one of the best choices he'd made. They offered quiet, soothing companionship, even when the people were scared, hungry, or hurting.

He eyed the supply of mealpacks in the corner, trying to talk himself into eating one so he wouldn't wake up famished later. With the loss of the dining hall and hydroponics section, the emergency mealpacks were the only available food. Fortunately, the *Faraón* was generously stocked, so no one would starve. Instituting extreme water conservation measures ensured they'd have enough to last the five days, especially since they'd discovered one of the intact cargo pallets carried hundreds of expensive, transit-stable wines. A few of the passengers hadn't been sober since.

The cargo master had determinedly cracked every single accessible cargo container to look for something that would have attracted two jack crews to fight over it. Jess could have told him the answer was in the comm archives.

At the *Faraon*'s first packet drop after Branimir, Liao had received a ludicrously high bounty offer on the ship's cargo, which was supposedly protected by extra guards masquerading as passengers. At their next stop, Winn-Prox Station, Liao had sent acceptance and supplied the ship's schedule along with a suggested attack point. She'd brought her cousin, Moon, in on the plot, and crudely rigged the system engine to shut down if the engine pod was sealed. That was just insurance for her primary method, which was simply to stall in the chosen packet drop area and let company policy of giving up cargo take its course. She hadn't counted on the captain ordering her to switch shifts with Malámselah so he could oversee Kane's spin-exit nav solution. Liao also hadn't counted on the glitched comm system that didn't purge her damning trail of messages like it should have.

Cargo bounties weren't unheard of for specific high-value targets, such as untraceable luxury items, illegal chems, or a passenger worth kidnapping. Shippers lied on cargo manifests all the time to deter thefts, skip taxes, or avoid ownership questions. Smart cargo masters scanned and measured the cargo carefully, but shippers continually developed new smuggling methods.

Jess-the-bomber believed the high bounty was one last attempt to kill Kerzanna. If her pursuers thought she'd left Branimir, the best way to target all possible departing ships would be to post a high bounty for a supposedly precious cargo leaving the planet, and let jackers do what they did best. Kerzanna hadn't agreed with his opinion, but she hadn't disagreed, either. He suspected she'd moved it off her survival priority list for the time being, since she was the real captain behind the scenes, despite the crew and passengers having crowned Bhatta as the hero.

Just as the least-objectionable mealpack he'd selected warmed in his hands, his earwire pinged a private message from Kerzanna. They'd had even less private time together than before the attack, and he missed her. Luckily, the shipcomp's AI successfully rerouted itself around missing nodes and stayed functional, or they'd have been well and truly lost.

K: Yarsulic suspects you know more about his engines than he does.

Jess subvocalized his reply between bites of pasteboard protein in gluey sauce. LZ, the orange cat, watched him attentively.

J: Only because the Faraón's flux drive is older than he is.

Jess suspected the engineer personality overlay had been created using the memories from a military engineer who'd been around for the birth of the Central Galactic Concordance two hundred years ago.

J: What's he unhappy about now?

He spooned a bit of pale-as-snow chicken into a small plate and set it in front of LZ. In the interest of galactic peace, he did the same for Igandea, who'd been pretending disinterest, but would happily steal from LZ, who took umbrage.

K: He found the siphon you and the crew installed on the nav pod to reroute its flux supply to the main.

That has been Jess-the-bomber using Jess-the-engineer's skills to save the flux for the main ship, and to make sure Liao, if she was still alive, wasn't going anywhere. The ensuing headache had nearly blinded him for several hours.

J: He'll forget once we exit transit. I don't know the system drive at all. How are you feeling?

She'd been using her illegal ramp-up system to keep herself awake and functional for long hours, like she would have done back in her active Jumper days. Jumpers refueled with concentrated nutrient streams and metabolism stim drugs. All she could do was eat mealpacks and sleep, and the continued high stress wasn't doing her waster's disease any favors. She was delaying a crash-and-burn, but it was coming. He planned to keep her safe when it did.

K: Malámselah died ten minutes ago. I need a nap before we exit from transit. Are we okay to be there together?
J: Yes.

He didn't care if it might crack their cover as distant cousins who didn't like each other much. He wanted, no, *needed* to be in the same room with her, even if he couldn't hold her, or comfort her for the loss of Malámselah.

"The very first thing I'm going to do when we hit ground zero is rent an entire bathhouse for the night," declared Bhatta over the private command channel. "As it is, they'll probably have to cremate my exosuit. It has its own ecosystem of bacteria by now."

Liao's clumsy sabotage of the system engine had damaged the ship's environmental controls. With Yarsulic's guidance, Jess and one of the passengers with integrated systems expertise had repaired it as best they could. All the crew had stayed in their exosuits the whole time, and most of the passengers had followed suit. Better stinky than dead.

"*Mine, too,*" agreed Kerzanna.

Bhatta and Yarsulic shared the engineering console, with Bhatta as the acting captain, strapped into the foldout seat, and Yarsulic standing, but tethered, in case the gravity compensators failed. Kerzanna, acting as navigator and weapons control, sat at the working weapons console.

After securing the cats' inflated and sealed orange habitat to holdfasts on the wall, Jess strapped himself into the seat of the nonfunctional weapons console, in the far end of the donut-shaped engine pod. No one could see him, and for once, his only job was to make sure the shipcomp did what was needed to help them survive reentry into realspace above the Mabingion orbital elliptic.

"This is Acting Captain Bhatta with your two-minute warning to transit exit." She sounded calm and competent over the ship's announcement system. She'd gained confidence in the last five days. *"Strap yourself in now, if you haven't already done so, and power up your exosuit, just like we did in the drills."*

Jess touched the controls on his suit, and the room went silent, but not for long, once the system drive engaged. He'd directed his percomp to use the suit's heads-up display to show him system status, so he could make sure the comm packets and emergency broadcasts went out on all available channels the microsecond the *Faraón* hit realspace.

The transition into realspace shook the ship with bone-rattling vibration, but their repairs and patches held. The crew member monitoring the inert nav pod reported no activity.

"Commencing active scan sequence," said Kerzanna.

"Acknowledged," replied Bhatta.

"Inverter coil six heating up," warned Yarsulic. *"If it gets to fifty, I will take it offline."*

The shipcomp signaled an incoming broadcast.

"Injured merchant Faraón Azul, *this is the High Command Cutter* Nove Planetan. *Please state the nature of your emergency."* The voice was an actual human's, but he sounded bored.

Jess kept his exasperated sigh to himself. Why had he gone to the trouble of including all the details in the emergency messages if the military wasn't going to read them?

Bhatta identified herself as the acting captain and succinctly told the man about the jackers, their escape, the ship's condition, and the nav pod problem.

A new voice came online. *"This is Commander Agostino. How many survivors are we talking about?"*

"Twenty-eight. No, twenty-seven. Our pilot died fifteen minutes ago."

"My condolences. He or she must have been a damn fine pilot."

Jess let out the breath he'd been holding. The command crew had agreed to tell everyone that Senior Pilot Malámselah had saved their collective asses, and Jess had made it so in the shipcomp's records. Bhatta didn't want to be fired for interstellar piloting without a certification rating, and "Laraunte Kane" and "Cadroy Joffalk" didn't want to be discovered by the ruthless people he supposedly owed money to. Yarsulic thought his good buddy deserved to be thought of as a hero because he'd saved them with the warning about Liao's betrayal. They'd transferred Malámselah to the only movable autodoc and stationed it in the engine pod. Bhatta said he liked being surrounded by friends, and maybe she was right, because he'd lived a lot longer than the autodoc predicted.

"We're too small to take your people on, especially since your airlock is gone. Can you make it to Mabingion Station?"

"I think so, but we have no positioning jets, so we'll need tugs," replied Bhatta. "And we don't know the stability of the nav pod."

"Tell you what. You continue nice and slow toward Mabingion, and we'll send over a few spare drones to get close-up scans to see what we're dealing with."

Jess wondered how many drones the cutter carried, because the *Faraón*'s sensors counted at least seventy of them swarming over and into the breached hull. Agostino obligingly sent a live feed back to the *Faraón* with the results. Unfortunately, the drones couldn't tell them anything about the nav pod, other than it was probably dead. No one in the command crew liked the "probably" part.

Thirty minutes later, the comm system intercepted a repeating ping.

"...ews. Hailing the Faraón Azul, *this is Bayonet Media News. We'd like to talk to you about your situation. This is Bayonet Media News. Hailing..."*

"How did they find us so fast?" Yarsulic sounded dismayed and disgruntled.

Jess fought the impulse to duck his head like a turtle drawing in. Kerzanna had mentioned it as one of the bomber's tells.

"Luck and opportunity, most likely," soothed Bhatta. *"I'll bet they monitor every known frequency. We're just lucky that the* Nove Planetan *was a lot closer. If we answer now, we control the narrative."*

"They'll be bees to honey. It will be a madhouse," Yarsulic grumbled.

Jess-the-bomber certainly hoped so, since he'd gone to the trouble to arrange it.

CHAPTER 16

KERZANNA WOKE SLOWLY to the sound of gentle snoring in her ear. Except it wasn't snoring, it was purring. The pillow under her head began bobbing up and down. She cracked one eye open to see a small, dark furry face with green eyes focused on her as the cat named Igandea kneaded the pillow next to Kerzanna's head.

The room was still shadow-dark, but that didn't mean anything, since it had no windows and they'd paid extra for do-not-disturb service. Kerzanna lifted her arm so Igandea could snuggle into the curve of Kerzanna's chest and under her chin. Joy palaces made their profits on up-charges, so they'd probably make them pay extra to clean up the cat fur.

She tried to go back to sleep, but her full bladder and busy brain wouldn't let her. Not until she determined their situation and confirmed the plan of action. Stupid Jumper brain.

She rolled onto her back and reached out to feel for Jess's solid form, but the space was empty and the bedding cool. It had felt both strange and right to share a bed with him again. Too bad she hadn't been awake to enjoy it.

"Chamber 3930, lights, twenty percent," she said out loud. The room comp obligingly raised the soft, ambient lighting to where she could see her way to the fresher without tripping over a cat.

Every joint creaked like a rusty hinge and every muscle felt tight, but not painful. Her hands seemed steady when she held them out. It could be the Jumper-rated pain patch Jess had thoughtfully saved for her, or it could be some new and delightful symptom of her ever-evolving waster's disease. Adrenaline was her enemy, and she'd been mainlining it for five days straight.

Since Jess had paid an outrageous amount for "Tatyana Vasil," and her new cohab, "Ziad Edisson," to do whatever kinky things they wanted for four days in their guaranteed-private room, Kerzanna indulged herself in a long, hot shower. Dreary, incompetent, ungracefully aging Ridderth hovered near the bottom of anyone's list of perfect cities, but at least it had water in abundance.

Twenty minutes later, the forced air of the solardry frizzed her longer, now red-streaked hair into a tangle, but she'd tackle that problem once it finished drying. It was time to put more red color drops in her eyes, and the mirror told her she'd need to reapply the skin-matched permaseal over the Jumper tattoo on her neck to keep the lighted parts from showing. Fark, she was collecting beauty regimens.

"Chamber 3930, list messages," she said as she padded out into the front room in search of her clothes. She'd been one IQ point above comatose by the time she and Jess had sealed themselves into their supposed love nest, so her memory of anything after that was hazy at best. She'd been stumbling with exhaustion, hanging onto Jess to stay upright; the staff probably thought she was chemmed. She did remember he'd destroyed both their percomps soon after they'd left the *Faraón Azul*, so they couldn't be traced. The man was hard on percomps.

"*Text message for Madam Tatyana Vasil from Master Zee Edisson from two point one hours ago. Shall I read it to you?*" The room comp's lifelike synth voice was sultry and tinged with a British Isles accent, in keeping with the joy palace's theme of a huge preflight Western Earth castle. The staff and sex workers all wore fluttery, fanciful versions of fairytale clothes that looked extremely impractical for any activity she could think of.

"Yes, please."

Computers didn't care if she thanked them, but the politeness made her feel better. She found her new underwear and bra on top of a neat stack of her striped pants, long ruffled blouse, and bolero-like vest, suggesting Jess had straightened up after her. She remembered he was a folder. She was a draper, or a hanger, or a drop-clothes-anywhere kind of person, especially when she was tired. It probably drove him crazy.

"*From Master Zee Edisson: Coming back with food and drink. Don't start without me. End message.*"

"Delete message, please."

"*Certainly, Madam.*"

She wouldn't be starting anything without her boots. Wherever they were, she'd bet her socks were with them, unless LZ dragged them into the orange cat habitat wedged into the corner of the bedroom. The yellow tabby was inexplicably fond of rolling in and drooling on smelly socks.

During quiet moments, she felt a nagging conviction that she'd forgotten something big, something vital, something urgent. Since the annoyingly elusive sensation had only started after Varemba gifted her with the locked message packet in her mind, she assumed it was her non-minder's brain trying to accommodate the foreign object, for lack of a better word, lodged in her memory. She owed Varemba for healing her, especially since the "aftermarket" ramp-up she'd so casually repaired had probably saved lives on the *Faraón*, but Kerzanna was more than ready to be done with playing courier.

"Chamber 3930, display weather forecast and news, please."

As the wall opposite the gigantic bed lit up, she checked her internal chrono for the time. Great gods of chaos, Jess had let her sleep twenty-one hours.

So much for their original plan to sleep a few hours, then slip into the Ridderth afternoon rush and find accommodations in a less glitzy part of town, where people were better at minding their own business.

She needed to be planning farther ahead than the next meal, but too many unknown variables bogged her down—she wasn't a minder forecaster, able to see the patterns in seemingly unrelated data and predict likely future scenarios. Her thoughts kept circling back to Jess. He was fast becoming as necessary to her as breathing. Her hormones alerted her to his nearness even at the most inappropriate times. He settled her. He made her laugh. The prospect of returning to her solitary life was increasingly bleak, but she'd rather space herself out the nearest airlock than make him watch her die day by day.

Kerzanna licked the powdered sugar off her fingers. "It was clever of you to create the media feeding frenzy to cover our departure, but did you have to make it a named story and the number one newstrend in the galaxy?" After nothing but cheap mealpacks, the fresh egg-soaked, fried flatbread tasted sinfully good. Jess had brought back enough food to stock a small restaurant, and they'd already eaten half of it. Well, mostly she had. She was still replenishing her reserves after nearly continuous use of her "aftermarket" ramp-up system to help keep the *Faraón* flying. Her bones would probably ache for days.

Jess shrugged one shoulder. "The 'Rescue of the *Faraón Azul*' must have hit a slow news cycle. I remembered Ridderth has flocks of independent journalists, especially after that Ridderth media company broke the 'Mabingion Purge' story. I hoped they'd create enough of a crowd for us to get lost in the mix once we got on the ground. I didn't expect them to send out ships to livecast our progress and make a planetwide drama out of it."

Kerzanna speared a cube of fresh peach from the bowl on the table between them. "Bhatta is too much in the spotlight for us to send the cats to her now."

Neither she nor Jess had trusted the pet-intolerant military or the negligent Mabingion spaceport authority with the welfare of the two cats, but people on the run couldn't provide a suitable home for them, either. The friendly, fearless cats deserved to be on a ship with passengers to indulge them and crew who could care for them. Bhatta already adored them.

"Ridderth's government systems are still as porous as ever, so I inserted records for an obscure city ministry that's responsible for small animal veterinary health and quarantine. When we leave tonight, it'll deliver the cats to her." He fished a piece of orange melon out of the mixed fruit bowl and put it on a small plate on the short table behind him, where Igandea sat waiting. Kerzanna suspected he'd miss the cats as much as she would.

"Did you have any pets growing up?" she asked. His expression flatlined, and she sighed. The oddly domestic atmosphere, with familiar echoes of their briefly blissful life together four years ago, made her forget how any questions about his past made him shut down. "Sorry."

It still hurt when he shut her out like that, even though she knew better than to ask in the first place. She picked up the temporary bracelet-style percomp he'd given her. He was building better ones for them both. As "Tatyana," she had an affinity for color coordination, currently centered on bright red. She slipped the bangle onto her wrist and pretended to admire the contrast to her shiny glitter-gold fingernails and ultra-feminine filigree skin art she'd let the body parlor talk her into, in celebration of her new cohab. Her mother would have been so pleased.

For his new "Zee" persona, Jess had adopted a fondness for shiny metallic jewelry and stylized lightning-patterned face art, shorter red-streaked hair to match hers, and his eyes were now icy electric blue, which made his brown skin seem more golden by comparison. His sweater and scarf made his shoulders look wider, and his tight pants and high boots drew lots of eyes to his memorable thighs and backside. And lucky woman that she was, she had plenty of old memories of seeing him naked to keep her warm when the waster's disease inevitably claimed her and made her body a statue.

Jess abruptly stood and walked away from the table, then turned back to her. "I don't want to have secrets from you." He looked frustrated. Neither of his eyes twitched, so it was just Jess talking.

"I don't think it's altogether your choice." She pointed to her temple to indicate the "friends" that could immobilize him with seizure-like symptoms to keep him quiet. Besides, they had no future because *she* had no future, and he deserved so much more than she could give him. "You don't owe me anything."

He wrapped his arms around himself as he took a deep breath and let it out slowly. "I am an orphan child of Rashad Tarana."

His words sank in, and she felt her jaw drop. She'd have sooner expected him to tell her he had a group marriage and twenty children, or was an alien spy from the Andromeda galaxy.

It made an appalling kind of sense that he'd volunteered to serve in the Citizen Protection Service. The CPS had rescued the six thousand shattered adult citizens and became the guardians for the nearly three thousand equally shattered orphaned children. Who better than top CPS minders to help the survivors recover from the ordeal and heal the post-event stress trauma? And who better to recruit than people who saw the CPS as their saviors?

She didn't know whether to apologize to him on behalf of the civilization that had destroyed his homeworld, or ask him for details, which was like asking an accident victim to relive their trauma. She shook her head. No wonder he didn't tell anyone about his childhood. And no wonder he'd been able to buy property on Branimir without meeting the stringent residence requirements. No member planet of the Central Galactic Concordance could or would refuse immediate full citizenship to a Rashad Tarana survivor.

His inscrutable look might have fooled others, but she saw worry and resignation, like he was afraid his admission would change how she thought of him. She stood to face him. "You are not your past." She crossed her arms to quash a selfish impulse to reach out to him, to hold him tight and get lost in the warmth of his embrace. He'd think she pitied him, or wanted comfort. "You're the strongest, most resilient person I've ever known."

He looked at her a long moment. He drew breath to speak, then closed his mouth. Finally, he shook his head. "You always surprise me."

Kerzanna raised an eyebrow. "Says the man hosting a frelling *convention* in his brain."

The tension eased in Jess's shoulders and a corner of his mouth twitched. "You have a point. It's a fair cop." His accent was pure British Isles.

She sat back down at the table and poured herself more kaffa, the sweet, lightly stimulating warm drink to which she'd developed a slight addition. "So, Master 'Edisson,' how do we go about finding one man in a sea of twenty million so we can meet with him and deliver the goods?" She pointed to her head.

He gave her an amused grin. "We go fishing, of course."

Of course his method involved percomps and Ridderth's local data net. He'd spent almost every waking hour on the *Faraón* developing loosely organized drifts of code snippets that combined and broke apart seemingly at random, but queried all public systems for key phrases of interest, such as Tuzan the Janitor. He'd sent them out at each comm buoy and space station, and ever since, they'd been busily harvesting potential data points and squirreling them away in unused corners of the public net. Now that he was hooked into the local net, he'd collected his gleanings and sent out better-tuned queries. At least, that was Kerzanna's simplistic view of the technical process Jess had patiently but fruitlessly tried to explain to her. She'd have a better chance understanding the inherent strengths and weaknesses of the Central Galactic Concordance government's expansionist economic policy.

While he sat hunched over three disposable percomps he'd acquired, she brushed and played with the cats, took a nap, organized a mid-afternoon meal for humans and felines out of leftovers, and reintroduced her body to the meditative strength and stretching exercises she'd skipped while playing Laraunte Kane. Her regimen might or might not be helping slow her waster's disease, but at least it gave her the comfort of doing something about it. Once she and Jess were in something larger than a cozy plush playroom, she'd return to the work-in-progress martial arts form she'd invented for herself, designed to accommodate the limitations caused by her waster's disease.

The meditation also gave her the chance to make mindful decisions, instead of just reacting with instinct and emotion. She'd survived two attempts on her life, but it was still the right thing to do to stay in a crowded, crime-ridden city she swore she'd never go back to, and deliver a mysterious information packet stored in her mind to an unknown man. She and Jess were obviously pawns in Neirra Varemba's long game, whatever it was, but it had reunited her with Jess, and Kerzanna owed her for that. Varemba's death only strengthened Kerzanna's determination to carry out the woman's last request. After that, she wanted to go back to Branimir and figure out why people were trying to kill her, and stop them.

Lastly, but most importantly, she wanted to do right by Jess, because she owed him more than anyone. She selfishly wanted him in her bed and in her life, but that wasn't necessarily doing right by him. She couldn't continue to make choices for him, like she'd done when she'd tried to leave him on Branimir, but he needed all the facts first.

She went to the bedroom to pack up her toiletries and check the news and weather. The weather hadn't changed—Ridderth was perpetually cloudy and rainy—but the demons of chaos were meddling again.

"Jess," she called out, "come see what you think, but I think we're going to have to change our plans for the next few days."

When he came to the bedroom entry, she pointed to the display of the top newstrends for the whole planet.

"Faraón Azul Flight Logs Tell Tale of Extraordinary Skill of Injured Pilot, Crew, Passengers"

"Pilot Who Betrayed Faraón Azul Died of Exposure to Transit Space; Mystery Duo Saved Doomed Ship"

"Who Really Saved the Faraón Azul? Passengers Point to Missing Cousins"

"Shipping Company Offers Reward for Info on Missing Crew Member, Passenger"

"Have You Seen These People? Cousins Wanted for Questioning in Faraón Investigation"

The last story featured an artist's interpretation of what she and Jess looked like, based on what journalists had gleaned from passenger descriptions, since Jess had thoroughly twisted any shipcomp records that involved either of them. About the only thing they got right was gender and height, but it was enough.

"Any tall male-female couple in Ridderth is probably being chased down the walkway by swarms of cameras." Ridderth banned the use of flying camera eyes, but enforcement was a joke. Celebrities and politicians invested in aggressive tech suppressors to maintain a modicum of privacy, but even those couldn't stop the long-range visuals. "We'll be on planetwide broadcasts within half a day, tops. We can't stay together."

Jess's shoulders jerked and his left eye twitched, but he shook it off and moved close enough to touch her arm. "The bomber was wrong four years ago. I was wrong. I never should have left you."

Four years ago, she'd have agreed with him wholeheartedly. Ruthless honesty made her realize she'd been wrong. She reached up to palm the side of his face, wishing she could erase the remorse and pain from his expression with a simple brush of her thumb. "You made the best decision you could at the time, but you didn't know everything." It was her turn for revelations. "Remember the stolen hypercubes with ten years' worth of CPS veteran case-file data? The theft that the police used to justify the raids, but never found any trace of? The missing data Davidro asked you about?"

"Sure," he said. "It was the heart of the 'Mabingion Purge' story that proved the CPS had been instigating city riots on multiple planets for years, using false pretenses like 'stolen data' to cover up getting rid of troublemakers and whistleblowers."

She touched her breastbone. "I have them."

His eyes widened, but he didn't pull away from her as she'd half expected he would, or the bomber would. "Do tell."

"First of all, the Minder Veterans Advocates didn't steal the data, they developed it over ten years by interviewing tens of thousands of Minder Corps actives and veterans. We promised anonymity and security, and they gave us their stories and their records. By the time I got involved, the MVA had strong evidence that the Minder Corps was lying about the so-called 'enhancement' drugs and their effects on minders. Since Ridderth's net is as secure as an unlocked, unwatched airspeeder, and half our volunteers were likely CPS informants, a small committee came up with creative ways to hide and protect the data. Because it's Ridderth, it was easy to find a no-questions-asked body shop that could upgrade my Jumper processor and quadruple and encrypt the storage space. Gave me full control of the dormant tracers, too, meaning the CPS couldn't use them to find me later." She'd had to pretend for days that her rebuilt sternum and the replacement biometal didn't hurt like frelling hell, or the medic part of Jess would have insisted on treating her, and then she'd have had to tell him why. "I knew there were other copies, but not how many or who had them. Interrogation telepaths and sifters can't make you share what you don't know."

She looked up into his brilliant blue eyes, and missed the familiar mismatched green and brown. "I made a bad choice in not trusting you to tell you what I was doing. I think your Nordic friend suspected I was a risk, and helped you make the hard, better choice that saved you. Saved us both."

He didn't look convinced, but he was no longer radiating despair and regret. "Did the CPS know what you had?"

"No, or they'd have sent better hunters after me." She gave him a sardonic smile. "Craftiness and paranoia didn't come built in to the Malory Solis identity. I had to learn them on my own." A darker possibility occurred to her. "Either that, or the CPS twister who gifted me with the awful memory of your death also twisted my other memories, too."

"Can you access the hypercubes?"

She nodded. "I've added to them since." Starting with her own records, because Jumpers deserved the truth, too. Particularly those that didn't know about the terrible price they'd be paying.

"Then the twister didn't know about them, or you wouldn't be here. That's a much bigger prize than protecting me."

She hadn't heard this theory before. She raised an eyebrow. "Do tell."

His mouth twitched with humor, acknowledging her salvo. "It's the only scenario that makes sense for the CPS sending someone to muck about in your mind. Which likely means Dixon Davidro ordered it, because he found out you'd started sharing my flat. He thinks I'm asexual, and slow and stupid, but he had telepaths at his disposal. The bleedovers make me hard to read, but not impossible."

"So they made me think you were dead so I wouldn't undermine their neat little story of where you were when the city exploded?" Her temper flared, and she took a calming breath to contain it. "That's warped."

"And Davidro made me think you were dead so I wouldn't look for you." His jaw tightened. "I would have."

She wasn't sure what he wanted at that moment, but she wanted to hold him tight, make love with him, maybe cry on his wide shoulder for the very different star chart they might have created together back then. Unfortunately, every second longer they stayed together now increased the likelihood of them being discovered. She made herself step back, away from temptation, even though doing so hurt worse than the fiery shrapnel that had cost her part of a leg.

He must have recognized and agreed with her resolve, because he nodded once, then tilted his head toward the trending headlines still rolling silently on the wall display. "Give me thirty minutes to activate new IDs for us and get the courier here for the cats."

"I'll get them and us ready to go." She started for the fresher, then turned. "Where are we going?"

"You knew the city better than I did. Where do you suggest?"

She pictured the sprawling city in her head and unearthed memories she'd tried to bury. "*Guógē Shān* district for you, I think." His blank look reminded her that he didn't speak or read Mandarin. Someday, she'd have to ask him why not, because he spoke the other common languages fluently. "Anthem Mountain, in English. Freelance laborers used to live there, probably still do. Play the dim farm boy and you won't stand out. Maybe someone will offer you a janitor job." She sighed. "I tank at undercover work." He opened his mouth to protest, but she interrupted. "No, you know I do. Malámselah suspected I was a lot more than a Class 1 navigator, or he'd have called Yarsulic, not me, after Liao's attack. And Yarsulic will probably work it out, once he has time to think, even if Bhatta doesn't tell him what she knows." She made a face. "I never thought I'd say this, but I think the Canals is the safest place for me. Lots of little sub-sub-sublet rooms if you know how to find them. I interviewed a lot of Minder Corps veterans there, back in the day. Without the 'Tatyana' glamor"—she waved her glittery long fingernails—"I'll be just another twitchy, self-medicating ex-Jumper with waster's, looking for odd jobs and cheap chems."

He nodded, but his expression flatlined. She wasn't happy with their choices, either. But safety was an illusion, and the gods of chaos didn't give a flying fark what two fleeting sparks in the solar winds wanted. All they could to was go along for the ride, and try not to flame out before their time.

CHAPTER 17

* Interstellar: "Chi'imarro" Ship Day 2 * GDAT: 3242.017 *

DIXON DAVIDRO SAT on his heels on the floor in front of Georgie, his pet savant forecaster, who huddled in his chair, wrapped in a blanket despite the sauna-like temperature of the commercial ship's large stateroom. Dixon dripped with sweat, and his nearby enforcer Renner was practically sweating rivers, but Georgie's pale skin was parchment dry.

The emergency trip to Ridderth for him and his entire team of active and reserve independent contractors, or pets, as it amused him to call them, cost a small fortune. However, when ordinarily sunny, childlike Georgie turned darkly apocalyptic, Dixon knew from painful experience to listen. The one and only time he hadn't, he'd lost more than half his pets, including the best bodyguard-shielder he'd ever had, and had come within a nanometer of being caught and sent to the penal restitution system he'd worked for before the CPS. He also knew from experience that Georgie would stay in "Armageddon is coming" mode until the danger was past.

Three of Georgie's high-powered comps displayed constantly morphing shapes of data. The fourth, his favorite, displayed a holo image of a damaged sphere-shaped merchant ship. He stroked it as if he could actually touch it. "Pretty little Blue Pharaoh." His lower tone sounded almost adult. When he got like this, he barely ate and had to be tricked into taking his CPS enhancement drugs. Most forecasters didn't need them, but like all his pets, Georgie was special. Georgie had been his happy, burbling self until he heard about Neirra Varemba's death, and the next thing Dixon knew, Georgie was forecasting the destruction of civilization as they knew it, starting with Dixon.

Dixon had no idea how Georgie figured out a fleeting, media-manufactured drama above the planet Mabingion meant that Nevarr and Orowitz had again slipped through the kill-net, or that they'd gone to ground in stinking Ridderth instead of prudently escaping to anywhere else. But Georgie was rarely wrong about such things, which was why Dixon protected and indulged him.

Vahan's laudable idea of posting rewards for the return of stolen containers of "fully loaded anonymous cashflow chips" on an unknown ship that had left Branimir on a given date had resulted in good business for jack crews who trolled the transit points near Branimir. Good business for the insurance industry, too, who'd likely see increased policy purchases, especially after an under-insured interstellar passenger liner had suffered so many casualties. Best of all, Dixon hadn't needed to pay the reward, because not even mythical phantoms of the pirate clan could recover cargo that didn't exist.

Dixon still puzzled over how or why Nevarr and Orowitz had connected in the first place. His best guess was that Nevarr somehow found out about the ex-Kameleon's considerable bank balance and latched onto him for that, because it certainly wasn't for sex, companionship, or intelligence.

Dixon infused as much warmth into his voice as he could. "Georgie, where do you think Nevarr is now?"

Lamis bel Doro, Dixon's one and only official CPS employee, had supplied Georgie with everything she could dig up on Nevarr, as well as all their records on Orowitz.

Georgie frowned, still caressing the ship image with one hand and manipulating his highly customized computer interface with the other. A skulljack wasn't an option for him. "I told you," he said peevishly. "Ridderth, where it starts. She'll tell them everything she knows, and the rains will turn red." He turned fever-bright, dark-ringed eyes to Dixon. "Nevarr's heart nurtures the seeds of change. You will be white dust. I will be dust." Georgie turned to look at Renner. "You will be covered in our dust." Renner ignored him.

Dixon hid his exasperation behind an attentive smile. Happy Georgie babbled like a brook, but the babbling contained useful information, once Dixon had learned to interpret it. Apocalyptic Georgie's metaphoric pronouncements made the nonsensical poetic quatrains of the Ayorinn Legacy prophecies seem like a detailed instruction manual by comparison.

"George, sweetie," he said, gently pushing a filthy lock of hair off Georgie's face, "how do I find Nevarr? Will she dump Orowitz, or keep him?"

"Parallel." He held up his two index fingers next to each other. "When their streams cross…" He made an X with his fingers, then imitated the sound of an explosion and splayed his fingers like fireworks. "Pretty."

Finally, something else actionable beyond "find Nevarr or die horribly." Dixon smiled and kissed Georgie's cheek. "Thank you, darling, that's very helpful." He stood and pulled out his tunic several times to fan himself, then looked to Renner. "Tell Ms. Sachin to get started tracking Orowitz in Ridderth. We'll hire crew in town. He's an obsessive creature of habit, so he'll probably go back to his old stomping grounds, or maybe where hick farmers hang out. He'll be our bait to reel in Nevarr."

"Now?" Renner's voice sounded huskier than usual, making Dixon realize the analog mechanical collar around the man's neck must have ratcheted tighter. Sure enough, Renner's sweat-soaked white sleeveless tank was pink with fresh blood. Dixon hadn't intended to punish Renner this time; he'd just had his hands full with Georgie.

"Yes, Mr. Renner, tell her now. When you come back, I'll loosen your collar." Dixon fanned himself with his tunic again.

Renner turned and exited the stateroom. His unique, deadly minder talent made it impossible to use ordinary CPS-secured percomps, and he knew better than to leave a conversational record in a commercial ship's comm system. Renner's talent wasn't controllable by any normal means in CPS's arsenal, and he had an unfortunate contrary streak. Dixon finally commissioned a skilled fixer to build Dixon's design for an intricate, entirely mechanical collar to ensure that Renner stayed close and had a deep and abiding interest in keeping Dixon alive and well. He was rather proud of his solution. The collar ratcheted tighter every two hours unless Dixon personally loosened it. Any attempt to use the wrong sequence, or to cut, burn, or freeze the collar, would trigger one of several failsafe mechanisms, any of which would kill Renner instantly. Dixon had made sure not to disclose all the collar's features to Renner. The man wasn't patient or smart, but he was very, very stubborn.

It was too bad Renner had never learned to embrace his fate. It made him constantly surly and angry, but his resulting propensity for violence had served Dixon well over the years. *You really ought to take better care of your tools*, Dixon chided himself.

Dixon had already taken steps to limit Nevarr's and Orowitz's options. He'd issued orders to freeze any and all accounts for Orowitz and Nevarr, but it had taken nearly seven days for Branimir to begrudgingly comply, and the tiresome planetary government had agreed only to monitor Nevarr's business accounts because hers wasn't the only name on them.

As far as Mabingion, Dixon had easily gotten approval for a planetwide detain-and-restrain order on Orowitz. On the rare occasions when ex-Kameleons shattered, the aftermath was usually sordid and always newsworthy, at least in Ridderth. The CPS base that served as the primary headquarters for the Kameleon Corps program shared facilities with the large regular military base. The CPS might not officially acknowledge the Kam program, but it was an open secret in Ridderth. Bad publicity about Kams was bad for everyone.

In the meantime, Dixon had the full resources of the CPS at his disposal, but he'd have to use them judiciously. The emergency trip's purpose was to enforce the security protocol of the CPS's black-box, ultra-secret research project, code-named Charisma, not expose its existence or agenda to every CPS field office on Mabingion.

Which reminded him of the other vexing problem on his plate. Senga Si'in Lai, his assigned third-generation test subject, was deteriorating. The CPS researchers and partner pharmas in the Charisma project were already back at the design boards, coming up with a better alteration procedure to try out on compatible minders.

He should have terminated her back on Branimir, after she'd gallingly embezzled funds from one of his personal accounts to pay for the deaths of everyone on the Branko Regional Business Council. He admitted he'd let his pride and ambition influence his judgment. In his project reports, he'd painted too rosy a picture of his success, where all the other handlers had failed with their subjects months earlier. He'd been in the middle of cleaning up his records to reflect his careful narrative of Si'in Lai's abrupt decline when Georgie had gone off the skytrack.

Dixon had initially planned to bring Si'in Lai with them, so his pets could keep her in line, but Georgie had wailed about certain death, forcing Dixon to leave her behind. He'd reluctantly left her in the care of a local contract shielder and a squad of mercs to keep her iced until he got back. He'd given the merc company permission to bring in sex workers from the three largest joyhouses to keep her busy and distracted for the week he planned to be gone. CPS black-project protocol said her death had to look like an accident, and he only trusted his own pet independent contractors to do it right and not talk about it. The best pet he'd ever had for arranging fatal accidents had been Taliferros Radomir, but he'd also been an out-of-control serial killer who he'd been forced to have Mr. Renner put down not too long ago. Renner lacked Radomir's artistry and planning skills, but the end result was the same.

"Red earth and sparks," murmured Georgie. "The conflagration is coming."

Despite the room's heat, Dixon shivered.

CHAPTER 18

JESS CAST A jaundiced eye at the roiling, blue-gray clouds above the city and resisted the urge to walk faster to avoid the coming rain. One of the tricks to making himself invisible was not to call attention to the ground-eating stride his long legs were capable of, which would call attention to his unusual height. He sat whenever he could, but Ridderth's metro transports didn't have many stops in the poorer parts of the city. As "Petero Bo'totunde," itinerant day laborer with a strong back and sullen attitude, he'd taken an afternoon gig shoveling out a decrepit warehouse in exchange for an anonymous cashflow chip and a cold meat pie so awful even the rats wouldn't touch it. None of the workers knew the name Tuzan.

Part of his urge to walk faster owed to Jess-the-bomber's increasing pressure to move on. Four days in Ridderth was three too many. The longer they stayed, the easier it would be for Kerzanna's enemies to find her. If they had a telepath interrogate her before killing her, he'd be next on their hit parade. And those were the cheeriest scenarios the bomber came up with.

The rain came on quickly. Jess pulled his wide hood forward and shoved his hands in his pockets. His deliberately scuffed and stained overcoat was warm and waterproof, but his boots weren't. The sun was just setting when he got to the building where he'd rented a glorified sleep pod of a room. He paid for one minute's use of the louder-than-a-flux-engine solardry in the building's lobby, then trudged up the two flights of stairs to his room and ducked inside, after verifying his physical telltales hadn't been disturbed. He sat on the foldout, too-short bed and stripped, draping his clothes everywhere so they'd dry. It reminded him of Kerzanna, and made him laugh ruefully. He even missed her bad habits. His body ached for her.

He wrapped himself in the bedraggled robe he'd salvaged from the recycler and sent a ping to "Erielle Courchesne," the new ID for Kerzanna. He didn't control the Ridderth comm nets, so even with his highly customized privacy protocols, they had to use code phrasing, but it was better than nothing.

J: No luck finding work. You?

After a long enough time that he'd started to worry, she responded.

K: I have lead on a real job. Interview tonight.

Jess stood up so fast he nearly bumped his head on the overhead light dome. "Real job" was their agreed code for contact.

J: Lucky you. Where?

K: Forwarding the name and location ref. Favor? Check with your Nordic friend to see if it's legit.

He opened another connection to the highly encrypted shared dataspace he'd created for them to use. It had a flat photo of a handwritten note on a slightly wrinkled paper napkin with a time later that evening, coordinates, and a good drawing of a sweeper. It wasn't Kerzanna's handwriting. He memorized the data and erased the file, then sent his code snippets to scrub the dataspace clean. A quick net query said the location was a pub called Decknav Green Go that served food and the usual drinks, chems, and alterants. Its name and proximity to the sprawling Ridderth military base suggested it catered to regular gunnin from the Ground and Air divisions.

J: How did you hear about it?

K: Canals kid.

J: Hang on.

Jess allowed himself to become Jess-the-bomber to weigh the risks. Kerzanna's enemy hired others to create believable accidents, so luring her to a military bar wasn't their style. The story about the ship-saving missing cousins had been supplanted by a juicy scandal involving a failed public works project that looked like the tip of a very corrupt iceberg, but not all journalists were so easily distracted. A minder with a finder talent who specialized in missing persons could conceivably have made the correlation between his and Kerzanna's successive identities. However, anonymous notes and midnight meetings were too twisty for Ridderth journalists, and as far as he remembered, they wouldn't be welcomed in a military bar.

City maps and images said the standalone building had a lot of windows, three entrances, a flitter stacker on the roof, and was close to two public transport stops. Jess-the-bomber sourly admired the choice of location as being difficult to contain and easy to get out of—one he would have chosen for a meeting.

Jess let the bomber slip away and rubbed his left temple to soothe away the incipient headache.

J: *Nordie says okay.*

K: *Thanks.*

He'd bet his only pair of dry socks that Kerzanna was already on her way to the pub, and would only have diverted if his "Nordic friend" had given her a good enough reason. She hated inaction even more than the bomber did. He dressed quickly while fishing in his mind for any overlay remnants that would help him blend in with the Decknav Green Go's regular patrons. Often, it was better to let such requests loiter in the sidelines of his thoughts than make direct demands.

He let Jess-the-bomber back in for a few minutes to help him choose which weapons to take with him from the collection he'd amassed. He still had the unfortunate Engine Tech Moon's phaseknife, and the four different beamers that came from the hidden armory he'd discovered on the *Faraón Azul*, but he'd also made a few more unconventional weapons in his spare time since then.

In the end, he decided to take everything. It never hurt to be prepared to commit mayhem.

Jess slipped into the deep shadow of the giant glass pillar, the solitary surviving evidence of the never-replaced overhead pedestrian walkway. Ridderth was full of infrastructure gaps caused by the heavy-handed tactics of the police during the Mabingion Purge and previous riots. He pulled his wide hood forward and hunched into the protection of the overhang, just another civilian waiting for the current torrents to ease up.

He'd scouted around the neighborhood and watched the pub for an hour. He hadn't seen Kerzanna enter yet, but he could have missed her. The meeting wasn't for another two hours, but his feet were growing numb from the miniature icy swamps inside his leaking boots and his pants were soaked. As he walked toward the entrance, he pulled together the military persona he cobbled together from bits and pieces, as he'd done with Cadroy Joffalk, the romantic gambler. He let his instinct guide him, straightening up his posture, as if military marching had been drilled into him, and automatically cataloging his surroundings, sort of like Kerzanna did when she was flying.

The pub was welcoming, and the enclosed solardry in the vestibule meant he actually felt warm and almost dry for the first time in days. He hung his overcoat and tough waterproof bag on the locking anti-theft clamp and pocketed the token. He glanced at the tables and booths as he made his way to the bar, meeting any casual gazes with a friendly but neutral nod. The bar was half full, with maybe twenty-five adult customers, since it was too late for kids to be up. The decor looked homey, with soft, patterned textures and bright splashes of color, a departure from the usual past-glories memorabilia in typical military bars. Perhaps that was the point.

"Half pint of light ale, whatever's in the line," he said to the bartender as he placed a cashflow chip in the slot. It flashed a high enough balance to pay for his evening, but not enough to attract trouble.

"Any dinner with that?" The bartender had a high tenor voice with accent-free English and perfect diction. Jess tentatively categorized him as presenting male, but wouldn't want to bet on it. The man had shiny bronze skin, slender musculature, and no visible hair. His shimmery, draped caftan, kohl-lined golden eyes, and multiple heavy gold-chained earrings and bracelets made him look like a wish-granting *djinn* from classical tales. Jess's current persona was fanciful.

Jess smiled. "Got anything that beats a mealpack?" He gave his English a slight lilting accent that went with his current family name of Bo'totunde. Some of his bleedovers had spoken Swahili and left a few fragments of its vocabulary and rhythm.

The bartender looked amused. "What doesn't?" He tilted his head toward the menu display on the counter.

Jess ordered a sandwich and sipped his ale while he waited for a table to open up. All he could see from where he stood was the big common room, but he knew from his research the pub had several smaller meeting rooms along the north side next to the kitchen, plus storerooms and offices. A short, sylph-like server, who looked all of about twelve years old until he saw the front half of him, moved through the tables with ease. He felt himself relax a bit when he realized even the loud, exuberant bunch in the southwest corner didn't grab or harass him. Behavior like that overrode his objectivity.

"New in town?" asked the bartender genially.

"No, but it's been a while." He tilted his head toward the silent newstrend holo above them, showing highlights from an armed clash between Ridderth police in riot gear and a Canals street gang in makeshift armor. "That's new. Used to be bricks."

The bartender frowned and shook his head. "After the Purge, the gangs leveled up."

Jess could hardly blame them. While the CPS may have fomented the week-long riots so they could round up Kerzanna's veterans' group and other so-called "enemies of the peace," the brutal Ridderth police took advantage of the chaos to inflict serious damage against the "criminal element" in the Canals and other troublesome parts of town, not caring how many innocent people they hurt.

The inside entry door opened to let three men out and admit two tall women who were laughing together. Jess took a sip of ale to hide his smile. Kerzanna could make friends anywhere. Under the guise of considering the recently vacated table, he looked for anyone taking particular note of their arrival, but saw nothing out of the ordinary.

Both women wore their hair short or up and their necklines open enough to display their Jumper tattoos with pride. Jess-the-medic noted that the sea-green-haired woman with Kerzanna had cybernetic eyes and hands. The CPS's Jumper body shops could never get the eyes to look quite right. Kerzanna's tanker-gray tunic and newly dark hair and eyebrows made her skin look pale and gaunt, in keeping with her chem-addict cover. Jess assumed the lumpy pockets of her cargo pants contained some of the smaller weapons she'd collected from the Branimir mercs. Both women exhibited the slight movement hesitation symptomatic of waster's disease. Jess-the-bomber shoved aside Jess-the-man's distress and watched the women place their chem orders out of his peripheral vision as he pretended to be looking at the news. He settled on one of the adjustable-height barstools so they could take the vacant table.

An hour later found him and his long legs crammed into one of the tiny, two-person booths, pretending his head didn't hurt, and nursing a glass of fizzy fruit juice while letting the pub's pleasant ambiance wash over and through him. The golden-eyed bartender had left thirty minutes ago. His replacement was a big and burly, very alpha male who looked more like a bouncer than a bartender, but he smiled easily and knew his customers.

Jess took on the appearance of someone mulling over a big decision and who wouldn't be good company. In part, it was true. If the meeting didn't pan out, he wanted to get off Mabingion that night, even if he had to buy his own interstellar yacht, but he had Kerzanna to consider.

Superficial, coded pings gave him no clue as to what she was thinking. He'd only seen her from afar in the past four days, and she'd probably kick his ass if she knew he'd sometimes trailed her around the Canals instead of looking for the "real job." Not that she needed his help. The previous evening, she'd efficiently and effectively fended off a pair of chemmed, would-be muggers and left them unconscious in an alley. He'd wanted to ask her about it, but then he'd have had to explain how he knew.

Kerzanna's green-haired companion, whose name he hadn't caught, stood and stretched, said something to Kerzanna, then headed toward the front door. Kerzanna idly toyed with her bracelet percomp and stared moodily out the window at the rain.

Jess's hidden earwire pinged a message.

K: Another napkin. Freshers. Now.

Jess drained his fruit juice and transferred a small tip from his cash flow chip to the server, then threaded through the tables toward the back. The slender server intercepted him and pointed toward the open office door behind him. "Use the employee fresher through there." He made a face. "I hate wet cleanups."

Jess lingered, as if uncertain, until he saw Kerzanna out of the corner of his eye, then trudged slowly toward the door as he listened to the server give Kerzanna the same instructions.

The lights came on as he stepped into the room. Beyond the nondescript table and chairs and a tiny kitchen area were four closed iris-style doorways. He stopped and looked to Kerzanna, who wordlessly went around him and headed for the second-to-left door. She pulled a napkin out of her pocket and held it up to the lock. The door irised open to reveal a motley collection of cleaning supplies and sweepers. She stepped in, and Jess followed. Her body language said she was confident about where they were going.

The door irised closed behind him. She held the napkin up to what he'd taken to be a wallcomp, but turned out to be controls for a lift, which took them down.

Kerzanna caught his hand and stepped closer to speak quietly. "The server is a telepath. He gave me instructions. We'll take a forty-meter tunnel to the building north of us, then go to the second floor. I'm sorry, but he picked your face out of my mind." She closed the distance between them and wrapped him in an embrace. His arms went around her of their own volition, and the world stopped for the long moment he held her and soaked in the warm feel of her against him.

In that moment, he knew he would never leave her again.

"They'd have had to see me eventually. I have the key." He drew in her scent, the one that amped his hormones every time. His body stirred for her, even though the timing was terrible. "How are you?"

"Tired of being cold and wet. Tired of telepaths waltzing through my thoughts at will." She squeezed him a little tighter, then let him go and stepped back and caught his hand again. "Glad to see you're all right, though I can't say I'm fond of the orange stripes."

"Bo'totunde has distractingly bad taste in hair color and makeup," he agreed.

She snorted and opened her mouth to speak, but the lift stopped and the doors irised open.

By tacit agreement, they didn't talk as they walked purposefully through the tunnel. Someone had money to spend, because Ridderth's shallow water table made subterranean structures difficult to construct and maintain, and the lighted tunnel's finished interior was warm and dry. Another, almost identical lift, sans cleaning supplies, took them to a conventional office building hallway. Silence prevailed once the lift irised closed behind them. All the doors were closed and dark except one.

Jess casually slid his hands in his vest pockets as they walked, and powered on the small beamer as they stepped into the office that had no signage on the door.

"Greetings, Subcaptain Nevarr. Please don't shoot me, Mr. Orowitz. Neirra Varemba went to a lot of trouble for us to meet."

The distinctive voice belonged to the golden-eyed *djinn* of a bartender from the Decknav Green Go.

CHAPTER 19

TELEPATHS MADE KERZANNA uncomfortable. A hazy memory from her time with Neirra Varemba said Tuzan, if that was his name, was one. She blanked her expression as she sat in one of the expensive adaptive chairs he'd offered to her and Jess.

He could have pulled their real names out of her head, but the clandestine contacts and meeting arrangements had taken time, so his claim that Varemba had pinged him about meeting them seemed plausible. More importantly, Jess's subtly rounded shoulders and eye twitches said his paranoid bomber persona was up front, and so far, he seemed willing to listen.

"You are very hard people to find." Instead of sitting behind the desk, Tuzan sat a few meters away in the small office's third guest chair facing them. It made her think the office was borrowed for the occasion. His bare feet, loose, baggy pants, and long tunic disguised but didn't diminish his exotic looks and natural charisma. She'd initially thought he was barely thirty, but something in his eyes now said he was far older.

Jess gave him a thin, humorless smile. "So are you."

Tuzan waved graceful fingers. "I had the advantage of knowing when and where to look for you. Even so, it took days for my very good finder to see the pattern of anonymous queries and trace them from Joffalk and Kane, the heroes of the *Faraón*, then to a joy palace, then to the Anthem district."

Jess nodded, but didn't seem unduly concerned. When she thought about it, she knew why. He'd wanted to be found, to distract attention away from her. She'd made contact by luck.

Tuzan turned to her. "I received part of a key for Neirra's message packet. Do you have the rest of it?"

"I do," said Jess. "I'm her insurance." The warning in his voice was unmistakable.

Kerzanna took a deep breath and held onto her temper. "Jess, just give him the key. Varemba trusted him." She tapped her brow. "The sooner he gets the farking message out of my mind, the sooner we can get the hell out of here." She turned to Tuzan. "I'm tired of being a token in someone else's game. I don't like telepaths in my head, but I can't stop you, so just do it."

Jess's expression flatlined, but he nodded once. His shoulders straightened and his right eye stopped twitching. He spoke a short series of numbers and letters that sounded like location coordinates.

Tuzan nodded once, and all of a sudden, he was in her mind. He must be a high-level telepath if he didn't need to touch her.

I promise I won't go anywhere you don't invite me.

She pushed an ugly memory back into its closet. *Just take your packet and get the hell out.*

She had a fleeting impression of hurt feelings, but she couldn't control her rising fear. She knew it was different, that she wasn't the terrified teenager being compelled to kneel before the short, reeking man in the alley, but just like the memory of Jess's death, it had power over her intellect. Tuzan seemed to recognize it, and quickly said Jess's code and another in her mind, then pushed it at the black box that had been sitting in her memory like a neutron star.

She reeled as overwhelming sensations, emotions, facts, images, memories not her own, and phantom pain flooded into her. She somehow knew what it was like to have an articulated metal parasite on her back actively trying to kill her. She felt warm, motherly affection for a big, angry, anguished man covered in blood. A heartbreakingly beautiful brown-faced little girl with a cloud of wavy hair held up her arms and demanded a goodnight kiss. She hugged a different version of Tuzan as he cried. Her vision doubled, and she realized she was also seeing her body from Tuzan's point of view, arching and falling back in the chair as if in seizure, and seeing Jess's alarmed expression morph into lethal anger. Desperation shot through her.

Tuzan! Control me or Jess will kill you!

She felt her body relax and her eyes close, even though her brain was still trying to send panicked, garbled orders to both fight and run. She reached desperately for the quiet, anywhere-but-there place in her mind that would let her come out of this with her sanity intact.

Sorry. The packet is big. It's spilling over. The walls around Tuzan's mind thinned, giving her glimpses of his struggle to keep control.

The deluge in her mind eased, depositing smaller nuggets of data. Like the impression that Neirra's long game had started when the Ayorinn forecast had first ignited the original Ridderth riots thirty years ago. That Neirra wasn't just a top-level healer and a telepath, she was a twister. That she'd met Kerzanna once before.

Whatever Tuzan was doing now was rubbing her mental fur the wrong way. It felt like mopping up, and it came to her that he wasn't just a telepath, he was a cleaner, able to erase her memories at will. It didn't surprise or scare her as much as it should have.

Almost done. Another wave of apology accompanied his words.

She distracted herself by going through her survival checklist. She felt the nauseous aftermath of an adrenaline spike. Considering how many she'd already had in the last week, she'd worry about that later. Her internal chrono said only three minutes had elapsed since he'd first entered her mind, but it felt like hours. Her face felt wet, and she realized she'd been crying. Jumpers didn't cry, but she wasn't one anymore, so she allowed it just this once. Tuzan released her body right as one last surge of agony rocked her.

She heard a sound of pain and snapped her eyes open. "Jess, no!"

Jess had Tuzan in a headlock, holding what looked like an amped wirekey to the man's throat. "He was hurting you."

"No. Varemba stuck a big farkin' thorn in my mind. He pulled it out." She pulled herself to her feet, half surprised she didn't topple over. For once, her mind was shakier than her body. "It was just pain." She mustered up a challenging grin. "Jumpers eat pain for breakfast."

She willed him to read her face, to see that she was fine, or soon would be. He stared at her for a long moment, then let Tuzan back down to the carpeted floor and stepped back. He looked stubbornly unrepentant.

She caught Tuzan's eye. "Thank you." She knew he could have fought back but refrained.

"You're welcome." Tuzan took a deep breath, held it, then let it out in a rush of air. He gave them both serious looks and pointed to the chairs. "Shall we sit? We have some issues to discuss."

She sat, and after a long moment, Jess slipped the wirekey in his pocket, then pushed his chair closer to hers and sat on the edge, his back ramrod straight. No eye twitches, it was just Jess himself, feeling protective. She knew the feeling well.

"What issues?" Jess asked.

Tuzan sighed and rubbed his neck. "For one, you both know too much, and you're vulnerable." His lips thinned in annoyance. "Neirra took enormous risks to help people, but she expected them to be willing to do the same. She's given me—us—time bombs, ready to go off. She expected us to use them for the cause."

Jess's eyes narrowed. "What cause?"

A memory, or something like it, fell into place in her mind. "Ayorinn's forecast," she said.

With those words came a whole web of associations, like a neural net coming online. "Varemba was there, in the Ridderth Riots of 3209, when the Legacy was born. The forecast itself is older." She looked to Jess, then to Tuzan. "The CPS brought her in from far away to help deal with the conspirators, to twist them, make them think they'd been betrayed by their…"

Another not-memory opened, of sitting in a harshly bright room on the Mabingion Space Station, and Neirra's cool fingers caressing her face. She took a ragged breath, trying to hang onto her temper. "She twisted *me*. She gave me the memory of Jess's death."

She reached for his hand, needing to feel the solid warmth of the still living, still breathing man beside her. He clasped her hand in both of his.

Tuzan nodded. "Yes, under Dixon Davidro's direct order, but she also left you the real memory, hidden away in your mind. She gave me the key." He looked away, then back to her. "It'll hurt, and it'll feel weird for months until the true memory reintegrates. The twisted memory will always be there, competing with it, because she tied your emotions to the false one. The events around it will always be hazy."

"Personal experience?" asked Jess.

Tuzan sighed. "The riots were…" He shuddered delicately. "It was an awful time. A killing time. The CPS's favorite tactic is to turn minder against minder. Even under the control drugs, Neirra was a top-level multi-talent. She made them think she was impaired, that they controlled her. She used that trick and invented others to save a lot of minders, right under the noses of her handlers and the other telepaths. She saved hundreds of us—me and my sister included."

Kerzanna squared her shoulders. "If it means I get the truth, I'll take the pain." It couldn't be worse than that memory. Nothing was.

In her mind, Tuzan spoke what seemed like a random series of words in several languages, and her head split open. She gritted her teeth against the pressure behind her eyes, and released Jess's hand so she couldn't crush his poor fingers. As the worst of the pain subsided, she warily called up the memory of Jess's death, except it wasn't Jess, it was a bloody, battered woman she'd never seen before, frothing at the mouth with rage, who'd used telekinesis to crash a police aircar and kill its occupants. An angry police officer made her kneel and executed her on the spot, splashing her brains against the wall. It had little of the personal emotional trauma associated with the Jess memory, but it felt as nightmarishly weird as Tuzan said, because the police uniform morphed into a CPS Minder Corps uniform and Jess's image superimposed itself in parts, like a double exposure.

"Okay?" asked Jess quietly. She knew he was worried, though he hid it well. She nodded, more grateful than she could say that he was there with her. She'd spent far too long without him.

She wanted to be done with all of this and move on. "What time bombs, and how are we vulnerable?"

Tuzan's expression was a cross between disapproval and sympathy. "Neirra's last message asked me to bring you a gift." He splayed graceful fingers toward a side table to Jess's left that had a small box she'd assumed was decoration. "She said we're all sad, untrusting sea fish who would need proof."

Jess leaned over and grabbed it with one hand, then passed it to her.

Inside was a medical instrument for measuring and monitoring neuro-response in Stage Four Pelker Thomré Vadembo Syndrome. The tester for waster's disease.

She lifted the innocuous little unit, glad that her hand was steadier than her thoughts. It weighed so little. The tightness in her chest proved that despite rigid vigilance, hope, her nemesis, had somehow crept into her. Hope that Neirra had given her at least a few more years to be with Jess, if he wanted her. Hope that Neirra had succeeded in creating a miracle. The test results readout would change nothing... or everything.

Sternly telling herself to quit stalling, she pushed up her sleeve and slapped the tester on her forearm, like she'd seen other Jumpers do. It automatically wrapped around her arm. Her skin itched for a moment where microneedles pierced her skin and extended nanofilaments into her muscles and nerves. She'd have the answer in twelve minutes.

"You'll need all your baseline data for a meaningful comparison," said Jess, the slight French accent of his medic persona softening his consonants.

"I have it." To distract herself from watching the excruciatingly slow countdown, she focused on Tuzan. "What other bombs did I deliver?"

Tuzan looked to Jess. "She left a packet in your head, too. I don't know how, because Kameleon brains are a convoluted, fractured nest of vipers, but I have the key." Tuzan correctly interpreted Jess's sudden stillness. "Yes, I know all about Kameleons, and that you were one." He smirked a little and waved a circling hand. "I didn't always clean *offices* for a living, you know."

Phantom memories sparked in her head but flitted away when she tried to catch them. She wondered if this was what Jess constantly felt with the overlay *déjà vu* fragments. No wonder he was a little fractured.

Jess appeared calm, but his right eye twitched. "Do you know what's in the packet?" The Nordic accent said the bomber persona was again in the pilot's seat.

"Yes, because Neirra liked redundancy." Tuzan sounded irritated. "It'll mean more to you, though."

Jess glanced at her, and she nodded to let him know she trusted Tuzan, who'd passed up multiple opportunities to destroy them.

Jess's expression flatlined. "I'm ready."

Tuzan sighed and crossed his arms as he spoke a nonsensical phrase. Jess's expression didn't change, but his hands made fists. She knew he was riding out the pain and the flood of data as she had. She wished she could help make it easier for him.

After long seconds, Jess's hands slowly relaxed, and he blinked a couple of times. "The CPS's Charisma project for genetic alteration. Dixon Davidro."

More elusive phantom memories fluttered in her mind, but she ignored them.

"Indeed." Tuzan frowned. "And to think I once believed the CPS treated minders better than pet-trade experi…" His voice trailed off, his focus seeming to drift for a moment.

Tuzan abruptly stood up and crossed his arms, shoving his hands under his armpits. "I'm told my finder friend says someone with considerably less subtlety than you has been looking for Joffalk and Kane. The reward is ten times what the journalists are offering. The same anonymous cashflow account just offered the same amount for Orowitz and Nevarr, and the newly cohabbed couple, Vasil and Edisson."

She and Jess stood almost simultaneously. Jess spoke first. "They'll find the trail I left so you could find us." The Nordic accent was back.

Tuzan swore in a language she didn't know. "Remember what I said about being vulnerable because you know too much?" He pointed at Jess. "You're hard to crack, but"—he pointed to her—"*you* are an open book to any telepath who wants to know."

She frowned, not liking what she was about to say, but it had to be done. "Then clean my memory, and we'll go." If they could stay one step ahead–

"I can't," snapped Tuzan testily. "For one, I'd have to practically blank-slate Mr. Orowitz to get all the memory fragments his overlay personalities have already squirreled away. More importantly, your memory has to be intact, because if Neirra really did discover a repeatable technique for healers to cure waster's disease, you're our only proof, and you have the only other copy of the instructions. No one will believe us if you aren't whole."

So that's what Neirra had meant when she'd told Kerzanna she *was* the message. She hated that role.

"Us?" asked Jess.

"Yes, us." Tuzan blew out an exasperated breath. "You both know too much about me, now, too, which was exactly what Neirra wanted. She used you both as human couriers to force us to make a connection for our own good." He snorted. "Or for the good of the cause, at any rate."

Another phrase rose to the surface of her mind, and she shook her head. Distracting flotsam and jetsam from other people's lives was getting annoying. "Your shadow railway." Once again, as soon as she said the words, another web of information fell into place. It was a nickname for the organization Tuzan and his sister had put together to help minders escape the CPS, and it was part of a larger effort throughout the galaxy.

Jess's eyes widened, and his jaw clenched slightly. Apparently, Neirra had implanted the same knowledge bomb in his mind, too. The woman's talent was terrifying.

Tuzan looked back and forth at them. "That's just fabulous." He rocked side to side, as if he wanted to pace. "Neirra was a unique talent, but she was also driven and ruthless. She's risked a lot of lives to force me to be a good little dog and do what she wants."

Her new knowledge said the shadow railway helped minders—and sometimes their extended families—leave CPS Minder Corps service and disappear. She shook her head and looked to Jess. "We'll find our own way off Mabingion. Tonight, if we can."

"Yes." The fierce promise in his expression was unmistakable. She released the breath she didn't realize she'd been holding.

Jess proved to have been thinking more strategically than she was. "Why you?" he asked Tuzan. "Your shadow railway is a part of a bigger network than just Mabingion. She could have sent us anywhere."

Tuzan shrugged. "Who knows? Just my lucky day, I guess."

Jess's eyes narrowed. "You're lying."

Kerzanna raised an eyebrow. He was rarely so sure of himself when it came to people, or so confrontational.

Tuzan's lips thinned in irritation. "Because she knew I have a way to protect you."

Jess frowned. "What, a trusted shielder, to get us through the crowds?"

"No, your own permanent shields." Tuzan put his fists on his hips.

It was Kerzanna's turn to frown. "Some sort of tech implant?" New hardware was usually incompatible with her Jumper systems, and likely much less with whatever undocumented bioware was in Jess's brain.

"No, permanent *minder* shields." Tuzan held up a slender finger to forestall whatever Jess was going to say. "The thing is, it'll take a couple of days to arrange, because I'm not exposing my resources unnecessarily."

"I hate to point out the obvious," she said, "but we're not minders."

Tuzan waved her words off. "You don't have to be. That's why I kept it secret, but she found out somehow. To people like Neirra, it's just another tool in their arsenals. They don't stop to think of the cost or the risks." He looked at them consideringly, then seemed to come to a decision. "First, you have to agree to let me erase your memory of how this gets arranged and how it happens, or we'll stop here. Second, you'll need to go completely off grid and keep moving while we decoy the bounty hunters. I'll put you on the shadow railway."

"Yes," she said, glancing at Jess, who nodded his agreement.

Tuzan looked pointedly at her. "We communicate via minders—telepaths—and you'll have to be around them all the time, because I'll need you on call."

She appreciated the warning. "I'll be okay, as long as they don't compel me."

"And you," Tuzan said to Jess, "need a sifter to teach you how to handle your talent, or you're vulnerable. I don't know any I trust right now, but I'll look."

Jess shook his head. "Sifters can't affect the overlays." He lifted his arm and turned his wrist to show his percomp. "If you'll turn off the tech suppressor that's somewhere in here, I can help with the decoy effort."

Tuzan blew out a noisy breath. "What part about 'completely off grid' did you not understand? And I meant your sifter talent, not the personalities in your head."

Jess's expression flatlined. "I'm not a minder."

Tuzan seemed oblivious to Jess's sudden tension. "Yes, you are, because only sifters can tolerate the Kameleon process. Kameleons are rare and valuable. Low to mid-level sifters are so common, they're expendable. The CPS made sure to erase that from your memory the day you signed the recruiting contract, and rewrote your CPS Testing Center records to match."

Jess shook his head. "Even if that were true, why would they care if we knew?"

"My guess is they didn't want you experimenting during your downtime, or using your talent on your handler. Don't believe me? Ask yourself why you've always been good at knowing when someone is lying or is about to be violent, or why you hate crowds, or why you can sense when someone's a minder, or why most pain and sleep drugs don't work well or at all on you?"

Kerzanna looked at Jess, remembering how quickly he'd come after her in the Branimir Spaceport, even after she'd dosed him with two full dormo patches.

"And you know this because..." Jess trailed off, inviting Tuzan to fill in the rest.

"I was once a good little Institute-trained CPS cleaner. Tightly controlled, went where they sent me, did as I was told, including making brand new Kameleons forget they even knew what a sifter was." He thrust his chin out and stared at Jess. "Tell me I'm lying."

Jess held the gaze for a moment, then looked away, his face troubled. She could tell the idea bothered him.

Tuzan rolled his eyes, then looked at Kerzanna. "Where did you find the low-profile IDs to use? We might need two more of them."

She held up her hands in denial. "I'm just a Jumper. Jess is the data genius."

At Tuzan's questioning look, Jess took a long moment to respond. "I created them."

"But they have a histor... Oh, that's why some of the cubes and arrays disagreed—you found soft insertion trusts and twisted them." Tuzan's eyes gleamed. "Very slick."

A long monotone beep startled her. She'd forgotten about the waster's test unit on her arm. She looked at the blue numbers displayed on the tiny flat screen. She pressed the release sequence so the unit would let go of her arm, then showed the display to Jess and Tuzan.

31%.

Tuzan didn't know what it meant, but Jess remembered. "It's seven percent lower than her last test." Thoughtful, softhearted Jess knew Jumpers didn't cry, so he let one tear fall on her behalf before he blinked them away.

Tuzan started to smile, but Kerzanna squared her shoulders and shook her head. "One test isn't proof of anything. I'll repeat it tomorrow. And I need another test unit in case this one is defective." Miracles were for believers and magic was for fantasy fiction. "If we're going somewhere from here, I left a bag and coat in the pub, and Jess did the same."

Tuzan's gaze went inward for a moment, and then he was back. "We'll get them to you. You were smart to split up, and we'll keep it that way. My sister is looking for places for you tonight. I don't know about tomorrow yet." He caught Jess's eye and gave him a look of sly invitation, full of interest. "Before we go, why don't you and I create a little mischief?"

Jess looked surprised, as he always did when he realized someone was making a pass at him, but one of his overlays rescued him. "But of course, *monsieur.* What did you have in mind?"

CHAPTER 20

* Planet: Mabingion * GDAT: 3242.021

DIXON DAVIDRO HATED lists. They meant his life had become too complicated to manage in his mind, which meant he might be missing important things. He'd been plagued by the sensation of forgetting things ever since arriving in Ridderth.

The pale, monotone color palette and well-worn furniture of the rented business condo depressed him, but he could stand anything for a few days if he had to, even no sexual encounters or audiences for them. He'd reward himself after taking care of the people who had Georgie so worried.

Dixon pulled the list and his pen out of his bag. His CPS peers, and even his supervisor, teased him about his use of primitive technology. He encouraged them to think it was a whimsical affectation. He wrote in a code he'd learned so long ago that it was almost a second language to him. Even the most sophisticated intelligent scanners and powerful infiltration software couldn't sniff records that weren't in digital form. He'd learned the hard way that anything he couldn't control had a way of coming back to bite him when least expected.

He forced himself to sit calmly on a high stool at the kitchen area's counter and sip the real coffee he'd had to make for himself. Lamis was busy using her CPS authority to dig into local records, and Vahan, his shielder and backup enforcer and bodyguard, couldn't make a decent cup of coffee if her life depended on it. He'd sent her on a food and supplies run, since he didn't want deliveries being made to the condo.

The newest addition to his list worried him the most. Georgie, still in doom-and-gloom mode, had noticed a trending unsourced rumor in Ridderth about a mysterious government project known as Charisma. The project members had maintained perfect control for four years, and now suddenly, a few days after Nevarr and Orowitz lost themselves in Ridderth, information was leaking. Dixon didn't believe in coincidence, and the CPS sure as hell didn't. He needed to find and contain the leak fast, or the CPS would do it for him, making him as expendable as a dying ex-Jumper and a dumb-as-dust ex-Kameleon.

As a consequence, he couldn't just kill them, he had to get his hands on Nevarr to learn how she found out about the project and who she'd told. Dixon had initially underestimated Nevarr's un-Jumper-like subtlety and craftiness, but he had her measure now and would soon have her in hand, one way or the other. He also might have underestimated Orowitz's contribution to the pair's continued elusiveness. Kameleons had emergency survival routines built into their bioware, and Nevarr may have inadvertently triggered his. Fortunately, all Dixon needed was a sifter to shut Orowitz down, and Dixon had one of those. Then he'd have that sifter, Zerrell, and Xan, his slightly warped pet telepath, ransack Nevarr's mind. After that, he'd pay a local wetwork crew to dispose of both Nevarr and Orowitz, plus whoever else needed silencing, and be on his way.

To that end, he had Renner and Xan nosing about where Jumpers liked to congregate. Nevarr probably wasn't stupid enough to go there herself, but perhaps she'd been seen somewhere and recognized. Sachin, his cleaner, was out hiring the crew. Her addiction to helio, a highly illegal drug that bleached her skin to frosty blue-white and drained the color from her eyes, gave her instant credibility with the criminal element, no matter what planet.

Despite Renner's unsolicited opinion that it muddied the waters and invited freelancers to meddle in their business, Dixon had decided to continue offering the various rewards for information on the successive pseudonyms Nevarr and Orowitz had used. He'd also issued official CPS detain-and-restrain orders for them, with the best descriptions and images he had. The rewards and person-of-interest orders effectively turned the CPS offices and citizens of Ridderth into his personal surveillance network, though he'd had to pay extra for the service to sort through the inevitable flood of bad tips. As he'd pointed out to Renner, they didn't have time to be elegant.

Next on his list was how best to exploit the information that Renner and Xan had already uncovered about a ring of local telepaths who helped fugitive minders escape from the CPS Minder Corps and leave the planet. Breaking up the ring would look good on his record. However, based on Georgie's cryptic pronouncements, Dixon suspected Nevarr and Orowitz might have stumbled across them, too. Maybe he could send Vahan out to investigate first, though it left him without the protection of a trusted shielder. He wouldn't be entirely alone, but close enough to make him uncomfortable.

Several loud thuds over his head signaled the expected arrival of a rented aircar on the building's rooftop airpad. Zerrell was the last of the mobilized contractors to arrive. Dixon used to have more, but they'd proved too difficult and expensive to manage.

He turned his list face down and waited for the tiny lift to disgorge its passenger. Zerrell seemed older and grayer since the last time Dixon had activated him. The man was barely one hundred and ten, and he looked it. Really, there was no excuse for people letting themselves go like that.

"Pleasant trip?" asked Dixon.

"Are they ever?" asked Zerrell. He patted the bulky bag at his side. "Where am I staying?"

"Here. Lamis will show you later. Put your things under there for now." He waved toward the conference table they'd dragged into the kitchen for meals.

As Zerrell did so, Dixon briefed him on the mission status and current plans, and Zerrell's role in all of it. "How close do you need to be to trigger Orowitz's failsafe?"

"His what?" asked Zerrell, looking puzzled.

Dixon frowned. "I thought you worked for the Kameleon Corps?"

"I did, in the civilian intake department." He looked intrigued. "What does the failsafe do?"

"Emergency shutdown, in case one of the overlay personalities goes rogue." Dixon now wished he'd looked more closely at Zerrell's history before adding him to the team. An ugly thought crossed his mind. Sometimes, his staff didn't like their assignments, and Zerrell's loyalty was insured by fear, not willing cooperation. "You're sure you weren't trained on how to trigger the failsafe? It would be a shame to have to tell your family about your other career."

Zerrell stilled and his expression hardened. "I think I'd remember it." Bitter reproach laced his tone. "But of course, Xan can read me and check."

"Of course." Dixon sighed. He hated it when his staff—prima donnas, every one of them—got their feelings in a twist and sulked all day. He had no errands to send the depressing man on, to get him out of Dixon's hair… but wait, he did. Morose, conservative Zerrell would be perfect.

"I'm sending you undercover to infiltrate the ring for fugitive minders. The ring uses telepaths for communication, but Mr. Renner says the rest of their security is flawed." Dixon liked his idea more and more. "Your primary goal is to find Orowitz and Nevarr, but while you're there, use your talents to collect evidence on the whole operation, and get the names of other minders who have used it. Get each node to pass you on quickly to the next one."

"I can't do that and be here to interrogate Nevarr."

"I know that," Dixon said as patiently as he could, "but I don't have her yet, and in the meantime, you can be useful. Get Lamis to set you up with an identity." Dixon cocked his head, trying to see Zerrell as a suspicious stranger would. "Lose the autotailored business suit and percomp, and buy some set-size, local-style civilian clothes. And you'll need a waterproof coat and boots, because it's the rainy season." He pointed toward the deep-inked, intricate marriage tattoos on the back of Zerrell's hands and wrists. "No time to send you to a body parlor to get those removed, so we'll make you newly single after the tragic loss of your spouse. It'll be the reason you decided to leave the CPS." He snorted. "That, and because they just transferred you to stinking Ridderth."

"What do I do if I find Nevarr or Orowitz? Or find information on where they are?"

"Ping Mr. Renner or Lamis… no, you can't. The ring uses tech suppressors and confiscates comm devices." Dixon drummed his fingers on the counter and thought a moment. "Set up a passive drop—give Lamis the ping ref—and buy new disposable percomps between each node to send your reports. I'll have Mr. Xan contact you every few hours, or when we need you to come back." Xan's ability to find known mental signatures and phenomenal range alone had made it worth the trouble to save him and keep him entertained. "Ask Mr. Renner for a briefing on the organization and their security. He's escorting Mr. Xan." Only Renner, with his natural immunity to telepaths and his unique talent to deliver pain, could keep Xan on task. Otherwise, Xan exhausted himself, searching any mind he could reach for memories of sexual encounters, since he had none of his own. He couldn't bear to be touched.

"How is Georgie?" Zerrell's ordinary job, the one his family knew about, was providing therapy to traumatized children. People like Georgie were right in his star lane.

"The same. I gave him the northeast office on the second floor. You could drop in and see him before you go. Maybe you could get him to take a shower." Georgie disliked water, and hated the alternative sonic or mist options even more. Dixon smiled ruefully. "As it is, we're going to have to pay an extra fumigation fee when we leave."

Zerrell nodded once, then headed toward the stairs. Dixon had no idea how a children's therapist got along without a sense of humor.

Once Zerrell was out of sight, Dixon looked at his list again. Senga Si'in Lai, his failed Charisma subject, had gotten so bad that the mercs in charge of her had been forced to drug her to keep her quiet. He wrote a notation to check that he'd provided the list of approved drugs to use. The ultra-secret research treatment had skewed some of her physiology. Dixon didn't know why the CPS kept trying to go down the genetic alteration path. They'd only had one success, nearly two hundred years ago, and the procedure that created paracommando pathfinders—popularly known as death trackers—resulted from a lab mistake. Dixon wasn't supposed to know that part of the history, but he'd done due diligence before tying his rising star to the high-risk-high-reward Charisma project. He still needed to put the finishing touches on his final report of Si'in Lai's decline. After all, he had a reputation to maintain as the project's most successful handler.

Last on his list was a reminder to rent a secure storage unit, preferably within walking distance. A standard business condo was a poor choice for conducting interrogations and keeping bodies iced until the wetwork crew could pick them up. Dixon decided he'd take care of the rental himself, since he unfortunately knew Ridderth far better than his staff. Once again, the sense that he was forgetting something fluttered through his mind, but it wouldn't solidify, so he ignored it.

Since Zerrell didn't know how to trigger the Kameleon failsafe, Dixon needed to hire a sifter who did, so he added it to his list. At least they were in the right place to do it, near Kam Corps headquarters. Plenty of active-duty Minder Corps staff did a little moonlighting when they could get away with it. Because of Ridderth's history with the Ayorinn nonsense, the city was rife with informants, so he'd need Xan to weed them out, and Sachin to clean any inconvenient memories afterward. He really missed Neirra Varemba at times like these. Twisted memories were far harder to detect by the CPS telepathic auditors. But that ship had sailed and burned into a crisp, so he needed to move on. He quickly used his percomp to post a contract offer on a few selected nets. Considering the high fee he was offering, word would get around quickly.

CHAPTER 21

* Planet: Mabingion * GDAT: 3242.022 *

JESS-THE-LABORER ostensibly surfed the newstrends on his cheap but waterproof tablet while seated at the end of the outside bench at the public transport stop, waiting for the metro. He wore a cap over his buzz-cut hair and kept his maroon hood up, despite the prediction for a sunny morning, or what passed for one in Ridderth. The other people waiting at the stop stayed under the canopy. His excuse was the desire to avoid listening to a cantankerous discussion of the politics surrounding the spectacularly failing government headquarters project. Ridderth was a cornucopia of corruption, incompetence, and shady business, which was why so many journalists made a good living there.

The icon he'd been waiting for blinked. He moved so his body blocked anyone's view of the tablet, then called up the data sent by his motley array of stolen camera eyes. Jess-the-bomber had helped him hijack and take control of them, and Jess had used his own programming skills to rewrite their onboard protocols so they routed their feeds through a random net path to his tablet, masquerading as flat video segments from newstrends.

The composite images of his target, Castal's Corner, told him the diner was a popular lunchtime destination for a variety of clientele, from mid-level corporate types to starving students. They also confirmed that the diner's actual access points matched the records he'd been able to find. Unfortunately, like most public businesses in Ridderth, the diner used a tech suppressor that killed cameras, so he could only see the customers entering and leaving, and those who were visible through the windows.

Tuzan had slightly relaxed his "off the grid" requirement after Jess had proven his skills by showing how he'd customized his percomp. For once, Jess hadn't needed to simplify his explanations, because Tuzan turned out to have similar interests and expertise. And as with Kerzanna, Jess didn't have to hide who he was around Tuzan. Jess liked him.

He hadn't liked not being able to contact Kerzanna at all for the last two days, however much he agreed with the prohibition. They had to assume the deep-pocketed CPS was behind the lucrative reward offers, which was why he and Kerzanna had agreed on the need to stay apart. The CPS's involvement was also why Tuzan had agreed to let him use his untraceable migratory code snippets to insert the "rising trend" on the secret Charisma project. With luck, the news would distract the CPS, and if he managed to daylight enough of the project details that were now packed in his and Tuzan's minds, thanks to Neirra, the CPS wouldn't have a reason to kill them anymore. Besides, working on the code gave him something to do when he couldn't sleep. The only news he had about Kerzanna was a series of test results numbers from the two waster's test units. The units agreed, and showed another one-percent drop, but it could just be a temporary remission. If she still thought she was dying, she might leave again to protect him.

He also hadn't liked realizing that he was almost certainly a sifter. Even now, he felt the presence of the waiting passengers. If that had come out when he was still on Rashad Tarana, he'd have been publicly and literally crucified as a heretic, as he'd been forced to witness countless times by the time he was thirteen. The thought of being a minder of any sort terrified him on an instinctive level, but Tuzan was right in pointing out that not knowing how to control and use it made him vulnerable. It helped to think of the talent as just another bleedover personality to manage.

Right on time, Tuzan's small ground hauler arrived and parked near the diner's back entrance. Jess checked his camera feeds one more time, then pinged the "all clear" signal to Tuzan. After a moment, the hauler's back panel opened. Tuzan and Kerzanna got out, both wearing shapeless, hooded coverall jackets and carrying boxes of supplies. They closed the hauler's doors, then entered the diner.

The metro maglev train arrived at the stop, screeching to a halt. Maglev trains were ordinarily fast and quiet, but not in Ridderth. In case he had an audience, he glanced up at the train's designator, then back down at his tablet, as if he hadn't expected it to be the train he wanted. The waiting passengers boarded, and none got off.

He took advantage of his temporary solitude to direct the flying cameras to hide themselves but still keep watch. He stowed the tablet and headed toward the ground-level metro stop close to the diner. They'd agreed Kerzanna was more vulnerable and should be the first to get the permanent shields. Jess found it hard not to demand details, but the less that had to be cleaned out of his memory, the better. He was no happier than Kerzanna was at the thought of telepaths mucking about in his mind, even though Tuzan had so far proved trustworthy.

Forty-five minutes of no visible activity and no news left Jess jumpy and with a pounding headache. Only Jess-the-bomber had the patience to sit and watch the camera feeds. Jess-the-medic wanted to monitor Kerzanna, and Jess-the-military-gunnin wanted to be in the diner, leaving Jess himself to worry about the myriad things that could go wrong.

For example, the unexpected appearance of an automated medevac capsule that floated down to rest on the walkway behind the diner. A man in a medic's white jacket with a red armband arrived by groundcar. Instead of going into the restaurant, he stayed near the capsule.

Jess pinged Tuzan with the news immediately, but got no answer.

After another agonizing minute of waiting, he hastily directed the cameras to still hide but watch and record all the exits. He rolled and stuffed the tablet in his coat pocket as he all but ran toward the back of the diner. When he got close, he made himself slow down, and reached for Jess-the-engineer, whose natural body language made him look old and tired. Jess slouched and trudged around the corner of the building, gave the man dressed as a medic and the medevac capsule a dull, incurious glance, then entered through the diner's back door as if he'd done it a thousand times before.

Once past the entryway, he hesitated. He knew where he wanted to go, but he couldn't reconcile the noisy, bustling, hotter-than-blazes kitchen with the diner's floor plan. A harried line cook used his meat cleaver to point to one of the two wide, arched doorways. "Customer seating is through there, pal. Use the front door next time, will ya?"

Jess shrugged an apology as he opened his coat and threaded his way through the kitchen and into an empty hallway with several closed doors. The end of the cooler hallway led out to the customer seating area, where the tables he could see looked full. When he was certain no one was watching, he palmed open the first door on the left and slipped into the room.

Tuzan and Kerzanna sat in two of the private dining room's chairs. Kerzanna looked surprised, but Tuzan looked annoyed.

"Goddammit, this isn't the–"

Jess cut him off. "There's a medevac out back. That wasn't part of the plan, either." Kerzanna stood, and he caught her eye. "I thought it might be for you."

She smiled and moved around the table toward him. "I'm good, Jess." She slipped her hands inside his coat and wrapped him in an embrace, and he tightened his arms around her. His body had been starving for the feel of her, and her low, velvety voice got him every time. He inhaled her scent, and the world stood still for a moment.

"Enough," barked Tuzan as he got to his feet. "Time to go."

Jess let Kerzanna go so she could step back, and he stifled the impulse to close his coat against the sudden loss of her warmth.

The door slid open, and Tuzan turned, then jerked and fell stiffly backward.

Jess spun around and glimpsed a short, brown-haired, sallow-skinned man in a corporate suit as Kerzanna launched forward but stumbled and fell to her knees. The man looked at Jess's face, then gave him a wide, happy grin. "Jackpot!" he said.

Jess's internal bioware suddenly woke up and flared. The fire illusion danced along his skin. He gritted his teeth and took a step toward the little man, but his bioware seized control of his body and froze him in place.

"Nighty-night," said the man.

Flame. Shadows. Blackn...

CHAPTER 22

* Planet: Mabingion * GDAT: 3242.022 *

THE SOUNDS AND smells of Ridderth woke long forgotten memories in Renner. It surprised him, because none of his previous visits as part of Dixon Davidro's circus had done so. The drumming of evening rain on the uneven glass roadway, the scent of stagnant water, the steady, insidious drip overhead that signified a hole in the roof, the nose-stinging acidic stench of the antimicrobials used to combat mold in the walls, all evoked images from long ago. Dixon seemed to have forgotten that Renner had grown up in the hard streets and crumbling waterways of Ridderth. He remembered random names, places, and faces, and his own cocky sense of having the world by the tail, right before he lost it all.

The small, rented distribution warehouse had newer smells, too. Sweat, not his own, and blood, also not his own. The sweat came from Dixon, who had worked himself into a fury. The metallic blood scent came from the tall woman who was zip-tied to a metal chair in the center of the space, where the interior lighting was brightest.

Renner stood by the warehouse's regular door, hands in his jacket pockets. He had tendrils of his talent on every control in the building, from the door lock to the power bars, and he already knew which neighborhood grid batteries in a half-kilometer radius had charge he could use if needed. Just that afternoon, Dixon had made Lamis and Vahan rent a new townhouse for the group because Georgie had gone off the deep end again, insisting that fire would end them all if they didn't leave. In his new room, Georgie had collapsed into a deep sleep. Either that, or Dixon had drugged him to keep him quiet for a few hours.

Except for the battered, bloody Jumper in the chair, the tableau looked like one of Dixon's rare staff meetings. Sachin, the chalk-skinned cleaner, leaned against the wall, worriedly watching Dixon pace. Renner didn't blame her. If Dixon decided to withhold the uniquely customized drug cocktail that kept the helio poisoning in check, she'd be dead in a month. Xan, the telepath, sat on the foldout table. He held his sleeve up to stanch his bloody nose, a sign that he'd seriously overused his talent. The young man had little sense of self-preservation. Lamis bel Doro sat on a chair at the other end of the table, as did the prim shielder, Vahan, in her customary black corporate suit. Lamis looked bored, as usual. Renner didn't know Vahan well enough to tell if she was uncomfortable or not.

Renner sure was. On the rare occasions when Dixon actually lost his temper, instead of just modeling the behavior, his judgment got sucked out the airlock. Renner hated Dixon with the white-hot heat of a million super-giant suns, but his life depended on the man not getting himself caught by his CPS bosses, the internal inquiry auditors, or the very dangerous people he often did business with.

"Mr. Renner," said Dixon, "please persuade Subcaptain Nevarr to be more forthcoming." His angry tone belied the politeness of the words.

To each of Dixon's questions about the Charisma project, where Orowitz was, and who was helping her in Ridderth, she'd responded with inane, trivial questions of her own, such as asking if he preferred summer or winter, or if he'd considered meditation to control his dyspeptic temper. Dixon brought out his whole arsenal of tricks—cajoling, bribing, lying, flattering, threatening—but he didn't know which buttons to push. It wasn't like him not to have figured out her weakness in advance.

Renner had known Dixon's order was inevitable from the moment that Nevarr had awakened and proved to have mental shields that high-level telepath Xan couldn't penetrate, no matter how hard he tried, even though Dixon had "softened her up" with physical violence. Xan and Sachin both said they were shields, not a natural immunity. Vahan insisted that even if the shields had been placed by a top-level shielder, they should have faded after Nevarr was chemmed by the medevac capsule, and especially since Nevarr wasn't a minder. Unsurprisingly, Nevarr hadn't been forthcoming about her shields, either.

"We aren't waiting for Zerrell?" Renner asked. Xan had only recovered enough to connect briefly with Zerrell to tell him to come home.

"No." Dixon sucked on his bloody knuckles. He rarely indulged in personal violence, so he didn't know how to punch a face without hurting himself. "The local who found her may believe she was all alone, but I'm not waiting around to find out. I want to keep Zerrell on task tracking down that ring. Besides, her shields will probably hold against a sifter, too."

Renner stepped toward Nevarr and allowed his ever-simmering rage to flow, and with it, his talent. He didn't need emotion to fuel his talent, but it was easier.

Long ago, he'd reveled in his unique minder talent and used it often and unwisely for bad people, which got him caught by someone far worse. Dixon had an uncanny ability to set the right hooks to motivate and punish people, and had molded Renner into a weapon. Renner had fought his fate, and gotten himself a lethal mechanical collar around his neck for his trouble. After that, he'd lost himself in rage and grown numb to using his ability to control and direct electricity to punish, torture, or kill at Dixon's command. Then Neirra Varemba, Dixon's second oldest and most trusted pet, had decided he was more than a monster. She'd taught him how to think strategically and play the long game, how to manipulate Dixon and subvert his will. Unfortunately, those skills didn't help him avoid a direct order.

He met Nevarr's gaze. Despite her swollen eye, bruised cheekbone, and torn lip, she was a handsome woman. "This is going to hurt." He doubted she'd understand it was his way of apologizing. He admired her spirit, even though her mocking defiance goaded Dixon to the point of making impulsive, stupid decisions that endangered them all.

Renner had never worked on a Jumper before, so he sent a tendril of talent out to get a sense of her. In addition to the unique electrical signature that all animals had, her bioware systems hummed with latent energy, powered by the small but surprisingly powerful batteries for her cybernetic thigh and hip. He'd like to have explored further, but he had a job to do. Since the goal was to cause pain, not cripple her, he avoided her main systems and gave the nerves along her spine a sharp shock. Her back muscles contracted involuntarily, thrusting her shoulders back and chest forward. Her throat pressed hard against the tie round her neck, and her Jumper tattoos lit up briefly. He pounded her with four more pulses of increasing intensity.

She screamed an obscenity on the last one. When she lifted her head, she smirked not at him, but at Dixon. "That was fun. Can we go again, Daddy?"

Dixon frowned in irritation and waved at Renner to continue.

At the end of twenty minutes, with similar results, Dixon threw up his hands in disgust. "This is pointless. She's not going to give up an atom's worth of data. We don't have time to find the right leverage."

Renner relaxed his talent and let go of the current he'd been pulling from the city power node down the street, rather than draining the storage batteries that their warehouse and surrounding neighborhood depended on for powering building systems and comps.

Dixon stood and put his hands on his hips. "Ms. Sachin, ping the local disposal specialists you hired and tell them we have a package for immediate delivery." Sachin nodded and used her percomp, then asked Lamis for paper to write the location ref down, since Renner couldn't keep a percomp alive for more than a day. "Mr. Renner, after you take out the trash,"—he waved dismissively toward Nevarr—"your number-one priority is to find Orowitz and get him in here for a chat." Dixon turned and spoke to the rest of his staff. "That goes for all of you. We have to find the Charisma leaks and stop them, or there will be hell to pay." His glare said he'd make sure they'd be the first ones paying.

He stomped to the door and slammed his palm against the release, then stormed out into the night. The rest of the staff followed like remoras after a shark, leaving Renner alone with Nevarr.

After he checked the zip-ties to make sure she wasn't going anywhere, he opened the big loading door and ducked out into the wet night to retrieve the rented panel-sided ground hauler and move it as close as he could. He'd already found out the hard way that Nevarr was a lot heavier than she looked, and he didn't want to have to carry her and her chair through the rain.

He muscled her into the hauler, then strapped the chair to the holdfasts to keep it from bouncing around. He was done causing her more pain than was necessary. After strapping himself in, he fed the coordinates to the hauler's comp and told it to sync with the Ridderth traffic control system. He used the hauler's comp again to send a ping to the crew Sachin had arranged and told them he'd be there in twenty minutes with one package for disposal.

The collar around his neck ratcheted tighter, the click audible in the sound-insulated hauler. The next click would draw blood, though the scar tissue prevented him from feeling it, except as pressure on his throat.

Swiveling his seat, he turned back to look at his passenger. She seemed calm, almost serene. He didn't think he'd ever been there. Even now, his temper simmered, knowing her death would be pointless, and the failing Charisma project wasn't worth it.

She met his gaze, then dropped her focus to his neck. "That's a unique fashion statement. Your idea?"

Honesty wouldn't hurt him. Who was she going to tell? "Nope."

She nodded. "I saw something like it on the back of a remarkable woman I met in the Branimir spaceport." She shook her head and snorted, spraying a little blood down the front of her ripped and stained thin blouse. "Your boss is one massively warped control freak."

Long experience kept his thoughts off his face, but her words told him more than Dixon had gotten out of her in the past two hours. He only knew one person on Branimir with a mechanical leash on her back, which meant Nevarr was one of Neirra's children, as she liked to call the people she'd co-opted for her very long and deep game.

Which put him in a dilemma. He wasn't as dimwitted as he let Dixon believe, but he had no hope of figuring out all the pieces Neirra had put into motion, or what she hoped to accomplish. She'd told him he'd know when he was ready. Nevarr was a lot smarter than he was, and probably smarter than Dixon, so he asked her. "Are you supposed to live or die?"

"According to who?" she asked. She turned her head and looked at him with her good eye. "Are you religious?"

"No. The woman on Branimir."

Her eyebrows rose in surprise. "Live, I think, at least until the message gets delivered." She gave him a sardonic smile with the less damaged side of her mouth. "I'm the hope of PTVS Jumpers everywhere, don't-cha know."

He had no idea what the rest of it meant, but he understood hope. It had been Neirra's greatest gift.

He closed his eyes to think.

Renner grunted with effort as he carried the chair with Nevarr's limp body through the door of what turned out to be some kind of automated distribution center. Ceiling-high shelves took up half the space. Bots roamed the narrow aisles and used delicate metal fingers to select items to put in shipping bins.

Twin men, dressed in white protective gear that covered everything but their identical faces, closed the door behind him, then led him to an open office area. The desks and furniture were draped in shiny petroplastic, the material of choice for body disposers across the galaxy.

"Dead?" asked one as he pulled on a pair of safety goggles.

"She's big," said the other. "Might cost extra."

Renner grunted again as he set the chair down with a thud. He stood and pointed to her feet. "Need her boots and blouse."

The twins looked at each other and shrugged. The goggle-wearing man crossed to a table and opened a case that contained a medical bone laser, while the other began unfolding the first of a stack of collapsible crates on a gravcart.

Renner pulled his multitool out of his pocket, selected a blade, and sliced the ties at her ankles, then pulled off her boots. He sliced the wrist ties and started to pull off her blouse, then realized he'd have to release the zip-tie around her neck, too. The white-suited man setting up the crates sniggered at his predicament of having to support her floppy torso and limbs while he wrestled the blouse off her, and without the ties, her body wouldn't stay on the chair. One more task, and he'd have done all he could for the evening.

He collected her clothes and left her lying on the hard, frigid floor.

CHAPTER 23

KERZANNA WOKE TO miserable cold and the sound of a mechanical clicking. She'd had to let Renner use the hastily-purchased dormo patch to knock her out so the wetwork crew would think she was harmless. True to his word, he'd removed it when he'd removed her tunic and boots. They'd gambled she'd wake up in time before the disposal crew noticed or removed parts of her she was fond of.

It had been a surprisingly easy decision to trust Davidro's brutal-looking enforcer, once she'd seen beyond the massively ugly scars on his neck and the frosty eyes that seemed to barely restrain madness. He'd looked familiar from the first moment she'd seen him, but it wasn't until Davidro said his name that she realized she'd seen him in Neirra's packet of memories. She'd never heard of a talent like his before, but it packed a powerful punch. No wonder a cowardly twist like Davidro needed the cruel leash.

Even though her internal chrono said she'd only been there ten minutes, the freezing floor under her had already numbed her mostly naked chest, and her bones and biometal ached. She chanced a quick glance through the loose locks of hair covering her face to see the clicking sound came from a portable power supply, where a figure garbed in white repeatedly pressed a switch, to no avail. A gift from Renner, she guessed. The white-suited man swore vile oaths in Mandarin about the painful things he planned do to the lying, cheating monkey who'd assured them the unit was fully charged. Another man with a similar voice asked the first if he was doing it right, which engendered a bickering exchange about whether or not they could use the borrowed business's power and not trip any alarms.

Finally, the white-covered feet were together and facing away from her. She couldn't wait any longer, or shivering would give her away, and her half-cybernetic knee might fail. She flicked on her aftermarket ramp-up and rode the rush of power flushing through her Jumper systems as she gripped Renner's unexpected gift, the handle of the open multitool with a sharp blade. Slowly, so she wouldn't rustle the petroplastic, she raised herself to a sitting position, then got her feet under her. She waddled one step backward, then another, grateful Renner hadn't taken her socks. Her luck ran out when one of her would-be dismemberers turned and noticed their package had arisen from the dead.

She launched herself up and sideways to avoid his grasping lunge. The man with goggles swore and reached for his waist, but the coverall blocked his fingers. He spun and fumbled for something in a case on a table. The first man tripped on a fold of the petroplastic, giving her the opening she needed to quickly turn and side kick his unprotected face. Her attacker went down in a tangle of flailing limbs, causing her to leap awkwardly aside to avoid stumbling, but she slipped when she landed and lost the multitool in her effort to regain her footing. She took two long strides toward the man in goggles to grab his shoulders to pull him backward. A beamer ray scorched a line up the wall and onto the ceiling. She grabbed his wrist and squeezed until something crunched. He cried out and dropped the beamer. She spun him around and kneed his jaw, then flung him backward on top of his companion. She grabbed the heavy portable bone laser from the case and thumped the shooter's head, thereby ensuring the man would stay down and the laser would need repair. She scooped the biometric-protected beamer off the floor and hurled it with ramped-up strength to shatter against the far wall.

She shivered with cold and adrenalin as she picked up Renner's multitool. Her sports bra and socks would be poor protection against the weather, but at least she was alive to feel the discomfort. She pulled a large, clear trash bag from one of the crates and used the multitool's blade to cut rough holes for her arms and head, then pulled it over herself. She left the building through the side door, staying only long enough to make sure it closed behind her.

The empty, gently glowing road and walkway were shiny wet from the light, misting rain. She tried to orient herself based on the holomap of the area Renner had displayed using the hauler's onboard comp, but all she could see were tall buildings and reflections of the glass roadway's markings. She pushed her hair back as she walked as quickly as she could on the rain-slick surface to the closer intersection to her left and crossed it diagonally, then turned right. She locked away the awful, sickening memory of Jess collapsing and focused on her survival checklist. She couldn't hold the ramp-up much longer, and she needed safe shelter for a few hours. Her life, and probably Renner's, depended on her completely disappearing. Based on Davidro's questions and side comments, he didn't yet have a trace on Jess, but Tuzan's shadow railway for escaping minders was blown, or soon would be. Davidro hadn't learned anything about it from her because, miraculously, the mental shields she'd barely learned to operate had held up against sustained assaults from a high-level telepath, a shielder, and a cleaner. She had a vice-like headache, but her mind was her own. She wished she knew who to thank.

The ground-level businesses on this block were shuttered tight, but animated, colorful reflections at the intersection ahead suggested establishments that stayed open at night, likely frequented by people who might remark on a tall, bloody, half-naked woman in their midst. She started to speed up so she could sprint across the intersection, when she noticed a narrow, black doorway that gaped open. From the smell, even through the light rain, something had burned. The sound of an aircar overhead made her decision for her, and she slipped inside.

The wet floor was solid, but the acrid stench pervading the place made her eyes water, which hurt like hell in the swollen one. She used the weak light on Renner's multitool to pick a path through the piles of burned debris. She listened intently as she moved farther in, wanting to avoid a territory fight with any sheltering street rats. She supposed she was one now, too.

A dull cramp in her stomach warned that her ramp-up was running on empty, so she released it. She stumbled and clenched her jaw against the flood of pain messages that her ramp-up had masked. Along with everything else, her right foot felt like she'd fractured it in the fight. At least the cold, wet sock would keep the swelling down.

A black hulk in front of her turned out to be a slagged piece of machinery. Behind it, she found a doorway leading to a smaller room. Fatigue made her hand shake as she shined the light on scorched, deformed crates and a relatively unscathed padded heavy gravcart. The room smelled like an incinerator, but it was dry, and the gravcart was a damn sight better than resting on the sooty floor. She fished several charred segments of insulation out of the debris piles and took them to the small room. She folded her thankfully still attached limbs onto the gravcart, pulled the insulation pieces over her, and let exhaustion take her to oblivion.

CHAPTER 24

JESS BLINKED AND rubbed his neck, trying to keep his focus on the percomp in front of him. His brain ached from the inside; the new, mysteriously acquired mental shields felt raw and weird, like replacement teeth implants. Even his strongest bleedovers were subdued. The events of the past eighteen hours still had his head spinning.

"You're supposed to be resting." Tuzan's exasperation was plain as he came in and put a sack of food down on the counter near where Jess sat in front of a large display and two linked percomps. "Watching the trends isn't going to make them converge any faster." He took his dripping coat to hang it near the front entry and turned on the solardry.

"Couldn't sleep. Medic exam tables are hard. And short." And they didn't have cats or Jumpers in them, either.

When Tuzan returned, already barefoot because he hated shoes, Jess pointed to the holo display to his left. "The sniffers found another unmonitored interstellar comm relay, so I cracked it and added our packet." Incoming ships sometimes forgot to turn off their packet drop comm systems, and Jess was exploiting them, based on what he'd learned from the *Faraón Azul*. The more off-planet data sources they could seed, the harder it would be for the CPS to kill them all. The packets contained his clouds of unsegmented code that would temporarily assemble long enough to inject damning Charisma data into vulnerable systems, then fall apart and drift, looking for the next system. Tuzan not only understood it, he'd given the code snippets the ability to recognize each other and repair the inevitable coding replication errors that crept in.

He glanced up at the old-fashioned clock on the clinic wall that displayed a flat map of the planet, with creeping daylight and night zones to represent the passage of time. Galactic Date and Time said it was more than halfway through the day, but it was the break of dawn in Ridderth. He swiveled his chair to face Tuzan, who was lifting containers out of the damp, waterproof sack and putting them on the counter. "Targeting journalists with the Charisma data was a good idea. They like to gossip, so it's showing up in least thirty more feeds, none of them our insertions. I also tracked the reporter, Charrascos, who broke the Mabingion Purge story. She's been all over the galaxy before and since then, and has a lot of prime bylines for investigative stories. Guess who returned to Ridderth the day before the *Faraón Azul* limped into Mabingion system space, and published first on the planetary headquarters debacle?" What had started out as garden-variety mismanagement of a public works project had blossomed into a juicy tale of greed and corruption that seriously threatened the economy of the whole continent for the next thirty years.

"Let's hope Charisma is her type of scandal." Tuzan pushed a hot cup toward Jess and took the other one himself. "How's your head?"

"Improving," Jess said, more out of optimism than certainty. "How's yours?" Tuzan had taken a full stunner shot the day before, right before Jess had gone down. Stunners temporarily paralyzed the voluntary nervous system for a few minutes, but were particularly effective against most minders because they played havoc with their talents for hours.

"Clear as ever." He set his cup down and put his hands in the pockets of the vest he wore over loose, baggy pants that weren't in style but were perfect for him. He looked exotic even when he wasn't trying. "The shadow railway is closed for now, but we haven't connected with all the volunteers yet. My sister says we still have 'guests' in the system."

Something in Tuzan's face made Jess realize he'd been so focused on his own problems that he'd been oblivious to the needs of others again. Tuzan was worried. "Tell me about your sister."

"She's a CPS refugee, like me. The railway was her idea. She doesn't get out much, and it gives her the chance to feel like she's making a difference." Tuzan's too-bright smile covered more complex emotions that Jess couldn't read. "She's not good at saying 'no.'"

"Sorry," Jess said, feeling guilty. Jess-the-bomber persuaded Tuzan that they had to assume that the shadow railway was in jeopardy because Kerzanna had been forced to talk, or that her shields had failed. Jess covered the wave of despair that threatened to swamp him by reaching for the coffee Tuzan had brought.

Tuzan said she'd taken the shields well, but only had ten minutes to practice with them before two men had stuffed her into the untraceable medevac unit. Jess's motley fleet of cameras had recorded the action, but had been too far away to read the capsule's designator or discern faces.

Luckily for Jess, Tuzan had managed to get a distress call out to a telepath friend in the diner, who stopped the man trying to shove Jess's inert body into a serving cart. A telepathic interrogation of their attacker revealed he was a CPS Minder Corps sifter who had recognized Kerzanna because of a detailed description in an official detain-and-restrain order for her, but planned to get the reward money first, then tell the CPS where she was. When he'd made his move and found Jess, who he also recognized, he'd thought it was his lucky day.

Tuzan was vague on the details of what happened after that. The attacker was neutralized, which Jess took to mean he'd been cleaned or twisted. Tuzan had called in favors to have Jess awakened by a healer and stim drugs, which Jess remembered, because it was about as fun as being struck by lightning, and for Jess to get full minder shields, which he didn't remember at all because Tuzan had thoroughly cleaned the memory. Tuzan was able to show him how to use the shields because he had them, too. Despite his deep curiosity, Jess didn't ask for more. He understood more than most about the need to keep secrets, and he didn't want to force his new friend to lie to him.

Since then, Jess had spent every minute searching for evidence of where Kerzanna's capsule had gone, and the location of Dixon Davidro's temporary base of operations, because he'd bet anything the two were connected. Kidnapping instead of killing her meant Davidro wanted to interrogate her first. From what Jess recalled, Davidro had several contractors who would be delighted to inflict pain on his orders. Kerzanna's ignorance was as much a shield as the new ones in her mind, but Davidro behaved erratically when he couldn't control things, and once a sharp professional journalist like Charrascos dug in, the Charisma project's secrecy didn't stand a chance. Every hour without any news about Kerzanna added to the icy weight in his stomach. The coffee tasted like acid.

Tuzan took the cup from him and gave him one of the containers. "You'll be no good to anyone if you run yourself into the ground. Eat." He handed Jess a fork. "Now."

Jess complied with bad grace, bolting the food, while letting Jess-the-bomber in to help him think of other places he could look for Davidro and his circus. He owed Tuzan a lot, from calling in multiple favors to figure out how to revive Jess from the Kameleon failsafe shutdown, to finding a closed-for-vacation private medical clinic for Jess to stay in, to personally delivering high-powered comps and warm food. Not to mention, dropping everything to help Jess by using nova-hot skills with comps and networks that were probably better than his own.

Jess fed the empty containers to the recycler, then found Tuzan in the office he'd temporarily commandeered. Tuzan's habit was to stand and pace as he worked. Jess deliberately moved close and put his hands on the smaller man's strong shoulders. People tended to shy away from cleaners and twisters, meaning they didn't get much physical contact, and Jess had the impression Tuzan thrived on it. "Thank you. Sorry I'm a flatliner jerk."

"You're welcome, and forgiven." His face lit up with a wide smile. "I'd kiss you, but I think you're a one-lover-at-a-time kind of man, so I won't tease." His eyes twinkled as he rose up to the balls of his feet, which put the top of his head even with Jess's collarbone. "Besides, I'd need to stand on a chair to be tall enough."

Jess smiled, but couldn't hold it as he stepped back. "It's only ever been her." He looked up with a sigh. "I wish I'd told her that."

Tuzan's expression became determined. "Then let's do our damnedest to see you get the chance."

Jess stood and stretched his suddenly screaming back. It had probably been complaining for the last hour, but he'd only just noticed it. The wall clock said it was well past local noon, and he'd barely budged from the clinic chair, sending out new sniffers whenever he came across another social web whose members might know anything. Jess-the-bomber helped him design the algorithms that pinged alerts when they found promising patterns in the vast oceans of ephemeral data. One unexpected benefit of having his Kameleon reset button pushed, as Tuzan had characterized it, was the bleedover headaches were less intense than before. It probably helped that all the bleedovers loved the idea of having minder shields, even though Tuzan had warned that the shields might fail if a top-level sifter could get past them and trip the failsafe again, or because of some other hidden surprise in his Kameleon bioware.

He used the fresher and cleaned his mouth and teeth with the odd-flavored sample squib of orajet he found in the cabinet, then poured himself another glass of water.

He jumped when Tuzan's head appeared around the corner. "Got him!" Tuzan gleefully made a beckoning motion. Jess hastily put down the glass and followed him to the office.

The room was full of holo displays. "I remembered something you said, or maybe it was in Neirra's memories, that Davidro is a creature of habit, and monstrously egotisical. And he's tightfisted. I'd been thinking he was deviously clever and thorough like you, with your completely new IDs for each occasion, but that takes time and money." Tuzan pointed toward the big holo display. "A 'Dave Dixon' rented a business condo for a week, but left the next day and demanded a refund. The owner is a janitorial customer of mine." Tuzan rotated the holo. "Meanwhile, a 'Dax David' rented a ground-level warehouse a couple of blocks away and complained about having to pay for a whole month when only a week was needed, and yesterday, a 'David Rodix' rented a corporate short-stay townhouse with six bedrooms in the high-rise around the corner from the warehouse. One of my staff has a second job there as a maintenance tech. The two women who dealt with the site manager were as corporate as they come. Their coworkers were anything but, including a big man with a badly scarred neck."

"Sounds like Davidro's circus." Jess memorized the address of the warehouse, because Jess-the-bomber insisted Kerzanna would be there, rather than the townhouse. "Send me any data you can—cashflow accounts, ping refs, whatever—for my tracers."

Late the previous night, Jess had vetted and selected several discreet merc companies that could mobilize quickly. He'd also discovered that his and Kerzanna's primary financial accounts on Branimir had been frozen, undoubtedly Davidro's work. Fortunately, one of Jess's first acts of rebellion during his Kameleon service had been to siphon funds away from his official, CPS-monitored financial accounts and invest them elsewhere, because his childhood had taught him the devastating cost of being at someone else's mercy. Seeing how Davidro treated his contractors in the later years had made him redouble his efforts to ensure his financial freedom. The temporary unavailability of his Branimir accounts was a minor inconvenience.

Jess all but ran back to his comp setup in the clinic area to rent transportation and send the requests for fast bids to the merc companies, using various untouched but well-established and well-funded identities he'd created just for this. He also checked the other arrangements he'd been readying, such as a private medic clinic, and multiple avenues out of Ridderth and off the planet. As much as he disliked Mabingion, he was now grateful for its status as a major transportation hub. The CPS would find it difficult to interdict outgoing traffic in time.

He ordered his ragtag collection of stolen camera eyes to fly to the warehouse location, but it would take them at least thirty minutes to arrive, and he'd probably lose some to accidents and equipment failures along the way. He kicked himself for not thinking of buying and programming his own fleet. And for not remembering Davidro's habits. Once his handler had decided Jess was zero-witted, the man had been carelessly lax in conducting non-Kameleon business in Jess's presence.

He went to Tuzan's office again. "Where would I go to hire local crew for a hostile pickup and delivery job?"

Tuzan blinked. "You want to kidnap Davidro or one of his staff?"

"No, I think Davidro dangled a payment-on-delivery contract for whoever could produce Kerzanna or me. That way, he only pays for results. It was just luck that the CPS sifter saw us first." Jess had another thought. "If the contract is still open, I can use it to get me inside Davidro's base."

"Bad, bad idea." Tuzan crossed his arms. "Ridderth's crews are an order of magnitude more dangerous than when you were here last. They'll kill you just to see the funny look on your face." Tuzan frowned. "But I can see you're going to do it anyway."

"She'd do the same for me."

Tuzan snorted. "Of course she would. She's a Jumper." He turned to one of his displays. "I'll get you a list."

Jess nearly jumped out of his skin when one of his queries finally popped on the identity of the medevac capsule that had taken Kerzanna. He'd spent the last two hours preparing to fall into the lap of one of the less violent crews, and using Jess-the-bomber's expertise to develop multiple contingencies to get him out of trouble. Between the surprising array of weapons that had been in Kerzanna's bag that she'd left in Tuzan's borrowed delivery ground hauler, and his own collection, he had a veritable untraceable arsenal. A brief trip to a local body parlor—owned by one of Tuzan's myriad customers—gave him the hair, eyes, and lighter skin tone that Davidro would remember. Jess completed the image by buying a farmer-style brown coat, pants, and boots. A rented airspeeder with a few premium features sat waiting on the clinic's rooftop airpad.

He quickly crafted a half dozen queries to track the capsule's location all the previous day. Whoever directed the capsule smartly had it changing

ID numbers between each of the Ridderth traffic system's tracking nodes, but hadn't bothered to change the speed, elevation, and size designation. Tracing its path on the holomap, Jess imagined a scenario where the sifter's accomplice sent the capsule into a holding pattern circling the city until he collected the reward from Davidro, then sent it straight to the rented ground-level warehouse eighteen hours ago. He had to get there now.

He hurriedly closed down the big comp and strapped the largest percomp on his arm. He grabbed his coat and bag on his way to Tuzan's office. "I think I know where Davidro has Kerzanna, and I'm going in." He handed the man the other percomp. "Source logic for the identity insertion code drifts. Consider it a donation to the cause."

Tuzan stuffed the percomp in his pocket, then hugged Jess tight. "You're totally fractured, you know. Good luck. Ping me when–" Tuzan suddenly arched back and screamed, his face a rictus of pain. "Majiril! No!"

He staggered sideways, then took off running out of the office and toward the clinic entrance.

Jess followed. "What's happening?"

"My sister!" Tuzan snarled. "Someone's killing my sister!" He frantically pounded on the emergency exit bar until the door opened, then launched himself outside and toward the small groundcar he'd left up the road. Jess grabbed the man's coat and boots and ran out into the rain after him. He caught up to Tuzan just in time to support his elbow and save him from falling.

"Where is she?" asked Jess.

"At home. Golewoma District," Tuzan sobbed, fumbling at the groundcar's door lock. "She's in so much pain."

Jess knew it was easily an hour away by ground, and Tuzan's hysteria made him worthless to drive.

Sending an anguished, fervent prayer to Kerzanna's gods of chaos to protect her for a while longer, Jess pulled Tuzan away from the groundcar and back toward the clinic.

"We'll take my airspeeder."

CHAPTER 25

JESS HAD PICKED an airspeeder because they weren't required to use the Ridderth traffic control system, and therefore harder to trace. No autopilot meant he couldn't divert any attention to his passenger, or they'd be a splat on the front grill of anything bigger, which was everything else that flew. He pushed the speeder to its limit and got to the modest eight-story apartment building in the Golewoma district in thirteen minutes. A meter above the airpad, Tuzan scrambled out and tore into the entryway that led to the building lifts. Jess bounced the airspeeder and landed off the airpad in some gravel. He locked it and ran to the entryway himself, only to discover Tuzan must have taken the stairs.

Jess had to waste precious time cracking the security pad so the building would let him into the stairway. He wasted more precious time running through the halls of the top floor because he didn't know the apartment designator. He slowed when he finally saw an open doorway at the end of one cul-de-sac hallway and approached it cautiously, listening intently.

When he peeked once around the doorway, he saw Tuzan on his hands and knees near a woman lying on the carpeted floor. Something brushed against his tight mental shields, but he ignored it. When he peeked again, Tuzan was lying next to the woman, his arm across her stomach.

Jess pulled a shockstick from his left large coat pocket and cautiously entered the room. "Tuz–"

Movement to his right startled him into stepping left and raising the shockstick.

An older, sad-faced, gray-haired man wearing gray held his hands up. "Please don't hurt me. I'll give you anything you want. I didn't see anything. I'm just visiting."

Guessing the man to be one of the shadow railway's "guests," Jess started to turn back to Tuzan, when his mental shields were slammed by what felt like a pressure vice. Instinctively, he switched the shockstick to his right hand and thrust it into the man's chest, shoving him backward.

The man cried out and the pressure in Jess's head lessened. Jess spun and took two long steps to swing a fist at the man's unprotected jaw. The man fell, and the pressure vanished. Jess shocked him again to make sure he stayed down, then turned to Tuzan and his sister.

Tuzan's face was wet with tears as he groggily raised himself to his hands and knees. The painfully thin, ghostly pale Chinese woman who looked nothing like Tuzan appeared to be unconscious, and a pool of blood saturated the carpet under her head of very short black hair. The front of the woman's patterned pink blouse was torn open.

Anger rose in Jess like a runaway maglev train. He dropped the shockstick to pull the phaseknife out of his pocket. He flicked it on as he stalked toward the man who had tried to rape a defenseless woman who'd trusted him.

The man on the floor must have recognized Jess's intent. "It was an accident! She tripped, and I tried to save her, and she hit her head on the table!" It had a ring of truth.

Jess slowed, but allowed some of Jess-the-bomber's ruthlessness into his expression. "Talk fast or die."

"I know who you are, Mr. Orowitz. What you are." The man smartly stayed on his back, with his hands still and visible. "Dixon Davidro sent me to hunt you down, but he wanted information on the minder escape ring, probably to make his boss want to keep him instead of deep spacing him for screwing up the Charisma project."

"Why did you hurt the woman?"

"I didn't mean to. Davidro uses me for interrogations because I'm a sifter and a telepath. I thought I had her well controlled, but she fooled me and got a message out to her brother, then tried to compel me." He shook his head, shame and guilt plain to read. "I panicked and pushed her away. She tripped backward. I grabbed onto her blouse to save her, but it tore and she fell." He briefly pointed toward the table.

"Why didn't you run?"

"I couldn't. Even though she was hurt, she froze me, compelled me to stop using my talent. Contained me." Consternation flitted across his face. "Sort of like a shielder, but more. Anyway, she finally passed out, and then your friend came barreling in. He didn't even see me sitting there. He's got shields like yours, but he was distracted, so I got through them to subdue him. Then you came, and you weren't distracted."

As far as Jess could tell, the man had told the truth. "Can you fix T...

my friend? Revive him?"

"Yes, but I need to touch him. I'm nearly burned out." Again, it seemed like the truth, but if the man was a sifter, maybe he could fool other sifters into believing he spoke the truth.

After a long moment, Jess took a deep breath and let it out. "If you hurt him, I'll kill you instantly."

"I know," the gray man said quietly. "I'm Zerrell, by the way." He sat up slowly, then equally slowly, scooted closer to Tuzan's foot. He reached out slender fingers and put them on the exposed skin above Tuzan's boot.

Jess thought he felt something flare, but it could just be his imagination. Within a minute, Jess could already see improvements in Tuzan's alertness.

"Why do you work for Davidro?" asked Jess.

"Because he'll destroy me and my family if I don't." Zerrell's frown deepened. "I was Minder Corps. Listed as a commerce auditor in the official records, but it was really a covert interrogation unit. After I retired, I made a deal with an ex-Minder Corps healer, and we helped each other get off the addictive enhancement drugs and start a therapy practice for traumatized children. I married into a blended group, but I didn't tell them what I had really done for a living—they'd never have accepted me out of fear that I'd betray several of their very talented kids who had deliberately failed their CPS testing." Zerrell shook his head, looking defeated. "Davidro found me somehow and threatened to tell them, and the parents of my patients, if I didn't do occasional assignments for him. When he pings, I tell everyone I got invited to a conference."

Jess-the-medic pushed at Jess to get medical treatment for Tuzan's sister immediately, but Jess would have to leave before they got there. "Have you seen Kerzanna Nevarr?"

"No. Davidro had his telepath call me home last night, but by the time I got there, he'd already interrogated her and got nothing. She really got under his skin, so he sent Renner to dispose of her. Renner reported that Nevarr was dead, but he was lying. I think he helped her."

Jess remembered Renner as a violent man with a volcanic temper, and loyal to Davidro. "Why would he do that?"

Zerrell shook his head. "I can't even guess. I think I've underestimated him for years." He pointed to a chair with a questioning look, and Jess nodded. Zerrell carefully slid into it.

"Look," he said, glancing to Tuzan and back to Jess, "you're probably considering killing me, or detaining me for a while, which is as good as killing me and my family, so I have an offer for you. I can permanently disable the failsafe shutdown in your Kameleon bioware. I'll leave here and go straight to my family, tell them the truth so they can protect themselves, and then I'll disappear."

Jess wanted to pretend ignorance, but mindful of the futility of lying to a sifter, he opted for keeping a blank look on his face. He needn't have bothered.

"I know exactly what you are, maybe even better than you do. The first five years of my service, I worked in the Kameleon program. I picked up all sorts of things I wasn't supposed to know about the bioware. I can disable the other default warning and control routines, too, if you still have them. When I was there, it was policy for the out-processing staff to 'accidentally' leave them active, in case Kams went rogue. I doubt it's changed."

Disagreeing overlays squabbled in his head, but he ignored them all. "Sorry, I can't trust you."

"Yes," came a high, breathy voice behind him, "you can." Tuzan's sister was awake.

Tuzan sat cross-legged by her side and held her hand. His face was still wet with tears as he tore his eyes away from her and looked up at Jess. "Majiril is never wrong about the people she deep reads."

"Trust your talent, Jess," she said, holding his gaze. In her eyes, he saw the resemblance to Tuzan. "Feel it in Zerrell. Feel it in me. No haze. No static."

Her words explained some of what he'd been feeling. Jess-the-medic pushed harder at him. "You need immediate emergency treatment."

"No, it's far too late." She squeezed Tuzan's hand until he looked at her again. "One last gift, *Gēgē*. Let me die."

Tuzan moaned softly and shook his head violently. Tears poured from his eyes.

Her voice sounded threadier. "I'm a burned out husk of what I was. My talents are gone. I don't sleep and I can't taste anything. The shadows... I hurt all the time. No healer can fix that, not even Ayorinn himself. I love you for sacrificing your happiness for mine, but I'm a danger to... All of you need to live... help those I can't..." She took a slow, rattling breath. Her eyes drifted. "The conflagration... is..."

Tuzan cradled her hand against his chest.

Jess felt her die.

Zerrell looked as anguished as Tuzan.

Jess took a deep breath then knelt in front of Zerrell. "Fix me." He pushed up his sleeve and offered his bare arm. "Fix me so I can go find Kerzanna. Then find your family and run."

CHAPTER 26

THE NOONDAY SUN cast weak shadows through the perpetual haze that hung over Ridderth. The rare clear day had people out in droves, pretending they lived in a sunny climate where they didn't have to carry powered umbrellas or wear hoods. Renner pulled his dark scarf up to his chin and ducked his head as he leaned against the wall, waiting for the laughing group of people to pass. His quarry was more than just in the middle of them, she was the center of attention.

He loitered like a tourist in the crowded media business district in Ridderth because something Georgie said had caused Dixon to pull Renner from the priority search for Orowitz and send him after the blue-eyed, red-haired journalist named Charrascos. She'd published a short teaser story with more innuendo than fact about the Charisma project, but Georgie said it was Dixon's doom. Dixon wanted her dead, but quietly and discreetly, which meant he couldn't kill a whole crowd just to kill her.

Renner had occasionally wondered what it would be like to die, and unfortunately, he had a feeling he was soon going to find out. Dixon was losing control of everything. Zerrell had come back to base because of Xan's message, and Dixon had sent him back to the fugitive minder ring instead of keeping him to be ready to interrogate Orowitz. He hadn't asked for details on Nevarr, for once simply taking Renner's word that she was dead. Dixon hadn't yet connected the news story about the capture and arraignment of the two notorious crew, nicknamed "the Gravediggers," who'd been discovered unconscious in a distribution center. Vahan secretly sent her credentials out, looking for another job, not realizing that Dixon would never let her go. Dixon forgot and gave Sachin an extra dose of helio counteragent, and forgot to loosen Renner's collar until Lamis reminded him. Georgie looked like death warmed over and talked about fire and ash.

If Dixon self-destructed, Renner would be dead within days. Quicker, if he had the courage to trigger one of his collar's several failsafes, instead of waiting for it to slowly strangle him to death. His long-game plan to escape had been more of an idle fantasy. What he'd really wanted was to go down in a blaze of glory that took out Dixon and as much of the CPS as he could with the afterburn.

He knew from his hasty research that the well-traveled and prolific Charrascos was actually in her late thirties, but in person, she looked closer to twenty. The vids he'd seen of her didn't tell him she was so short, or that everything and everyone interested her. In her three forays out of the Novo Granica Media building, each time for food, she'd never been alone.

The only time he'd been able to get within three meters of her had been in a restaurant that morning, when she and a group of her chattering coworkers at the news magazine with waited for a table. He'd snaked out a tendril of his talent to get a feel for and memorize her unique energy signature, so he could track her later from a greater distance. Unexpectedly, she'd seen him looking at her, and instead of turning away, she'd smiled wide as if she recognized him as an old friend. It froze him on the spot. The moment passed when someone else demanded her attention, and he'd quickly moved away and pulled up his hood. He was used to being feared, or as unnoticed as a piece of furniture, so her focused interest had been disturbing.

Now he followed the laughing group to the Novo Granica offices and watched them go inside. He'd already cased the building for other entrances, but found none, and the rooftop airpad was several stories up and well secured. Journalists had learned the hard way over the years that in Ridderth, extra security saved lives, usually their own. He hadn't had time to figure out where she was sleeping.

He found a public comm center with private booths and used the disposable percomp Dixon had made him take. He used CPS security protocol to ping Lamis for instructions. Dixon came online instead.

"Did you take care of the problem yet?" Even in the poor-quality holo display, the man looked harried.

"No, it's too crowded. How much latitude do I have?"

"No headlines," snapped Dixon, "or we may as well launch ourselves into the sun right now. Why are you pinging?"

The man really was going downhill. "It's thirteen hundred. Check-in time." If the collar wasn't loosened by that evening, the blood would be noticeable.

The reminder seemed to focus Dixon's attention. "Stay on Charrascos four more hours, then come home." For a moment the old Dixon was back. "We'll regroup at eighteen hundred and…" He shook his head. "Be home by eighteen hundred." The connection went black.

Renner was at a loss. He unexpectedly had the freedom to choose how he wanted to die, and he couldn't decide on quick or slow. This must be how captive-bred animals felt when kept in a pasture the day before slaughter. He shook his head, then shook himself again, hard. He wasn't usually the macabre type. Georgie's downward spiral had infected Dixon, who was now affecting Renner. He resolutely marched back to the Novo Granica Media building to watch for Charrascos and do his fucking job.

Renner found a bench in the small, ten-square-meter green patch that someone had audaciously labeled as a "park" and ensconced himself on it, as if bound and determined to enjoy a day outside without the ubiquitous rain. Dixon had trained him to stand, so sitting for any length of time hurt his hips and back, but the bench gave him a clear view of the building's ground-level entrance across the busy roadway. Wherever he could, he zapped the image-capturing abilities of the annoying flying cameras that swarmed like mosquitoes throughout the media district. He hated having his picture taken. His collar ratcheted, but he hardly noticed. He was testing the limit of his talent, to see if he could insinuate a tendril into the building and use the building's current to feel for Charrascos's unique energy signature. He couldn't tell if it worked or not, but it helped pass the time.

At a few minutes before fifteen hundred, he felt the building's systems energize. It took him a minute to realize it was some sort of alarm. If the fire suppression system failed, people would evacuate, and maybe he'd have his chance at Charrascos after all. He stood and stretched, then took the pedestrian bridge to the other side of the road. By the time he got to the building, a few groups of people had exited, but not as many as he'd have thought. He smelled fresh blood from his neck. He pulled up his scarf and drifted toward the closest group.

"…three drills in thirty days isn't going to…"

"…bomb warning tone sounds just like the fire tone…"

"…don't care… gets me out of the building…"

The stream of people exiting the wide double doors increased. He moved to the side of the building and leaned against the wall, head down but talent up, feeling for Charrascos. What he got instead was the feel of two recognizable energy sources, moving closer from the walkway behind him. More tendrils of his talent told him two people carrying multiple weapons were headed his way. Energy weapons weren't common in Ridderth. He chanced a brief glance up but didn't see the police uniforms he'd expected. Instead, he saw a man and a woman in tourist clothes, who slowed when they came upon the first clusters of people standing on the walkway. Their body language said they were more alert than they pretended, and their upright stance suggested military or mercenary. The woman, subvocalizing into an almost invisible earwire, slowed to a stop almost directly in front of him. She grabbed her companion's sleeve.

"Let's wait here," she said.

The man stopped and turned. He pulled a tablet-style percomp from out of the small bag strapped across his chest and looked at its display, but didn't power it up.

From fifteen meters away, the unique energy signature he'd been waiting for exited the Novo Granica building.

The man put his tablet away and reached into the pocket of his puffy pink vest. The unmistakable signature of a beamer weapon lit up Renner's talent. A moment later, he felt a second beamer power up from inside the woman's frilly jacket pocket. A few seconds later, they began purposefully walking toward the Novo Granica entrance. They were clearly a hit team, probably mercs.

It would be just Renner's luck that their target was Charrascos. She'd made new enemies with her stories on construction kickbacks to politicians. The mercs presented another dilemma. If he let them do the job, Charrascos would be dead, but the well-known reporter's splashy death would be the opposite of quiet and discreet, and Dixon had emphasized no headlines. If Renner intervened, he risked calling attention to himself in a crowd of curious journalists, and the scars on his neck alone made him memorable. After a moment, he pushed himself off the wall and checked that his scarf was still in place as he followed the man and woman. He sent tendrils of his talent to search for other weapons in the crowd, and found one other powered beamer signature, moving toward the door from the opposite end of the walkway. Mercs relied heavily on technology as a force multiplier, so maybe he could defuse the situation. He reached out to the farther solo merc and pulled the stored energy out of every power source he could find, including the communications earwire. He did the same for the pair he followed. He could tell the moment they lost their communications because they both faltered and reached up to tap their earwires. He risked moving closer.

"Abort or go?" the woman asked.

"Go. We can't leave Trout hanging. I'll track Cha… the target." The man pulled out his tablet again, then swore a vile oath in Arabic. "My percomp is dead."

The two mercs slowed even more. After a moment, the woman said, "So is mine. New kind of targeted tech suppressor?"

"Too many unknowns," the man replied, then shook his head. "I say we find Trout and abort."

"Agreed," said the woman. The pair abruptly veered right and picked up speed. Renner stayed on his straighter course and tracked them with a tendril of his talent. He pulled up his scarf as he extended another tendril, trying to find the merc named Trout again.

He ran into someone and reflexively murmured a raspy apology. His talent flared unexpectedly. He ducked his head and doggedly sped up to a fast walk, because he'd just run into Charrascos herself. Calling himself brain dead in a dozen languages for not keeping a tracking tendril on her, he nearly ran into a tall, beefy man with the electrical signature of the missing merc. Trout's companions evidently hadn't found him in time to stop him from going after Charrascos.

Dammit, this was the clusterfuck he'd been hoping to avoid. He stepped around an oblivious clump of people, then turned so he could watch with his peripheral vision. The mercs were pissing him off, because Dixon would probably blame Renner for their meddling.

Trout pulled his beamer out from under his coat and dropped his hand to his side. He was smart enough to avoid looking directly at his target, but his body language said he was primed for action.

From out of nowhere, a young woman from Charrascos's usual coterie of coworkers grabbed onto Trout's left arm. He reacted instantly, raising his beamer to shoot her torso. He didn't even get the chance to find out that it had no power, because another of the coworkers, a slender, bearded man, reacted with blinding speed and knocked the beamer out of the merc's hand, then followed up with an elbow jab to the throat. Trout's knees buckled, and the slender man, obviously a ramper, held the larger merc up by main force.

People in the crowd were starting to register the events. Renner stepped back and to the side, then turned and walked away at a leisurely pace, not the quick march his instincts urged on him.

He figured his failure in achieving Dixon's objectives was worth the possible recriminations, because he'd learned that whoever was providing security for Charrascos was subtle and thorough, and obviously had no prejudice against hiring minders. Trout's fate could easily have been his if he'd been similarly rash. He'd have to come up with another way to get Charrascos, who was probably a minder herself, if he wanted to survive the encounter.

A vibration on his arm startled him. He'd forgotten about the percomp. He rounded the corner at the end of the block, then waited for a lull in foot traffic to read the ping telling him to call in immediately.

He found a nearby ground-level parking garage and used his talent to kill a monitoring camera eye, then ducked into a corner and pinged. Dixon answered.

"Hello, Mr. Renner. You haven't ended Charrascos yet, have you?" In the holo, Dixon looked happy and relaxed.

"No," said Renner warily, wondering what had brought back the old, confident Dixon.

"Good." He beamed broadly. "I want you to come home immediately. One of our new friends caught our elusive fish, and we'll have him soon. I'm having him delivered to the warehouse. Xan and Zerrell will find him a much easier nut to fracture."

"Do you really need to interrogate Orowitz?" asked Renner. "Kill him and let's get out of here."

"We don't need to be hasty. The story Charrascos published today proves her Charisma information couldn't have come from us. It turns out a project special investigator has been here for days, tracking the problem." Dixon waved airily. "While I'd like to be on the next interstellar out of the Mabingion system tonight, we must be thorough." Dixon's thoroughness usually correlated to the proximity of his bosses. "I still need to know how Nevarr found out about the project, and if we're lucky, how a non-minder got those very interesting shields." He smiled and made grabby motions with his fingers. "I want me some."

Renner didn't like it, but Dixon would dig in his heels if he thought Renner was raining on his parade. "What does Georgie say?"

"Oh, Georgie's been much better ever since I told him Nevarr was dead. He even had a shower this morning." Dixon looked thoughtful. "But just to be safe, I'll mention Orowitz to him and see what he says." He smiled again. "Once we clean up the little Charisma mess we left back in Lhionine, the fugitive minder ring information will be my ticket to finding a new project suited to my skills."

All Renner could do was nod. When Dixon was giddy with imagined future glories, there was no denting his confidence in his own judgment. Renner was afraid he knew the future all too well. He was dismally aware that his only good deed to honor the friendship of Neirra Varemba and the courage of the Jumper had likely doomed them all. After being dragged all over the galaxy, it was darkly poetic that he'd end up dying on the planet of his birth.

CHAPTER 27

KERZANNA HAD NEW sympathy for the undead.

She'd done all she could think of to let Jess know she was alive and trying to connect with him, but so far, absolute zero, and it was breaking her heart. It was too dangerous to stay in Ridderth another night. The "Erielle Courchesne" ID might not be on anyone's scanners, but as it turned out, Kerzanna Nevarr was.

Some of it was her own fault, for going back to the Canals, because it was the only place she could think of where a beat-up, off-the-grid ex-Jumper could blend in. She'd nearly been seen by someone who knew "Eri" from the charity shelter where she'd asked for a cleaning job, and nearly recognized by an old volunteer for the Minder Veterans Advocates group who thought she looked like Kerzanna. She'd managed to duck one and mislead the other, but the longer she stayed, the thinner her cover got. The reserve on her emergency anonymous cashflow chip could get her a body makeover or a one-way trip off Mabingion, but not both.

The rare clear day in Ridderth drew people outdoors, meaning that instead of walking, she'd had to stick to sitting in the back of the ground-level metro as she made her way across the city. It was just as well, as she was still recovering from the evening of torture and miraculous escape.

After awakening in the burned out building yesterday morning, she'd accessed the well-hidden compartment in her cybernetic thigh to get the cashflow chip she'd carried with her ever since she'd left Ridderth the last time. She'd saved it all those years because it had been Jess's last gift to her before leaving.

Ridderth abounded with street kids, because the incompetent city government tanked at providing the Concordance-mandated social services safety net. She paid a too-thin, sharp-eyed boy with a recycled shirt, coat, and boots for buying the same for her. The coat's concealment let her ride the cheapest ground metro to the Canals district, where she'd scrounged a scarf to cover her tattoos, eaten three charity surplus mealpacks, and found a cashflow-only, no-questions-asked medic to treat the worst of her injuries, including the broken bones in her foot and her fractured cheekbone. The bruise-wash ports and portable bone knitters made her look like an evil cyborg from one of the popular adventure sagas, but they did the job. She spent the rest of that day acquiring a disposable percomp to read the newstrends and put out virtual breadcrumbs for Jess's algorithms to find. She also acquired weapons, because she was still just an ex-Jumper dying of waster's disease. Probably.

That afternoon, she'd visited the succession of locations her messages said she'd be at for given time ranges. She'd used a variety of public social nets and the simple "job hunt" references, but adding names and references only she and Jess would know, hoping he'd think to look for them. It was the best she could do. Devious thinking wasn't in her star lane, much less the subtle data games that would get Jess's attention the way his tricks had led Tuzan to them. Each failure weighed on her, and added to the fear that Jess might be dead, or have been caught by Davidro. The universe didn't care whether or not she and Jess stayed together this time, but she wanted it—wanted him—for whatever time was left to her.

Her internal chrono said it was time to go into the last pub on her list. If Jess or Tuzan didn't show, she'd take her worldly possessions—the messenger bag slung crosswise over her shoulder and the clothes on her back—to the spaceport and buy an empty berth to almost anywhere but there. Leaving Jess again was the second-to-last thing she wanted to do, but getting either of them caught or killed was the last.

Kerzanna had never been in this particular pub before, and a second after she passed beyond the boring entryway, she was sorry she'd chosen it. The old-fashioned name, Windrose Point, was innocuous enough, but the decor and memorabilia said it was frequented by Jumpers, which significantly increased her chances of drawing the kind of attention she couldn't afford. Jumpers were a chummy, inclusive lot. Even if her currently black hair and eyes, and fashionably blue-tinted skin, kept her from being recognized as Subcaptain Nevarr, who'd trained hundreds of pilots back in the day and pulled off a semi-famous combat miracle or two, some well-meaning Jumper would try to buy her a beer or engage her in a darts game, just to make sure she was okay. Jumpers looked after their own, because no one else would.

Still, this pub was her last hope for finding Jess. She might or might not be the farkin' Jumpers' hope, but Jess was hers.

She made her way through the tables, noting the layout as she went and looking for anyone familiar, then asked the bartender for the freshers. She took the long way to look at the rest of the patrons and maybe a quiet booth, but the interior designer favored big communal tables. She stayed in the fresher as long as she dared, then found a barstool at the end of the bar and ordered fizzy water with lime. She didn't bother to hide her Jumper tattoos, because she still tanked at undercover work, and she'd give herself away in five minutes. She acknowledged friendly nods, and pretended she was just waiting for a buddy, but it wasn't in her to be rude to a fellow Jumper.

"Love the blue," said the tall bartender with a neck full of Jumper tattoos, denoting thirty years of service, and the intention tremor of a man in Stage Four waster's. He leaned closer. "Hides the bruises well."

The subtext of his observation was to ask if she was in trouble and needed help.

"I'm good," she said with a smile, then shook her head ruefully. "Too slow to get out of a bar fight that turned into a melee." All ex-Jumpers knew "slow" meant waster's disease.

The bartender nodded and started to speak, but got called away.

She kept her eye out for the buddy she told everyone she was meeting. At the end of the hour, after being approached three more times by people worried about her bruises, and propositioned for hot-connect sex in an autocab, she pretended to receive a ping that said her buddy had gone to the wrong pub. She pulled on her coat and bag, waved a casual farewell to her new friends, and slipped out the pub's back door and into the early night.

She stopped a moment at the top of the ramp to marvel at the stars visible in the sky. It was such a rare event in Ridderth that people were probably out on the rooftops and airpads, flooding the social nets with vids and stills of the stars. She'd seen millions of stars from all vantage points, but they still sparked a bit of wonder in her, the same wonder that had made her chafe at the restricting comfort of her family and sent her out into the universe to look for her place in it. And she was about to create a new exploration log.

She pulled her scarf out of her pocket to wrap around her neck and hide her tattoos, then ordered her suddenly dragging feet to get a move on to take her to the nearest transportation stand to order an autocab to the spaceport.

A small scrape of metal against metal said she might not be alone in the alleyway.

She casually turned away from the light to put her face in shadow and slid her hand into her large pocket to grab the handle of the concealed shockstick.

A voice spoke in the darkness. "I hoped you'd come out the opposite way you went in."

Her knees threatened to buckle, but she was a Jumper, dammit. "This very clever man I once knew said it was a good habit to get into."

She stepped off the ramp toward the voice and watched Jess emerge from the shadows. He pushed his hood back, then flicked a glance toward the bag hanging at her side. "Going somewhere?"

She held out her hand to him. "Not without you, if you'll have me."

He closed the distance between them and gathered her into his arms. She melted against him, and the imbalance she'd been feeling righted itself.

"I love you, Subcaptain Nevarr." His breath tickled her hair and sent a shiver along her back and thighs. "I always have."

She pulled back enough to cup his face in her hands, delighting in the chance to look into his familiar mismatched eyes. "I love you, Just Jess. I never stopped." She kissed him softly, intending it to be a pledge, but the smell and taste of him instantly put her in desperate need of more. He returned her kiss with interest, pulling her hard up against his solid warmth. They only broke off the kiss for need of oxygen.

"How about we continue this someplace else?" she asked. "Someplace horizontal."

"We have to take care of something first." He brushed a light caress over her still swollen cheekbone, worry crossing his face. "How are you feeling?"

She leaned into his touch. "Green go, as long as we're together."

He kissed her, nibbling at her lower lip. She met his tongue with hers and reveled in the heady masculinity of him. A rush better than adrenaline fluxed through her. He groaned as he pulled away from her. "I've dreamed of this for days. Weeks. Of kissing you, of feeling you. Loving you." He sighed. "My timing tanks."

Kerzanna chuckled. "Mine is no better. I nearly dragged you into the nearest closet a couple of times on the *Faraón*, even though we were in exosuits, and supposedly hated each other, and each time, something else would go wrong with the ship systems, or Bhatta needed me." She snorted.

"And when we finally got to the joy palace and a bed big enough for six, I slept twenty-one hours straight, when I could have been hot-connecting with you, telling you how much you mean to me."

"You needed the rest more." He quirked a smile. "Besides, Bhatta's new cats would have probably tried to help."

She laughed and kissed his smooth chin. "So what's this thing we have to take care of?"

Jess's eyes gleamed sharply. "Data retrieval."

CHAPTER 28

* Planet: Mabingion * GDAT: 3242.024 *

THE REMAINS OF an excellent delivered dinner had been cleared, and Dixon surveyed his staff with satisfaction. Sachin, Vahan, and Xan sat at the rented townhouse's dining table, watching him attentively. Lamis settled weakened Georgie and his favorite percomp tablet into the soft chair they'd dragged in for him, since he was still recovering from his self-induced trip to hell, then went back to her chair at the table. Renner stood near the arched room divider with arms crossed, muscles bulging, looking angry as always. A rivulet of red blood dripped slowly from his neck.

Only two problems vexed Dixon at the moment. The first he could fix easily. He beckoned to Renner. "Come, Rexium." He pointed to the floor. "Down." It was amusing to tease Renner by calling him popular names for attack dogs. The staff liked the levity that nicknames brought.

Renner stalked toward Dixon, then stopped a meter in front of him, turned, dropped to his knees, and bowed his head forward. Dixon had gotten so used to Renner's bad temper that he no longer even noticed. He pressed today's correct sequence to loosen Renner's collar to its maximum circumference. He patted Renner on the head and smiled. "Good dog."

Renner got to his feet and moved back to his place. The man had done well this trip. Perhaps Dixon should reward him with a visit to one of the galaxy-famous Ridderth body shops to change his look again. Skin the color of ebony and predator-red eyes, maybe, and a bit taller but a little less muscular. He made a mental note to sketch some body art designs. He'd have to work around the neck scars, of course, because the collar couldn't come off.

Dixon's other vexing problem was the disappearance of his pet sifter, Zerrell. He'd been so preoccupied that he hadn't noticed Zerrell's lack of contact until that morning, and Xan said he wasn't in Xan's ninety-kilometer range. The man could be hurt or dead, or he could be betraying Dixon's trust and running. He'd give the man until midnight to ping, but after that, Dixon would have no choice but to shatter Zerrell's career and family. Dixon would lose the respect of the rest of his staff if he started playing favorites.

"Ms. Sachin, please tell us what you found out about the crew that contacted you with Orowitz."

"Their prime lines of business are enforcement and construction graft, forced insurance, and wetwork on the side," she said. "The chief is Wutala."

Renner looked startled. "Gezi Wutala?"

Sachin nodded. "That's her. She picked up the pieces after a bloody coup about eight years ago, and has expanded their operations and areas of interest since then."

Something clicked in Dixon's head, and the memory that had been hovering just out of reach for days finally surfaced. "Did you know her, Mr. Renner? Back when you grew up here?" If he'd remembered that earlier, he might have watched Renner more closely, but no harm done. Renner's original past was dead and cremated long ago.

Renner's expression settled back into barely contained rage. "I knew *of* her. She was a pain specialist. Giving and receiving." He gave Dixon a pointed look. "I wouldn't cross her. She gets off on violence."

Dixon didn't need to be told how to deal with criminals. He hid his irritation behind a pleasant smile. "If she delivers the package, I'll pay in full." He would, too, even though the crew had demanded an excessive finder and delivery fees on top of the reward. He needed to wrap up the loose ends and move on to the next project he had in mind. He'd already booked an appointment with the new CPS base administrator to present his idea. He was fed up with working on other people's doomed programs and carrying the weight of poorer performers.

Lamis had already sent the delivery details to the staff, and printed out a version for Renner, who had once again managed to fry his percomp. He gave his staff their assignments and told them not to leave the townhouse until it was time.

At close to midnight, Dixon's determined good humor was nearly iced. His staff members were sniping at each other. Renner had twice offered unasked-for advice about how to handle the package transfer. Zerrell still hadn't surfaced. And to top it off, the crew's delivery was three hours late and counting.

Finally, *finally,* the ping arrived that said the crew would be at the warehouse in ten minutes.

"The Solstice Day present is here," he announced gleefully. He stood and grabbed his coat from a hook near the front entry. "Let's go, people."

Renner opened his mouth to say something, but Dixon cut him off. "I don't need you to tell me how to handle thugs. I was an assignments officer in the criminal restitution system before you were even born." He started to reach for the door, then turned back to Renner. "You know what? Change of plan. You stay here with Georgie, Xan, and Lamis until we need them, and Vahan will come with us instead."

Dixon ignored Renner's thunderous glare. "Vahan, get my beamer from the bag in my room. A little extra firepower won't hurt."

Vahan nodded and bounded up the stairs two at a time. By the time she returned, Sachin had armed herself with a stunner and a mister, in addition to the forceblade she usually carried. Dixon pocketed the beamer, wishing now that he'd replaced the outrageously expensive but unstoppable Davydov beamer that had been destroyed nine months ago. He nodded approvingly as Vahan expertly checked her beam rifle, then slung its strap over her shoulder and concealed it under her cloak. He had to admit she was settling in nicely, and decided he would keep her. He could gladly accommodate her fondness for watching things go up in flames, and maybe even sell her arson skills to replenish his slush fund.

"Lamis, if Mr. Zerrell should decide to grace us with his presence, have him wait here, then bring him when we call for you and Xan."

Dixon ignored Renner's deeply disapproving look and opened the door to let Vahan and Sachin precede him.

The walk down the block and around the corner to the warehouse was almost pleasant, for Ridderth. In this quasi-industrial district, the walkways were in good shape and well lit. And for the moment, delightfully dry.

He frowned and stopped when he saw a small, paneled ground hauler parked halfway down the road near their warehouse doorway, and a long-coated, hooded figure leaning against the wall. "Ms. Sachin, please find out why our package isn't being delivered by medevac capsule as promised."

Vahan stayed with him while Sachin continued walking, hand in her pocket. After a brief exchange, she came back halfway. The streetlights made her mottled skin look downright eerie. "The package was too tall to fit in the capsule. They had trouble getting the capsule in the first place, and didn't want to make you wait for another one."

"Very well, proceed." Dixon could believe they'd had trouble. Orowitz towered over everyone except Jumpers.

Sachin opened the big warehouse door, and the hauler backed in. Sachin closed the big door just as he and Vahan entered through the normal door.

The long-coated driver turned out to be a tall Asian woman with raised pictograph tattoos where her hair should be and studs for eyebrows. Two more long-coated men lifted an invalid's gravchair out of the back of the hauler and set it on the floor of the warehouse. The gravchair's occupant was covered in an ash-gray religious purity cloak and a full-face hood. Straps held the body up, but the head lolled forward.

"Authorize payment, please." The driver held out a portable display.

Dixon gave her a relaxed, professional smile. "Show us what's under the lovely gift wrap, and we will."

The driver nodded to one of the men, who untied the hood and pulled it off. The head was unexpectedly bald and light bronze.

"Face, please." Uneasiness curled in Dixon's stomach.

The man with the hood put his hand under the chin of the bald man and lifted. The unconscious face wasn't remotely familiar. The man let the head drop.

"Payment, please." The driver held out her portable display with more force.

"That doesn't look like my order." Dixon hated when people tried to cheat him. "I'll need biometric confirmation."

"Biometric matches." The driver stabbed a finger toward Sachin. "Ghost woman confirmed and approved the order."

Sachin shook her head. "The image you sent wasn't of this man. This is the wrong package."

The driver stabbed at her display, and then turned it to show Dixon. In a photo taken from a high vantage point, the bald man leaned against the wall of an office door that said "Yujimu Full Body Artistry."

Sachin raised her arm and activated her percomp, then showed a holograph of the face and shoulders of Orowitz, with his brown skin, black hair, and mismatched eyes. "You sent this." She tilted her head toward the gravchair. "It's not him. If he's had a makeover, we need biometric confirmation."

Suddenly, the images in both devices began to morph from pictures of two very different men into the same photo of a young, pretty, green-eyed

Chinese girl wearing an old-fashioned double-helix-style decoration in her black hair. Sachin and the driver stared at the images in consternation.

The driver's "What trick is this?" overlapped with Sachin's "Who the fuck is that?"

"My sister," said the man in the gravchair, who was no longer unconscious and was glaring at Dixon with naked hatred. "You killed her."

Dixon started to order Vahan to shoot him, but suddenly, energy beams stabbed the air and Dixon had to dive and roll for the cover of the table. By the time he could look again, one of the two men by the gravchair was down, and Vahan was trading shots with the other man and the driver from around the ground hauler.

The man in the gravchair glared at Sachin, who was staring back in terror. "No, no, no!"

Dixon drew his beamer and shot the bronzed-skin man in the center of his chest. The cloak burned away, revealing flexin armor underneath. The man's gloved hand raised a beamer, and Dixon ducked back behind the beam-proof table just in time to avoid losing an ear.

Time to alter the playing field. He pushed back his sleeve to access the wrist gauntlet he wore and keyed a control. The charges he'd had Vahan install in the corners of the large warehouse door made satisfying explosions as they blew the door out into the roadway. That was the flash that covered the bang that opened the hidden back door of the warehouse. A woman's voice cried out in pain, but he couldn't stop to see if it was the driver or one of his people.

"Sachin!" he yelled, pulling the table to shield him as he scooted toward his new exit. "Clean him and let's go!"

He risked a peek around the table. Sachin had dropped to one knee, and she was holding her ears, chanting, "Get out, get out, get out."

He took her at her word. He scrambled out of the doorway and into the back lot of the adjacent manufacturing plant. He used his beamer to melt through the gate's lock, then ran as fast as he could through the alley. He had no idea who the crazy man was, but he was probably a minder, the equal of Sachin or better. Dixon tore around the corner and made a beeline for the townhouse's front door.

A whistling, whining sound was the only warning he had before the front of the building shook with the impact of an incendiary urban combat round. He stumbled backward and ducked behind a decorative pillar. The townhouse's morphglass windows were shattered, but the scorched glass brick looked intact.

An amplified woman's voice boomed out and echoed off the walls.

"Trying to leave without paying, Mr. David? Or is that Mr. Rodix?"

"I'll pay when you deliver the right package," he shouted. Where the hell was the weapon mounted?

"No, you've proven to be untrustworthy. Pay first, then we'll deliver." The woman laughed. *"If the price is right, we'll deliver the fucking Continental Governor of Ridderth."*

Something metallic glinted on the roof of the building across the roadway. Too far away for his beamer. He needed to lure the attacking crew closer. "I think there's been a misunderstanding here," he shouted. "I have several thousand in activated cashflow chips in the townhouse that I've saved for a rainy day. They're yours as an inconvenience fee, and we can figure out what went wrong."

The woman laughed again. *"I do love doing business with a reasonable man."*

Two men and a woman emerged from the shadows of the alley across the roadway and stood, waiting. Dixon pocketed his beamer and moved into view slowly, his hands out, showing he wasn't holding anything. The woman tilted her head toward the front of the townhouse. Dixon started walking, and after a moment, they followed suit.

As he passed by the gaping window, Dixon hesitated. "I have a dog in the house. Please don't shoot him."

"We aren't monsters, Mr. David," said the woman, clearly amused. Her black skin was the color of the night sky, with a winking constellation tattoo splayed across her very large, almost fully exposed breasts. "What kind of dog?"

"Just a mutt. Found him in the street when he was a puppy." Dixon gave her a little shrug of embarrassment. "Bitey little thing. No one claimed him, and I found I kind of liked having him around."

He reached for the door pad, then hesitated, showing her he was waiting for her permission. She nodded, and he pressed his palm against it. The door slid open. He stepped inside several steps. The front room was smoky, but undamaged, except for the glass.

"Rexy?" Dixon called out. "These three nice people are friends of mine." He looked up the stairs and whistled. "Come on down, Rexy."

* * * * *

Renner knew they were in big trouble the moment whatever it was hit the front of the townhouse. He ordered Lamis and Xan to take Georgie out the back door and go to the all-night café on the next block. Georgie started to wail, but Xan grabbed hold of him telepathically and compelled him to be quiet and march. Lamis gave Renner one last look, then scurried out the door herself. He hoped Xan had enough self-preservation instinct to protect them all with his talent.

Renner stood in the shadowed corner between the lift and the stairway and drew massive amounts of energy from all the sources he'd already found. It gathered on his skin like sharp pins and needles, wanting to be free, and he had to concentrate hard to keep it away from the collar and its lethal failsafes. The natural hair on his arms and legs charred and burned in tiny little puffs of smoke. He'd learned the hard way when he was young that pubic hair and his talent didn't mix, so at least his armpits and genitals weren't burning, too.

He heard Dixon's warning about the dog in the house, and sent tendrils out to locate the three similar-sized people with him. From the voice, at least one was a woman.

"Rexy?" Dixon called out. "These three nice people are friends of mine." He whistled. "Come on down, Rexy." His tone turned to baby talk, like he sometimes used with Georgie. "They promised me they won't shoot you with those nasty-looking stunners."

Renner appreciated the warning, but he'd already found all the power weapons and drained their energy, adding to his store. It hurt like hell to keep the power contained.

"I guess the noise scared him," said Dixon. "The cashflow chips are upstairs in the safe. Who's coming?"

"Stay alert, boys," said the woman. "If I'm gone longer than a couple of minutes, you know what to do." The menace in the voice was unmistakable, and he realized it was Gezi Wutala herself. Back in his day, crew chiefs sat in their lairs and let the expendable crew—like him—do the dangerous work.

Dixon kept Wutala talking as they walked up the stairs. The moment Renner figured they were out of sight, he edged out along the side of the stairs until he was close enough to the two enforcers to strike simultaneously. He didn't have time to be subtle. He hit them with enough power to scramble their nervous systems and stop their hearts. He heard their bodies fall with soft thuds. He crossed stiffly to a blown out window, smashed glass crunching softly under his feet, and sent tendrils out, looking for more trouble. He found it in the form of two more enforcers. He lured them closer by using a bit of his power to make the glass walkway lighting flash like chaser lights on a marquee. He dropped both enforcers like he had the first two. Doing so expended most of his extra charge, making it less painful to move, but his skin was likely to be sore for days from talent overuse.

He ran toward the back door and sent tendrils out, but found no signs of life. Just as he ran back toward the stairs, he heard a woman's voice cry out in pain, followed by several thumps. His tendrils couldn't tell him what was happening, and Wutala was too close to Dixon—anything Renner did to Wutala could hurt Dixon.

More thumps and the sound of breaking glass, and then Dixon came pounding down the stairs, carrying his bag. "I threw her out the window. Where are-"

Renner interrupted. "I sent Lamis, Xan, and Georgie to the diner up the block. No Zerrell."

"Fuck him." Dixon grabbed the railing to swing himself around. "Back way?"

"Clear." Renner ran to the back door and slapped his palm on the pad to open the door.

Dixon pointed at the table behind them. "Bring Georgie's percomp, or he'll be unmanageable." He ran out the door.

Renner grabbed a dishtowel and wrapped it around the percomp to protect it from his talent, then headed for the door. The pad suddenly sparked because of too much power on Renner's skin, and the door slammed shut.

Desperately, Renner dumped the rest of his gathered energy into the grid, then slammed the emergency exit bar with his hip, but it stayed stubbornly closed. The back windows were tall but too narrow for him to fit through.

He sent talent tendrils out the front and didn't sense anyone, so he ran toward the front door, hoping he hadn't fried that control system, too.

A whistling sound announced an incoming round. Renner's feet skidded as he changed direction. The whole building shook with the impact, knocking Renner to his knees, embedding pieces of glass into them. The lights went out. He scrambled up and staggered toward the back door again, still clutching the wrapped percomp, away from the assault and falling debris. He bumped into the dining table, sending him off balance right as another round hit the front. He fell to one knee, but determinedly got up and stumbled toward the door. He aimed a kick at the emergency exit bar and thought he felt some give. The door nudged open a few centimeters and let in a thin shaft of light. Renner stepped backward to the table to give himself a running start.

The loudest sound Renner had ever heard blew his world apart.

He fell sideways, twisting, and landed on something sharp that stabbed through his back. The ceiling crumbled and rained down on him. Something smashed onto his legs, followed by something bruisingly heavy on his chest. He couldn't feel his arms, or even turn his head to look away from the back door. He heard another impact, but he couldn't feel the vibration. Somehow, he'd ended up under the dining table. The shaft of streetlight from the door illuminated clouds of dust.

His thoughts floated, free at last from the prison of his body and the talent that had made him a prisoner of Dixon Davidro. He mourned the lost chances to hurt the man as he'd hurt others, and to damage the agency that turned a blind eye to the abuses against all the others like him. He missed Neirra, and wished he believed he'd meet her again in some afterlife to tell her he'd loved her, too. He'd been afraid to admit it in life, because Dixon would have used it as a lever.

He heard another whistling impact, and saw the bones of the building break apart and cave in toward him.

He smiled.

At least he wouldn't die from the motherfucking collar.

CHAPTER 29

DIXON STAYED ON his hands and knees a moment and shook his head, trying to clear the ringing in his ears. The third incendiary round had been bigger than the others, and sent him stumbling forward. Either Wutala had survived the fall, or her crew was avenging her death. Either way, they'd want him dead. Like Renner probably already was.

He pushed to his feet and re-slung the shoulder strap of his bag, then started jogging down the alley, putting as much distance between him and the townhouse as he could. He couldn't afford to be questioned by any emergency responders descending on the scene. Up ahead on the roadway, traffic was already starting to slow as the city's traffic control system reacted to the trouble. Just as he was crossing an intersecting alley, two more rounds hit the townhouse. He needed get to the safety of the diner and his people. He made a split-second decision and turned left.

It looked familiar, and he realized he'd made a mistake. He was now headed toward the warehouse where the evening's trouble began. He turned around to go back. Before he'd taken two steps, a red-and-white airspeeder flashed by overhead, probably using the alley as a quick shortcut to the townhouse.

Dixon turned forward again and slowed his pace. He pulled his hood up, wishing for the cover of the detestable rain. He'd be just another midnight pedestrian, using the alley to avoid the bunching traffic. He felt almost naked, and it took him a moment to realize that it was because he was alone, like he hadn't been in decades. He didn't even have Renner. How very like the stubborn, contrary man to get himself killed at the least convenient time. Dixon knew there'd be no replacing him. Just like Neirra Varemba, Renner had been one of a kind. He'd just have to deal with his loss and move on.

The shadow of a decorative pillar startled him. *Get a grip*, he admonished himself. Thumbing on the beamer in his pocket made him feel better. It wasn't as shocking an equalizer as Renner's talent was, but could definitely ruin some mugger's night. He pushed his hood back so he could hear better, and walked at a steady pace. It was too risky to stay on the planet any longer. Wutala's crew knew too much about his business, and the bronze-skinned man from the warehouse wanted vengeance for some imagined wrong, even though Dixon hadn't personally killed anyone in years. Once he collected his staff from the diner, and Vahan and Sachin, if they were alive, he'd use his CPS authority to book a priority flight out–

A swarm of stinging pebbles hit his face. He ducked sideways and threw his hands up protectively. Something whistled past his ear and touched his neck, and every nerve in his body erupted in pain. He cried out as he fell to the ground and curled into a little ball, but it didn't help. The universe burned, and agony turned coherent thought to ash.

After uncountable seconds or minutes or hours, the pain eased, leaving him with spasming muscles and no clear memory of what just happened. His face and pants were wet. He smelled urine. Reality felt... unreal. He groggily pushed up into a sitting position and had to swallow convulsively to keep from throwing up. He took a deep, shuddering breath, and noticed two pairs of legs standing a few meters away. It surprised him hardly at all to see that one pair belonged to the bald, bronze-skinned man, and the other to the man who *should* have been in his Solstice Day package earlier that evening.

Orowitz's expression was remote, except for the freaky mismatched eyes. The bronze-skinned man's eyes gleamed with feral intent. He held Dixon's percomp and gauntlet.

"Okay, you got me," Dixon croaked. He cleared his raw throat. "But if you kill me, you'll spend the rest of your lives looking over your shoulder. The Citizen Protection Service takes care of its own."

The ringing in his ears got suddenly louder, and he realized it was high-pitched, booming laughter, coming from the bronze-skinned man.

"Oh, you poor, dimwitted sod. You're already dead." He laughed again. "We all are."

Dixon felt movement at his back, and then a woman's voice breathed in his ear. "You won't be needing this in the afterlife, Mr. Davidro." The comforting weight on his thigh lifted, leaving him cold. His bag.

He turned to look at her and saw the smart-ass face of a woman he intensely disliked. "But you're dead."

Nevarr was amused. "I get that a lot."

She walked over to Orowitz and handed him the bag. Her other hand held a neurowhip, which explained the mind-numbing, debilitating pain. They were good for riot control, and left no mark, unless the victim wore a lot of metal… like a spinal control mechanism the CPS used on rebellious healers who got burned up in their own spaceships. It had to be coincidence that Nevarr used a neurowhip on him.

Orowitz gave her a brief, soft smile, then opened the bag and pulled out one of Dixon's ornately bound paper journals. "These are his real records."

Dixon tamped down his fear with the comfort that only he knew his coded language. They'd have to keep him alive long enough for that, which improved his chances for being rescued by one of his staff, who definitely would want him to live.

"You really *are* a fool," said the bronze-skinned man, chuckling. Dixon was beginning to hate the sound of his derisive laugh. "You've leashed, blackmailed, drugged, and abused minders all your life, and now you think they'll save you? Your staff in the diner think you're dead. Your cleaner and shielder really *are* dead, so you're on your own. Even a low-level telepath could walk right into your exceedingly warped little null brain and pluck the code right out."

"Besides," said Orowitz, "we already have it. A willing gift from one of your staff. Along with a comprehensive list of account numbers, which we've already zeroed, thanks to you sharing your biometrics with us while you were busy pissing yourself." Orowitz smiled, and something deeply unpleasant came into his expression that said he'd enjoy watching Dixon burn. He'd seen the look countless times on dozens of Kameleons. Somehow, Orowitz had hidden the fact that he'd left the Kameleon Corps with parts of one of the most dangerous personality overlays intact. Then the expression smoothed, and it was just Orowitz, but with a presence and intelligence he'd never had before.

"Why are we talking, then?" asked Dixon wearily. "Kill me and get it over with." He dropped his head, and noticed the cord of a leather dogleash on his chest that led to a nearby gatepost. He fumbled at his throat and felt some sort of loose collar around his neck. How unoriginal of them.

Orowitz shrugged. "Not worth the trouble. I expect the CPS's special project team will do it for us. That *is* protocol for security breaches, isn't it?" He snapped his fingers, as if remembering somthing. "Oh, by the way, you're the celebrity of the week. All the newstrends can talk about is a woman named Senga Si'in Lai who poisoned an entire joyhouse full of workers and clients, then recorded a very newstrendy suicide note about the Charisma project, full of names, especially yours and your staff's, and the researchers who kidnapped her. It seems she wasn't happy being torn from her previous life as a regular Minder Corps social worker to become an unwilling experimental subject. She posted it on every social net she could find, right before throwing herself off the tallest tower she could find." Orowitz patted Dixon's bag. "The media are going to love this." The sharp smile surfaced again. "I figure you have maybe an hour before the flying cameras find you."

The three of them turned to walk away.

An impulse shot through Dixon, and he acted on it without letting himself think about it. He slipped his hand in his coat pocket and fired the beamer, right through the fabric.

Nothing happened. He pulled it from his pocket and fired again. Nothing.

The high-tenor laughter he hated rang out and echoed in the alley. "So, what do you think, Mr. Davidro? Did we discharge your beamer while you were twitching in the dirt like a sad little fish, or did your collared monster Renner leave you a final, screw-you parting gift before you left him to die?"

Nevarr turned and walked backward a few steps. "I really hope it was Renner." She gave him a smart-ass smile, then turned forward again.

They vanished into shadows, leaving the alley dark and empty.

Dixon waited until he was sure his legs would hold him, then stood. His left knee was swollen and hurt like hell, but it was functional. It took several minutes for him to get free of the dog collar because his hands shook so badly and he had trouble with balance.

He'd had contingency plans for a day like this, because planning for the future was what he did best. He learned from his mistakes and moved on.

The press would be trouble, but he knew how to stick to the buildings with tech suppressors and find free transport. If he could get to the private body shop where he had prearrangements and access the fluxed savings account he'd never used, he knew how to make it off Mabingion before the lumbering local CPS figured out where to look. Then he could start a new chapter of his life and never look back. Vengeance was for fools, and despite what the sneering bronze-skinned man thought, Dixon wasn't a fool.

He pulled up his hood and began limping down the street. Until he acquired a new shielder, one he had under his complete control, he'd be vulnerable to minders, so he needed to be where they weren't. He'd heard of a few religious enclaves that refused minders, but isolated communal living had never been his style, and too many of the planet of Purencia's various religious groups encouraged minders to join. A better choice would be a frontier planet. Some of them hated minders, and could use someone with people skills like his. Alternatively, pharma companies knew how to control minders, a skill he needed to get better at, and pharmas paid well, too.

The universe looked after those who looked after themselves.

Chapter 30

JANE PENNINGTON-SMYTHE, the newly appointed CPS base administrator for the Minder Corps, frowned at CPS Covert Operations Regional Supervisor Hujuru, who had insisted on delivering the bad news in person. Hujuru probably wanted to make sure she wasn't blamed.

"Only *one* of Mr. Davidro's independent contractors is still alive?"

Hujuru nodded, sending her cascade of variegated ringlets bouncing. Hujuru was *atarashī Nihon*, new Japanese, with only hints of her heritage in her features. Like so many people in Ridderth, considering the body shops on every corner, she was older than she looked. "My teams are still verifying the police reports, but it looks like everyone except the forecaster Jorge Enero-Baca either died in the warehouse skirmish or the townhouse incident." That was the approved wording for the press release. Much more soothing than "violent, murderous combat between vicious criminals" and "destruction of half a residential block with a stolen military assault cannon popularly known as a hellrail."

Jane's research and recent personal observation said Ridderth was a roiling cesspool of territorial crew rivalries, so deadly battles were an almost daily occurrence, but thefts of military weaponry would bear looking into. "And the survivor? Enero-Baca?"

"He's still in the crisis center, being treated for illegal chems withdrawal, long-term malnutrition, and a deeply delusional mental state." Hujuru's lips pursed in exasperation. "Admin Assist bel Doro was unfortunately assaulted by a telepathic cleaner. Her last memory before yesterday, when we found her and Mr. Enero-Baca in the restaurant, is GDAT 3228, fourteen years ago, the day she was promoted to a delta four and assigned to Mr. Davidro. She's in therapy, and will probably never be the same. Memory removal is apparently very traumatic for mid-level filers."

Jane didn't miss the condescension in Hujuru's tone, and made a mental note to check the woman's background. In her experience, CPS

Institute-trained minders sometimes lacked compassion for lower-level talents, and harbored outright disdain for non-minders such as Jane herself. She didn't hide her lack of minder talent, but she didn't advertise it, either.

Jane tapped her opal fingernails on the heavy, ornate desk with its built-in secure comp that looked like stained glass when not in use. The previous base administrator's taste for excess was part of why the prestigious job was now hers. "How did Mr. Davidro get past the cordon?" Jane tried to keep the annoyance out of her voice, because she needed Hujuru as an ally, but Davidro was a significant, ongoing security risk. The newstrends had hourly updates on secrets that only he and his staff knew. Since his contractors were all dead, that only left him as the source.

Hujuru's expression soured. "We don't know that he got past it. The Ridderth Police produced evidence that his body parts are at the bottom of the Shohruz Swamps, but that's right out of week one of covert operations training. He's at the top of the detain-and-restrain list for the whole planet and the space station. In the meantime, we're going after his records and accounts. Unfortunately he had not just dozens, but hundreds, and we know we're missing some." She crossed her arms. "Up until the Charisma mess, he consistently got top performance ratings, so his supervisors overlooked his flagrant 'procedure variances.'" Deep disdain colored her tone. "What the hell good is the Office of Internal Investigation if they don't catch abuses like that?" She shook her head.

Jane nodded her agreement. The OII was overworked and slow, and not a plum assignment in the CPS. She herself had started in the Statistics Division, but she'd built her career in the Covert Operations Division, and made her reputation by fixing the messes left by others. In a way, it was what she was still doing, only this time, for the regular Minder Corps, and on a much larger scale. In the official records, she was administratively in charge of nearly twenty thousand active-duty minders, including the Kameleon program and the CPS Academy and Institute campus in Arazak, a smaller city to the north. Her actual mission was to undertake the gargantuan task of cleaning up Ridderth operations so that leaks like the Charisma project didn't happen again, and to find and eradicate once and for all the hidden, virulent cancer that was the Ayorinn legend.

First, though, she had to stop the hemorrhaging from the Charisma project, at least on Mabingion. "Any connection at all between the ex-Kam Orowitz and the Charisma project?" Davidro's last-minute flurry of detain-and-restrain orders on Ridderth made no sense, especially since all records said Orowitz hadn't been off Branimir in several years. "Or the people who saved that merchant ship?"

"Not that we can find. Of course, the Charisma project may have records we'll never know about." Hujuru snorted. "I'll bet the OII won't find those, either."

"I'll rescind the orders, then. I'd rather not have the local press asking questions we don't know how to answer. We can reinstate them later if we need to." She made a quick note on her list, then looked up. "What kind of cooperation can we expect from the body shops on telling us if Davidro approaches them?"

Hujuru snorted derisively. "Absolute zero, unless Davidro doesn't pay his bill. If he gets to a frontier planet, we'll lose him for good."

"Let's hope he doesn't slip through our fingers before that happens." Jane made sure her tone said she wouldn't tolerate screw-ups, but she'd wager Davidro was already gone, no matter what Hujuru thought. He was a preening, deviant narcissist, but he wasn't stupid. CPS headquarters had decided he was the Charisma project whistleblower, but Jane had her doubts. Based on how he'd treated his independent contractors, he had few scruples about controlling and using minders, so the forced conscription of volunteers for Charisma project wouldn't have bothered him. She suspected something far more complex was at work, and she intended to find out what.

Hujuru didn't know it yet, and would likely howl when she found out, but CPS HQ was about to issue an edict forbidding any use of independent contractors in the Covert Operations division. There were too many Davidros in the organization, and too many supervisors who looked the other way. The CPS was taking a beating in the press, right when they were trying to expand the minder testing program to catch the late bloomers who developed their talents after age seventeen. It was much too hard for the agency to fulfill its mission to keep the galactic peace when it couldn't even keep the peace in its own organization.

Three subtle flashes in Jane's left eye alerted her to the time. She was still getting used to the upgraded internal chrono she'd had installed on her second day in Ridderth, but she appreciated its more sophisticated interface.

"I'm sorry, but I have to leave soon for a meeting off the base." Jane stood, and Hujuru did as well. "I'm representing the CPS on the Planetary

Council Liaison Committee."

Hujuru made a face. "Better you than me. The Committee's construction project scandal has journalists circling like they're starving jackals after a wounded antelope."

"So they are," Jane agreed. She smiled. "What was the name of that good-for-burying-jackals swamp you mentioned?"

Hujuru laughed, then became more serious. "I'm going to give you some unsolicited advice, seeing as you've only been in Ridderth a couple of weeks. The people of Ridderth lionize and respect the local journalists more than any place else I've been. Some of it's because Ridderth is a hotbed of crookedness, which makes exposing it a very profitable business sector, and some of it's because they give generously to charities, but I think the biggest reason is because they can take on city hall and win. Ridderth's government is only marginally worse than the continental or Mabingion government at stomping on citizen foundation rights with gravity boots. Citizens see journalists as their only hope for justice."

"Thank you," said Jane. "That's good to know."

Jane saw the woman out of her offices, then visited her new admin assistant to go over her schedule. She could have done it via a quick call, but Jane was rather enjoying the luxury of developing long-term relationships with her staff, and being able to go home to her family via limousine, rather than interstellar ship. That made her think of Raneel, her ever-loyal and extremely patient wife. Impulsively, she had her assistant order and send flowers, with a simple "thank you" tag. Raneel would know what it meant.

All of her new colleagues either warned her or commiserated with her about getting involved in the piranha-infested waters of the Mabingion Planetary Council Liaison Committee, but she saw the opportunity hidden in the chaos. If she and the Minder Corps, with its legions of loyal employees and offices in every district in Ridderth, helped them succeed in salvaging the shambles of a project to refurbish and upgrade the woefully neglected Planetary Council administration complex, calls for the twenty-year rotation to skip Ridderth this time would go away. The committee and the city would then owe her and the CPS, and be more inclined to cooperate when the time came to burn out the Ayorinn sickness. It would be in their best interests, too, since the resurgence of the meme was giving unhappy people an outside enemy to blame—the government—instead of taking responsibility for their own personal failures.

It wouldn't be easy, but Jane was patient, thorough, and very good with details. The regular CGC military and the CPS, which was technically a military division, but operated much more independently than the Space, Ground, Air, and Water divisions, had considerable economic clout in Ridderth. It was time to put it to good use. With the added skills of the minders in her employ, she could help Ridderth live up to its potential. It would be a much more practical legacy than vague threats in jumbled lines of bad poetry.

CHAPTER 31

JESS LEANED BACK in the office chair and used his new customized percomp to scan through the names one of his algorithms had gleaned from the galactic data nets. "What about Millefleur?" he called out. Once again, he and Kerzanna needed new identities, and she'd said she wanted some say in her name this time. She claimed he'd misspelled "Laraunte," even though he showed her examples in use.

"Sounds like a perfume," she called back. "Jumpers aren't named for perfume." The disgust in her tone made him chuckle.

Decommissioned Jumper Subcaptain Kerzanna Nevarr and retired Minder Corps quartermaster Jessperin Orowitz were living quietly and separately in Branimir. They'd never met, and neither had left that planet in years. Jess and Tuzan were collaborating on fixing any records on Branimir or Mabingion that said otherwise.

Because of her declining health, Nevarr had just sold her business to two pilots and become a silent partner, and was retiring to a self-sufficient mountain cabin to escape the annoyances of city life.

Orowitz complained to Branimir's government about his frozen accounts. The financial affairs division readily believed the obnoxious CPS had mistaken his identity, and ordered his accounts released. He sold his farm to his neighbor and moved to a small flat near the spaceport, from which he might travel from time to time.

As Kerzanna had pointed out, her cybernetic thigh and her Jumper biometal precluded anything more than surface body mods as a disguise, and Neirra's miracle cure for waster's disease only mattered if the patient was an ex-Jumper. Her latest PTVS percentage was twenty-eight percent, a further drop of two percent, despite the stress of a night of physical torture, freeing herself from a murderous crew, searching for him, and helping Tuzan use Jess's idea to infiltrate Davidro's den and avenge his sister's death. The decreasing percentages still weren't definitive; only time would tell to see if the numbers kept dropping, and how long they stayed that way. And after that, they needed more than one person cured, or she'd be no different from the occasional exceptions the CPS liked to trot out.

"Aurore?" he called out. She'd asked him to stick to French-sounding names, because she still had a tendency to mutter in Novo French when she was irritated. She made a lousy spy, which was one of the things he treasured about her.

"Second paternal cousin and a second-line great aunt," she called. They'd thought it prudent to stay away from any of the Nevarr family names, but he hadn't counted on how many that eliminated. "Come see if you like this one."

He grabbed his empty coffee mug and went down the hall from the tiny borrowed office to the virtual real estate immersion room where Kerzanna was searching for a better place for them to live than hotels. She had more patience for it than he did. Tuzan had arranged the after-hours visit to the cozy broker's office. Jess was convinced Tuzan's various companies cleaned half the residences and businesses in Ridderth, and half the population owed him favors. Jess and Kerzanna were in the latter category.

"How many relatives do you have?" he asked. He put his mug down next to hers on the desk, then moved behind her to wrap his arms around her waist and kiss her ear. Escaped tendrils from her braided crown of blonde hair tickled his nose. He loved the smell of her, the flavor of her skin.

"If you count babies and marriage alliances, probably hundreds by now. Twins run in the family." She keyed the display and relaxed against him. The holos lit up and took them on a life-sized virtual walk-through of a modular flat that could be configured to have anywhere from six rooms to ten by simply telling the building comp to make the change. She pointed out the kitchen with tall cabinets and adjustable-height counters suitable for tall people, the high ceilings and adjustable lighting, the multiple secure access points, the rooftop airpad, and the nice view. "We could even have cats. Not LZ and Igandea, though. I saw a story today that had a clip of Bhatta carrying them with her onto her new ship. She's still a minor celebrity."

"Where is the flat?" He kissed behind her ear, and delighted in the catch in her breath. Her responsiveness fueled his, the way it had five years ago. It was even better now, because he could lose himself in loving her and not worry that some subroutine in his bioware would ruin the moment.

"A mid-rise in Yànzi Shān district. 'Swallow Hill' in English. Close to the Canals, which is why it's affordable, but being on a hill puts it above the waters." Ridderth's periodic floods overran the channelized canals, which is why only the desperate lived there.

They'd agreed to stay in Ridderth for a while, since they were no longer on anyone's hit parade. After leaving Davidro in the alley, they'd had a long talk with Tuzan, and an even longer discussion by themselves. She was the only living proof of Neirra's legacy to the galaxy. She was also the keeper of a treasure trove of minder health data, and wanted to share it with minders as the original Minder Veterans Advocates group had intended. Jess had the seed of an idea on how to accomplish it, but he needed Tuzan's help. And they had to decide what to do with the goldmine of information in Davidro's journals. They'd already shared some choice bits via Jess's "unsourced rumors" algorithms.

"If you like it, I'll buy it." He felt her twitch, and remembered their old arguments about money and favors. "Question. Why don't you like gifts?" He'd only come to realize in the past couple of weeks that she wasn't rejecting him personally; it had deeper meaning for her.

She turned in his arms and looked up at him. Her natural blue eyes always made him think of summer, his favorite time of year. "Are you up for this?"

They'd made a deal to continue asking the hard questions and answering the harder truths that they'd avoided four years ago. "Yes." He meant it, even if he had to put information-hoarding Jess-the-bomber in a chokehold in his head.

She smiled and palmed the side of his face. "So fierce." Her smile fell away. "My first maternal cousin Blandine and I ran away to the big city when we were seventeen, because neither of us fit the small-town, ranch-life mold. She was too lively, and I was too tall."

He kissed her forehead. "Not for the Jumpers."

"Yes, I fit in there, but that was later. You have to understand that even though Newellia is a Third Wave planet, terraformed and settled three hundred years ago, it's still in debt to the settlement company because the company cheated. They're about to lose the final court case on it, but for now, RSI still owns most of the exploitable natural resources, the smaller towns and cities, and the critical infrastructure. Everything has a markup. They lose revenue when families like ours pay off their settlement debt, so they make it easy to buy on credit, which never seems to get paid off. A rate hike here and a quick loan there, and pretty soon, the company owns you again. I was careful, but Blandine likes the finer things and got in over her head. I took a high-paying summer job at one of the few quarries not owned by RSI to make enough money to get her out of debt. It was, uhm, an educational experience, but it got me in shape and taught me how to brawl."

He could feel the tension building in her, but he couldn't do anything other than listen. Secrets nearly destroyed them last time. Nothing she could tell him would make him love her any less.

"To make a long story short, when I got back, Blandine owed twice as much as before, and had a nasty chems habit on top of it. The people she owed money to had me raped as a message to her. They couldn't take me in a street fight, but one of their enforcers was a telepath. He compelled me into a utility closet and forced me to do every warped thing he could think of."

Jess had to close his eyes and take shallow breaths for a few moments to get control of his overwhelming anger.

He felt her other hand cupping his cheek, and he looked down at her strong, beautiful face. "I'm okay. It was a long time ago." She smiled a little. "I told a couple of my Jumper squad mates about it, early on, and funnily enough, right after they took ground leave, I got news from home that the enforcer had died slowly and painfully in a freak accident."

He didn't know what to say, so he just held her for a long moment, letting the heat from her chest fill the hollow in his, letting the scent of her soothe him.

"So to answer your question, gifts feel like obligations with hidden terms." She took a step back and waved toward the looping holo around them. "I trust you with my life and my heart, and I admit I want to have hot-connect sex with you in every room of this flat, but buying it would be a big damn gift."

Even though they'd exhausted themselves making love a half-dozen times in the past two days, Jess's hormones stirred at her words. He pulled her in for a heated, open-mouthed kiss and slid a hand under her tunic to cup her breast. He brushed a thumb across her taught nipple through her thin bra. "We'll lease it."

She laughed. "I should have started my sales pitch with the sex." She kissed him and caressed his ass, then twirled away. Maybe it was wishful thinking, but Jess-the-medic saw a marked improvement in the mechanical fluidity of her joints in the three weeks since he'd seen her get out of the autodoc. She turned off the holo. "My turn for a question?"

He nodded.

She sat on the edge of the desk and crossed her arms. "Why don't you like being a minder?"

Instinctive fear shot through him, and he breathed through it. Thank the universe she was patient with him, because he hardly knew where to begin.

"Conditioning, I guess you'd call it. On Rashad Tarana, minders weren't considered human; they were demons in disguise who were trying to deceive their way onto *Ġenna Triq*, Paradise Road. Being a minder got you executed in the public square and your relatives sent to the Warriors' Crusade to be used as sex toys and fodder for field training. I think Prophet Al-Din was a minder himself, probably a sifter and some warped form of empath, and wanted to be the one-eyed emperor in the empire of the blind. He used loyal sifters as 'God's Lenses' to find other minders for purification." His hands hurt, and he realized he'd clenched them so hard, his fingernails were cutting into his skin. He took a deep breath and let it out slowly, and shook the tension out.

He glanced at Kerzanna to see how she was taking it. She nodded once, respectfully. "I'm glad you survived." She'd told him that Jumpers acknowledged pain for each other, to help ease the burden. It was curiously comforting that she considered him as strong as a Jumper.

"Because of the years of therapy all Rashad Tarana survivors got, I know, intellectually, that the first thirteen years of my life were filled with a shed-load of shite, but the fear still lurks in the back of my dinosaur brain, trying to protect me. Sort of like one of the bleedovers, in a way." He shook his head. "The Mandarin language has the same effect. It was the language of demons and, coincidentally, the planetary government the Prophet overthrew. My devout parents offered up my thirteen-year-old sister to be a Chosen One for the Leadership Circle's harem because her phenomenal skill with languages would help the other young 'tributes' adjust. She lasted eighteen months. Speaking Mandarin got her and her newborn baby crucified in the town square."

This time, he caught his tension early enough to shake it off before it bunched up his shoulders again. "It ended thirty-eight years ago, and it still twists me in knots. I really am a fractured mess."

Kerzanna crossed to him and put strong hands on his shoulders and began kneading them. "I told you before, you're the most resilient man I've ever known. Neither of us is our past." She stood on her toes to kiss him. "We make our future. I love you, oh delightfully tall and plasma-hot man who hasn't told me his name."

"Josh DiGuilian." He put his hands on her hips and pulled her closer. "Close enough to 'Jess,' in case you forget while in the throes of passion." He kissed her, then nibbled along her jaw toward her Jumper tattoos.

She laughed. "Good thinking, since I plan on enjoying lots of throes with you." She thrust her hips in slow grind against his growing arousal. It was his turn to catch his breath. She kissed his cheek and stepped back. "Come on, let's clean up and get out of here. Tuzan said dinner would be ready at eight, and traffic tanks this time of day."

She scooped up their mugs and headed toward the small sink to rinse them out. He copied the pertinent details on the flat she liked, then replaced the activity logs with blank ones and powered down the display, leaving it as they'd found it.

He grabbed their raincoats from the hooks over the solardry unit and handed hers to her. He helped her pull her hood up as an excuse to kiss her again. "What about 'Jumper Adorabelle'?"

She growled at him, and he laughed.

CHAPTER 32

THE EX-JUMPER FORMERLY known as Kerzanna leaned against the doorjamb and sipped wine while she watched Jess... oops, Josh and Tuzan argue good-naturedly about some arcane coding thing that was so far over her head that it sounded like a made-up alien language. They were good for each other. Some parts of Jes... Josh still had the social skills of a wolverine, and needed to learn how to be a friend. Tuzan still mourned his sister and needed that friendship. Not that he didn't have a million friends already, but only a few who didn't care if he was a scary top-level cleaner and telepath, and hardly any who he could be himself with, or conspire with on computer stuff.

Neirra's actions had forced significant vector changes on all of them. Je... dammit, Josh missed his farm. He said he didn't mind, but she could see that the crowded city sometimes bothered him. Or more specifically, his talent. Like the other categories of minders in the telepathic class, sifters had to learn to contain their talents so they didn't have to sense others all the time. The one good thing that came from the failsafe shutdown, and the horrendous chance he'd taken by letting the sifter, Zerrell, fix his bioware, was that using the overlays didn't hurt nearly as much, and his eyes mostly stopped twitching.

"Quit lurking, Soleil Benoit, and come back in," said Tuzan. He emphasized her new name and exaggerated the French accent with a smartass grin.

"Jumpers don't lurk," she said sternly. "We stomp in and kick ass." She crossed the soft, plush carpet to put her glass on the table and sit on the settee next to Josh. They were both barefoot because of house rules. He slid his arm around her shoulders, and she liked the weight of it, like it was her anchor to the real world.

Tuzan relaxed into the corner of the doublewide chair he sat on and smiled. "When is the flat-warming party?"

Josh laughed. "First, we have to furnish it." In the ninety minutes between leaving the broker's office and arriving at the doorstep of Tuzan's flat, Josh had activated one of his dormant companies on Mabingion, which he apparently had quite a few of from his Kameleon days, and leased the flat she liked as "corporate accommodations for visiting staff." It kept their personal names off the records, and explained the all-new contents and any number of guests. He'd also told her how much money he had—enough to buy his own moon—then dropped a bombshell.

"You have the same."

She snorted. "Not unless I won the galactic lottery while we were in transit, I don't." She'd already been thinking about what to do for a job so she could pay her half of the rent.

He took her hand and kissed the back of it. "You do, because I transferred half of everything I have to you."

"What?" It was a good thing they were in an autocab, because if she'd been at the controls, she'd have probably crashed them into the next high-rise. "When?"

"I started doing it the first day on Branimir, while you were asleep in the flitter. I did the rest in the *Faraón*'s packet drops and the first day here. It's in various sealed estate escrow accounts. The Branimir part is in the Nevarr name, so we'll have to deal with that."

He was serious. She forced herself to breathe. "Why?"

"Because it's what I wanted to do the day we separated four years ago. I let the bomber stop me, because I thought we'd have time later." He squeezed her hand. "The money meant nothing to me. You meant everything."

Jumpers didn't cry, so she hadn't, but something got in her eye.

"What style of decor do you like?" asked Tuzan. "I can introduce you to some wholesalers." She got the impression he loved shopping, which gave her an idea.

"I like *your* style." She waved her hand to encompass the eclectic mix of utilitarian and one-of-a-kind pieces that made his place into a home. "How about I commission you to work your magic? If you have the time, that is." She gave Josh a pointed look. "It seems Soleil recently came into an inheritance." She still wasn't comfortable with it, but if he could come to terms with being a minder despite his ghastly childhood, then she could learn to accept presents from the man she loved with all her heart.

From the sparking gleam in Tuzan's eye, she'd made the right choice. "I'll see what I can do." He glanced at her hand resting high on Josh's thigh and gave them a knowing wink and smile. "Starting with a bed."

She laughed out loud. "Oh, yeah. We discovered on the way over here that we're too damn tall to have sex in autocabs." Josh smiled and shrugged, and Tuzan guffawed.

"Did you have anything to do with the new story on Charisma this morning?" she asked. "The one by Charrascos?"

Tuzan shook his head. "No, we only targeted her with that first rumor because she'd written the 'Mabingion Purge' story. I'm not surprised she found where more of the unwilling subjects came from. She's tenacious."

"That she is," Kerzanna agreed. "She interviewed a bunch of my platoon once for a story on Jumpers. We usually ate reporters for breakfast, because they typically produced crap stories that fit whatever angle they'd already decided on, but Charrascos was fair. And fearless." She smiled at the memory of the tiny woman standing her ground in front of a bad-tempered mech-suited Jumper. "I liked her."

Josh cleared his throat. "I made sure she saw some teaser rumors from Davidro's journals about the independent contractors he collected. Most of them weren't willing, either."

Soleil patted his thigh in comfort, knowing it bothered him that he hadn't recognized the full extent of Davidro's abuses until reading the journals. It bothered her that the CPS had allowed it to go on for so long, or worse, hadn't even noticed or cared. It was a haunting echo of how Rashad Tarana had happened under the Concordance's nose.

Tuzan traced the decoration on his wine glass with his gold-lacquered fingernail. "Getting back to your new flat for a minute, would you be willing to take some of Majiril's things? I don't want to put them in storage, but I'm not sure I could handle them right now. If it's too creepy–"

"We'll take them on loan," said Josh. "They're yours whenever you're ready."

"Good." Tuzan's smile turned wistful. "She was fearless, too. I wish you could have known her before the riots. She was a professor at the CPS Academy and Institute in Arazak, and she loved teaching. She was a high-level polymath, meaning she had all talents—healer, teke, sifter, forecaster, you name it. Polymaths often develop late, so the CPS thought she was just another obedient multi-talent, like me. They'd have leashed her tight and never let her near impressionable young minders, otherwise. She taught them to think, to ask questions."

A phantom image flashed in her head. "Did she know Ayorinn?" She tapped her temple. "Neirra." That was their shorthand for the leftover memories that Neirra's various packets had left in all their minds. Random smells, sights, or music sometimes triggered them, at least for her.

"Probably. Majiril never admitted it, but I think she reviewed early drafts of the Ayorinn forecast, and it made a believer out of her. The CPS heard about the forecast and deemed it a clear and present threat to the galactic peace, so they stirred up the riots as an excuse for finding and purging anyone who'd read it. By then, it was far too late, of course, but the CPS didn't know that. During the riots, Majiril helped as many people escape as she could, but someone betrayed her. The top enforcement team for the CPS—they called themselves the Skullrippers—tried to pull her mind apart. Neirra caught them and stopped it, and together, she and I together cleaned and twisted them so they thought they'd succeeded. Neirra twisted my memories so I couldn't give anyone away, but she hid the real memories and later sent me the keys to unlock them. Majiril was never the same, though. She convinced me to help her build her shadow railway to help more minders escape so she could continue her mission."

"We're sorry for your loss, Tuzan." Jumper Soleil showed him her respect for his pain. "Part of why we wanted to come over tonight, other than because we like you and we're tired of restaurants, was to talk to you about the railway. We can help."

Tuzan shook his head. "I'm shutting it down. All it took was one long-range telepath and one sifter to compromise it and get her killed."

"We know the risks," said Josh. "We can improve the security."

Soleil thought about all Tuzan had done for them, and probably others. Insight hit her, maybe from Neirra, or maybe from her own intuition. "Majiril just wanted to save *you*. It was you who built the railway to help other minders. You even helped the telepath Xan, and cleaned bel Doro's memories like she begged you to. Are you sure you want to burn it down?"

Tuzan looked away, clearly troubled.

Soleil let the silence settle. To give him time and to distract her impatient self, she threaded her fingers through Josh's and soaked in the warmth of him by her side. She'd missed him for so long.

Tuzan stood and walked to the small side table where the wine bottle was, but instead of wine, he picked up a percomp. "What do you know about Ayorinn's Legacy?"

She looked to Josh, who shook his head. She turned back to Tuzan. "It's a bunch of vague, poetic quatrains that could mean anything. When my older brothers and I heard it was banned, we immediately tracked it down and read it, but we couldn't make heads or tails out of it." She shrugged. "But we weren't minders, we were just ranch kids."

Tuzan sighed. "The forecast isn't just for minders, it's for all of us. Ayorinn believed we're stagnating as a civilization, and that it's killing us. We're preserving ourselves in amber. We've curated our languages, our cultures, our family tribal structure, even our ecosystems, but we're not evolving new ones, and we try our damnedest to stamp out variances. His forecaster talent drove him mad with visions of a horrific future, so he spent fifteen years developing the forecast that would save humankind. Unfortunately, the cost to individual humans will be unspeakable."

"Did you know Ayorinn?" asked Josh.

"No. Majiril tried to keep me in the dark." Tuzan shook his head. "I liked the light too much." He sighed again. "The forecast scares the CPS for two reasons. One, because they never saw it coming and couldn't contain it, and two, because it's still unfolding, and they still can't stop it. The version you read is what, thirty years old? There are at least twenty or thirty more quatrains after that. They came out at random times, random locations, and it makes the CPS crazy that they can't find the source. There haven't been any new ones for the last four years."

He keyed something on his percomp, and his wall display lit up. "This came out two days ago, the day my sister died."

> Glowing nets must from shadowed ashes rise; fractures healed with found hope
> Grasp the tail and swing the comet at the chained amber chrysalis.
> Red sparks travel faster than light and swallow the dark flooded city.
> Cleanse your heart, change your fate, remake the world.

"What do you think it means?" asked Josh.

Tuzan took a deep, noisy breath. "That we will burn down the old shadow railway and build a new one." He crossed his arms. "Even if we don't want to, even if it's dangerous, even if it gets us all sent to the Skullrippers."

"If you truly believe we are instruments chosen by something bigger than ourselves," said Josh, "then we should take charge of what we can, and do it right. I let the CPS take control of my fate once, and I barely survived it." He squeezed Soleil's fingers gently. "Believe me, second chances are to be treasured."

Soleil had joined the Jumpers to make a difference, and she wanted to continue that mission, even if it wasn't the way she'd envisioned it. "People have been hurt and died for me. Hell, *I've* died for me—twice. Every day is a gift, and I'm trying not to fight that."

She smiled as she gazed into the mismatched eyes of the man she loved, then turned back to Tuzan and waited for his answer.

Tuzan turned off the display, then sat back down in his chair.

"I'm in."

EPILOGUE

RENNER WOKE, IF he could call it that, to a sound. It was a nice change from the phantom fireworks behind his eyes. He'd been fooled before, though, so he decided he needed a plan. He would wait. It was a good plan, as plans went, because he couldn't do anything else.

That was a lie. He could do one other thing. He opened his eyes.

Daylight again.

Still? No, again.

The sound bothered him. He should do something about it, but he couldn't think what. The universe was laughing its ass off. He'd been so sure of his death that he'd taunted it, and now here he was, dying of the motherfucking collar.

Unbelievably, a face appeared before his. Blue eyes. Red hair. He blinked, slowly, but she was still there when he came back. Angel of death, maybe.

Lips moved. Her lips. Speaking. "Hi, there, Mr. Renner."

A hand came into view holding a wad of fabric. It brushed his lips, and something painful hit his tongue. Moisture. His throat tried to work, but of course it couldn't. It was enough for him to move his lips. "Kill… me…."

"What? No, I won't kill you," she said, looking deeply offended. "I just met you."

The motherfucking collar ratcheted. The phantom fireworks returned.

The woman's eyes narrowed as she looked at the collar. "Be right back," she said, then vanished. He should have known she wasn't an angel, because angels didn't have freckles. She wouldn't make it in time, but he was mildly grateful that she was putting in the effort. He drifted into the dreamland of hypoxia.

Suddenly, her face was back in front of his again. Not a dream, then. "Hope you have high pain tolerance."

She had a butcher knife in her hand. Hope flared. Maybe she'd kill him after all. Instead, he felt pain in the muscles of his neck, the burned skin screaming. He felt his eyes water and was surprised they still could. She grabbed his collar with both hands and forced it forward, into the new wounds, but easing the pressure on his trachea and allowing precious air in. Why one of the collar's failsafes didn't kill them both was a mystery.

"I've got help coming. An emergency response team, and a fixer who owes me a favor."

The rushing sound in his ears made it hard to hear. He had the oddest feeling that he should know her, but the memory wouldn't come.

Her expressive lips parted. "How long until the collar tightens again?"

He remembered that. "Two... hours..." And something else. "Dixon... key...."

She frowned. "Oh, well, that's a bit of a problem." She patted his cheek soothingly. "We'll have to muddle along without him."

She moistened his mouth again with the rag.

"How... long..."

"How long have you been here? I'm guessing you went down with the ship, as it were, so it's been a little over two days. The table saved you. The front part of the building is history." An angry frown crossed her face, making her look much older and more formidable than he'd initially taken her for. "The police should have fucking found you."

Police? The last thing he'd remembered was baldly lying to Dixon about the Jumper being dead, and then... buried in rubble. He'd called for help, but no one listened. His eyes drifted shut.

He felt fingers on his cheek again. "Stay with me, Mr. Renner."

He opened his eyes. He didn't think he'd ever seen freckles that close up. Faint, reddish, like a pale reflection of her flame-colored hair.

She suddenly moved back and looked up. "In here!" Her voice was so loud it echoed.

She leaned in closer to him again. "My friends are here. They're going to help you." She leaned in even closer, her lips almost touching his ear. "Don't fry anyone, okay?"

It should have alarmed him that the red not-angel knew about his talent, but it didn't. "Can't... it's... empty."

"That's good. I mean, bad that you... oh, never mind."

Her face vanished and a new one appeared, a dusky lavender-faced man with shining purple hair. The man spoke to the woman in an accent he couldn't place. "Light here." He pointed, and she complied by shining a handheld. It dazzled Renner's eyes. He shut them against the pain.

The lavender-faced man began working with tools. He hummed and made burbling sounds, almost like an espresso machine, all while working on the collar. Finally, the man leaned back and said. "The maker did good work. Not as good as me, though." The man's hands went once more to the collar, and suddenly, the collar was looser than it had ever been. "May I keep it?"

"It's dangerous. Failsafes." Renner whispered, and breathed deep. He couldn't tell if he was successful.

"Oh, yes. Very nasty. I de-fanged them."

The collar came off in two pieces, and the lavender man dropped it into a clear bag. Renner wished he could see what his neck looked like without the collar. The woman's face came into view.

"That was the easy part. This next is going to hurt, I'm afraid." She looked resolute, but the finger that gently caressed his cheek was shaky.

She was right. Even with the painkiller patches the medic slapped on him, the extraction process was agony punctuated by excruciating pain and unbearable torture as the circulation came back to crushed and broken limbs. The motherfucking collar had saved his neck from breaking, probably because it wanted to kill him itself. They finally got him into a medevac capsule.

Her face appeared above him again. In the better light, he noticed the freckles extended down her neck and to her chest.

"Where am I going?" he asked.

She gave him a perky, smartass smile. "To the medical center, silly."

He awoke again in the halls of the medical center, to the sound of her telling someone that he was her cousin Brenner who'd been in a terrible construction accident, and she'd send them his medical history, but there wasn't much because he was a specialist who traveled a lot and didn't have a regular medic. Inexplicably, they believed her.

She stayed with him all the way to the surgical suite, up until the point where medics barred her. She leaned in and kissed him on the cheek, then whispered, "I'll be here when you get out. Try not to zap anything." She would have pulled away but he stopped her with his one good hand.

"I'm sorry, but who are you?"

She blinked in surprise, then smiled. "I'm Charrascos, the reporter you were sent to kill."

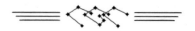

ABOUT THIS BOOK

Thanks for reading *Jumper's Hope*, book 4 in the Central Galactic Concordance space opera series. If this is the first book you've read in this series, welcome. As you might have gathered, the next book will continue with the events begun here, including how Renner and Charrascos fit into the picture.

By the way, if you haven't already read them, *Overload Flux* (Book 1) introduces the Central Galactic Concordance universe, and *Minder Rising* (Book 2) delves into the Citizen Protection Service. The short novella, *Zero Flux* (Book 2.5) is a short thriller and mystery, and *Pico's Crush* (Book 3) reunites characters from previous books for an explosive adventure on a paradise college campus, and you might recognize some characters who return in *Jumper's Hope*.

Please post a review of *Jumper's Hope* at the retailer where you found this book. Even if it's short and sweet, it really helps. Think of it as paying forward for the last time someone recommended a great book you enjoyed.

For news of upcoming releases, and to find out what's next in the Central Galactic Concordance series, please sign up for my newsletter at http://bit.ly/CVN-news. I promise not to send photos of my cats or vacations (unless it's somewhere off-planet).

I'd love to know what you think about the story and what you'd like to see in the future books. You can visit my website and blog at the cleverly named Author.CarolVanNatta.com and drop me a line, or connect with me on Facebook at CarolVanNattaAuthor.

I owe thanks to my friends and brave beta readers T3, Jill, Meredith, and Karen, who kindly pointed out ways to improve the story I wanted to tell. I am also grateful for the professional editing services provided by Shelley Holloway of Holloway House, and stunning cover design by Gene Mollica Studio.

ABOUT THE AUTHOR

Carol Van Natta is a science fiction and fantasy author. She shares her home in Fort Collins, Colorado with a sometime-mad scientist and various cats. Any violations of the laws of physics in her books are the fault of the cats, not the mad scientist.

Sign up for her newsletter at her website, http://Author.CarolVanNatta.com.

BOOKS BY CAROL VAN NATTA

Space Opera
Overload Flux (Central Galactic Concordance, Book 1)
Minder Rising (CGC Book 2)
Zero Flux (CGC Novella 2.5)
Pico's Crush (CGC Book 3)
Jumper's Hope (CGC Book 4)

Fantasy
In Graves Below
Shift of Destiny

Retro Science Fiction Comedy
Hooray for Holopticon (with Ann Harbour)

ORLAND PARK
PUBLIC LIBRARY
A Natural Connection

**14921 Ravinia Avenue
Orland Park, IL 60462**

**708-428-5100
orlandparklibrary.org**

CPSIA information can be obtained
at www.ICGtesting.com
Printed in the USA
LVOW10s1517100518
576717LV00011B/907/P